PRAISE FOR THERESA SCOTT'S HISTORICAL ROMANCES!

Broken Promise is an "excellent blend of fact and fiction that will keep you involved in an unforgettable reading experience. Outstanding!"

—*Rendezvous*

In *Dark Renegade,* "the passion is primitive and lusty....Kudos to Theresa Scott for an exciting and refreshing reading adventure. Superb!"

—*Rendezvous*

"*Yesterday's Dawn* is an entertaining read and an enticing beginning to the *Hunters of the Ice Age* series."
—*Romantic Times*

"Plenty of adventure and nonstop action....Readers who thrive on Indian romance should particularly enjoy *Apache Conquest.*"

—*Romantic Times*

"*Forbidden Passion* is a light, charming tale. Theresa Scott has penned a pleasant read for all those who love exciting stories of the days of old."

—*Romantic Times*

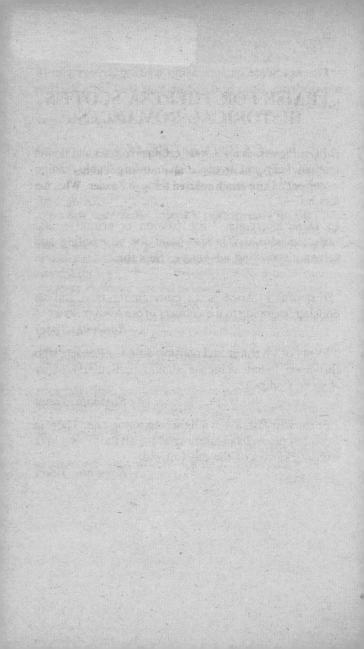

CAPTIVE LEGACY

"Now" —Dorie smiled—"take off your clothes."

"What?" Utter shock coursed through Zander. What the fool hell—

"Take off your clothes, Zander." Her voice was even, her blue eyes steady.

She couldn't mean it! He glared up at her, arms across his chest. "No." No one, and no little pistol, was going to make him strip off his clothes!

She leaned forward, the hand holding the pistol as steady as a rock. "Take off your clothes, Zander, or I swear I will shoot you right through your cold heart!"

His eyes narrowed. The fool woman who didn't know what the hell she was doing with a loaded gun now had the trigger halfway pulled! A cold sweat broke out on his forehead. "Don't shoot."

He started to unbutton his red flannel shirt. Her eyes followed every move of his fingers. Her pink tongue came out and delicately licked her lips.

He tossed the shirt to the ground. "Seen enough?" he asked indifferently.

"All your clothes, Zander." Was that breathlessness in her voice?

THERESA SCOTT

Captive Legacy

LEISURE BOOKS **NEW YORK CITY**

*This book is dedicated with love and affection
to my parents, Jim and Eileen Scott.*

A LEISURE BOOK®

January 1996

Published by

Dorchester Publishing Co., Inc.
276 Fifth Avenue
New York, NY 10001

Printed in the United States of America.

Special thanks to:

Cheryl Forcier, for consulting on horses; Sally Freeman, Park Ranger, and Curt Johnson, Chief Park Ranger, at Fort Clatsop, Warrenton, OR, for consulting on flintlocks; Christopher Johnson, PA/SA, for medical consulting.

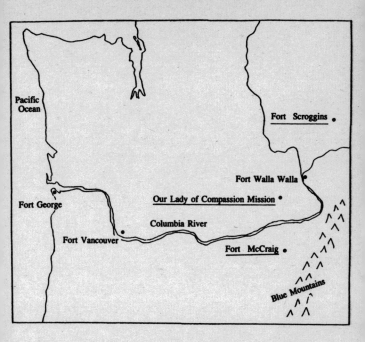

Oregon Territory in 1825.

Underlined places are fictitious

Prologue

Winter, 1811
Fort George
Oregon Territory

"Why can't we go in, Mama?"

A bitter, cold wind tugged at eleven-year-old Alexander Durban's thin body. He clutched his five-year-old brother's hand tightly as they waited anxiously on the porch of the Big House beside their mother, Elaine.

"No, Zander. We dare not!" she whispered.

Fat drops of rain splattered on Alexander's threadbare shirt as Elaine rocked the crying babe in her arms. The baby wailed loudly.

A heavy trapper almost tripped over Zander

as he filed past the small family and into the factor's house. A woman, her Indian-black hair and her white skin showing her mixed-blood heritage as surely as did the beaded, blue flannel gown she wore, laughed and flirted proudly with her escort, a burly mountain man clothed in a leather shirt and trousers.

Zander stared at the two. He knew the woman. She was his mother's favorite cousin. Why then, did she look away as she passed by them? And why did Mama turn away? What was wrong?

Zander frowned as the traders and clerks of the fort, the North West Company trappers, and the Hudson's Bay Company trappers strolled through the open door and into the light and music. Why were *they* allowed inside and he wasn't? This was the biggest wedding Fort George had seen in three years and he wanted to be there too!

Sweet violin music drifted through the open door of the manager's Big House and lured Zander closer. He eased his hand out of his brother's and edged over to the porch to peer through the factor's dearly bought, small-paned glass windows. Unfortunately, thick, flowery lace curtains barred his view.

A trapper clumped up from behind. "Elaine! Don't you go in there," he warned.

Zander whirled around, listening to the man.

"And keep your young 'uns away too. Archibald said he don't want you in there and he meant it!"

Zander watched as his mother dropped her head, her short, straight, black hair falling forward and hiding her face. Her shoulders slumped and the baby sniffled. "Mama?" he whispered.

"Good girl," said the trapper loudly. "You do as you're told. Why, when this is all over, you can come and visit me. *I* like Injuns—'specially the women." He laughed.

The trapper's blue eyes lighted on Zander and his brother, Willie. "'Course you can't bring your big boys with you. Bring the baby though; I don't mind babies." And then the trapper, too, opened the door and entered the room where the music swirled and loud, merry voices celebrated.

Zander didn't like the man. "Don't listen to him, Mama." He touched his mother's shoulder. "I'm a big boy. Let me go in," he urged. "It's wet and cold standing out here. Mama, please . . ."

Elaine's lips tightened. "We must not." She looked about to reprimand him.

"Why?"

Her lovely brown eyes softened as she looked at him. Finally she said, "I see you want to go in, Zander. But we must not. We must not!"

Zander dipped his head and stared at the

ground, stubbornness rising in him. He'd never seen a wedding before.

Another white man entered the building, then the heavy door closed with a solid *thunk*.

Behind that door, Zander could hear laughing and clapping. "Just one peek?" he begged. "Please. Let us go in."

"No, Zander," she answered firmly. "Take Willie's hand. We can watch from here. And remember, we must be very, very quiet."

Reluctantly, Zander took his brother's hand. But even with his face pressed against the cold, hard glass of the windows, Zander could barely see blurs on the other side of the curtains. "I can't see anything," he muttered.

Suddenly he released Willie's hand and ran to the heavy wooden door. He grabbed the handle and pulled the door open. Then he darted inside.

"Zander!" cried his mother hoarsely. "Zander! Come back!"

Zander entered on quick, silent feet and peered around the crowded, noisy room. He could have stomped into the room and no one would have heard him, he realized.

In one corner of the brightly lit room, three fiddlers played a rousing jig that shook the rough log walls.

Laughing men and women danced to the music. A huge fire burned in the dried-mud and slate fireplace. Against one wall stood a plank table with heaped platters of venison and elk meat, bowls of vegetables, and baskets of berries. Zander's mouth watered at the sight.

His mother suddenly appeared at his side and nudged him urgently. "Zander! We must go. We cannot stay. . . . "

But when he glanced at her, she was staring open-mouthed at someone. He saw that she was just as curious as he was. Didn't Mama want to see the fancy wedding too?

Zander darted toward a corner and hid behind a group of men and women. The violins ceased their wailing, and the crowd flowed over to one side of the room. Zander could hear murmurings.

He craned his neck to see what everyone was excited about. He tried edging around people, but they were all taller than he. Finally, frustrated, he returned to his mother. "I want to get closer," he said. "I want to see."

She touched his arm and whispered, "Only for a moment. But you must stay close to me. We may have to leave very quickly!"

". . . now pronounce you man and wife," said a loud voice, and Zander's attention was drawn to the rotund priest standing in the midst of the crowd. The priest raised his arm, and his black robes rustled with his excitement. "We need some room. Back, back!" he cried in a jovial voice. "We must make room for the happy couple!"

Zander moved away from his mother and brother and stepped closer to the priest. Oh, how he wanted to explore, to roam the room, eat the food, and dance to the music. A wedding!

"Zander!" He heard his mother's hoarse plea, but he ignored it. Willie could stay with her. Willie was still little.

Zander circled the crowd that stood between him and the priest and the "happy couple"—the bride and groom.

He sidled up close to the front. Suddenly Zander halted. Something was very wrong.

Whatever was his father doing here? And dressed like that, in a strange gray suit that seemed to choke him at the collar? And why was he holding the hand of that pale, brown-haired woman? She wore a long white dress and looked as if she had just sucked on a bitter berry.

"Father?" he asked, walking toward them.

Unaware of the silence that immediately fell across the gathered men and women, Zander continued to stare.

"Father? Sir?" His voice rang clearly in the silence.

Archibald Durban glared at him.

Zander's face flushed in embarrassment. It

was true that his father ignored him most of the time, but surely Archibald Durban could say *something* to him, could tell him what was happening. . . .

Archibald mouthed the words, "Get out!" Then he glanced back at the white woman, almost in fear.

She, too, glared at Zander. Then she glared at Archibald.

Zander's throat tightened. The "happy couple," he suddenly realized. No. It couldn't be. Why was his father marrying this woman? What about his mama?

He watched the woman's pale skin turn a rosy, mottled shade. "Do something, Archibald," Jane Potter hissed at her bridegroom. "Now!"

Archibald signaled with a nod of his head. Out of the corner of his eye, Zander saw a trapper move toward him.

Zander gritted his teeth and ran over to his father. Jaw tight, Zander clenched his fist and punched his father as hard as he could in the stomach. "That's for not marrying my mama!" he cried in a thin, clear voice.

A horrified gasp went up from the onlookers. One or two smothered chuckles could be heard. A woman screamed. Another woman fainted.

"Archibald, I will not have it!" shrieked the bride. "Get him out of here! He's one of your

Indian bastards, I know it!" Jane Potter yanked up a handful of her white dress, ready to chase after Zander.

Zander glared at her. "Who are you? You should not marry my father! What about my mama?"

His voice shook with anger. He glanced around at the sea of faces. Some of them looked horrified; one man snickered. A woman giggled behind her hand. Anger surged through Zander. How could his father do this? What would happen to his mama? To him?

"Get him out of here!" screamed the red-faced woman in lace. "Take him away! I never want to see him again!"

Archibald patted his new wife's arm to try and calm her. She shoved his hand away.

The trapper grabbed Zander by his arms and dragged him through the crowd.

"Well done," whispered a mixed-blood woman to Zander. "Your mama should be very proud."

"Hush, Sally," said another. "Look how angry Archibald is!"

Zander got one last glance of his father's furious face before the trapper pushed him out the door and off the porch. The door slammed and Zander was alone, sprawled in the mud in the pouring rain.

A moment later the door opened and his sobbing mother, clutching Baby Lena and little Willie, staggered through the doorway.

"And don't come back!" yelled the trapper. "You're not his true wife! You're only his country wife, do you hear? Only his country wife!" Then he slammed the door again.

Zander struggled out of the mud and winced as he crawled onto the porch. "What happened, Mama?" he asked, bewildered. "What happened?"

"Hush, you bad boy!" scolded Elaine. "You just ruined your father's wedding!" Then she started to weep. She fell to her knees and put one arm around Zander, one arm holding Baby Lena. His mother's thin body shook with her sobs.

"I didn't mean to, Mama! I didn't mean to!" cried Zander, sobbing with her.

She lifted her wet, streaked face. "Hush, child," she gasped, "it's not your fault." Then she burst into fresh sobs. Zander's face contorted with his tears and then Willie started crying too. The baby awoke and gave a loud wail. They all stood on the porch, crying, until the trapper came out and pushed them off the porch and out into the rainy night.

The next morning, Archibald Durban ordered Elaine and his children away from their small cabin at the fort. He told her they must never return.

Eyes red-rimmed, Zander and his mother and his brother sat listlessly on the wet grass beside the bedraggled, rotting weeds in the fort's garden. Zander held Baby Lena.

A traveling priest approached. When he asked Elaine what ailed her, she told him how she feared she would be unable to feed her three children now that their father would no longer help her. She begged him to take Alexander with him, so the boy could live and study with the Jesuits.

The priest consented.

At noon, Alexander Durban, back straight, eyes dry, said farewell to his mother and brother, kissed the baby on the forehead, and strode after the priest through the fort's open wooden gates. He never looked back.

Chapter One

Late Summer, 1826
Local Trappers' Rendezvous
in the Blue Mountains

"Who the hell is that?"

Alexander Durban dropped his playing cards on the plank table and leaned back to watch the white woman with the flowing blond curls sweep past him, trailed by two rugged trappers as escort. Her long blue dress, which could only have been made in St. Louis, clung to her generous figure. With every proud step she took, a huge yellow ostrich feather bobbed up and down on her blue-and-yellow bonnet.

Jacques Dupuis, a player in the card game,

glanced at Zander's cards.

"That," answered Pierre Renard, the third player, "is Dorie Primfield."

Zander's eyes narrowed as he watched her sashay past the gawking trappers and Indians. He knew he should be watching Renard and Dupuis' sticky fingers, but he couldn't take his eyes off the woman. Not just yet.

"And who," Zander demanded, "is Dorie Primfield?"

Renard slipped himself an extra ace and answered, "Why, *mon ami*! Dorie Primfield is the lovely young sister of Prudence Pomeroy."

Dupuis chimed in. "I 'ave heard the name. She is the wife of the clerk, is she not?"

"*Oui*. Mrs. Pomeroy is good wife to Leland Pomeroy, clerk at Fort Walla Walla."

"Well, that explains the lovely Dorie's presence, then," answered Zander sarcastically as he stared at her.

Renard smiled and slipped himself a king this time. "*Oui*, it does, *mon ami*." He laughed and took pity on Zander. "The lovely Dorie, as you so well describe her, is traveling to Fort Walla Walla to marry Clarence Biddle, chief trader at the fort."

"Haven't heard of him." Zander liked the way she walked. Her hips swayed with each step.

"I don't know much about him, either," admitted Renard. "In command at Fort Walla

24

Walla. Supposed to be a loyal Hudson's Bay Company man."

"Oh."

"Supposed to be a fair trader too. Unless you're Indian." Renard chuckled. "And for mixed-bloods like you, Zander, he charges extra on a trade."

Biddle sounded like an idiot, thought Zander. He brushed a strand of thick black hair back from his face. "Well, she's welcome to him," he snarled.

Dorie Primfield had halted her momentum through the crowd and was talking to one of her escorts. All heads turned to watch her as she leaned over the short, burly trapper, speaking earnestly with him. Zander wondered idly what she was saying as he stared speculatively at her lacy bosom.

"I see you and I raise you," said Dupuis, tossing two coins on the table.

Startled at the reminder of the game, Zander picked up his cards.

Renard plunked down two coins. "I see you and I call you," he said.

Zander laid two coins on the pile, peered at his cards, then shook his head in disgust. He slapped his cards on the table, but his eyes sought out the woman.

"I win!" Renard laughed as he hauled in the money.

*   *   *

Zander glanced around. All the way down to the river he could see the high cones of tepees. In the other direction, all the way back to the foot of the mountains, he could see the square shapes of trappers' tents. Cries and shouts punctuated the air as drunken trappers argued. Someone was singing a French ballad near one of the tents. A haze of smoke in the air stung Zander's nostrils. A loud yell from nearby told him another fight had started. He heard a woman's shrill scream and a man's hoarse laughter.

He pushed his way through the crowd of trappers and fur traders. The smell of unwashed skin, greasy leather, and wood smoke assailed his nostrils. The annual Trappers' Rendezvous had attracted a score of Hudson's Bay Fur Company dignitaries, two score trappers and three score Indians—all here to trade beaver furs for iron axes, rifles, blankets, and liquor.

Zander had attended the Rendezvous hoping to sell enough of his trinkets and trade goods to be able to settle down this year. He was tired of the trading trips back and forth from St. Louis. This was his third, and he hoped last year of making the long journey. This year he would pay back Sebastian and Monvay and be his own man again, owing no one. This year he would have enough money to be his own trader and he would set up a permanent trading post near

Fort George, far to the west at the mouth of the wide Columbia River. Fort George was his boyhood home. There he would receive his trade goods by ship instead of carrying them by mule and horse across leagues of wilderness. That was his plan and it was a good one.

Zander was taller than most of the trappers, and he easily spotted the yellow feather bobbing through the crowd. On a whim, he followed the feather until the sea of humanity suddenly parted and he came face-to-face with Dorie Primfield.

"Oh." Her blue eyes were, surprisingly, almond-shaped as she stared up at him.

He smiled and touched his leather hat brim. A touch of pink grew in her cheeks. So she was flustered, was she? "Good day, Miss Primfield."

"I—I don't believe we have met, sir." She glanced around and brightened. "Mr. Ross," she said, tapping gingerly on the shoulder of a short, burly trapper with a rifle slung across his back. "Do introduce me to this gentleman." She turned and smiled expectantly at Zander as she awaited the introduction.

Clifton Ross, trapper and sometime denizen of Fort Walla Walla, snorted. "That's no gentleman," he snorted. "That's Zander Durban."

Zander could feel his smile tighten.

Dorie paled. "I—I don't believe I've heard—"

"Nothin' to hear about him, Miz Primfield.

27

He's a horse trader and thie—"

"I've had the pleasure of besting Mr. Ross at trading a time or two," interrupted Zander genially. "I see he has not forgotten."

Ross snorted. "You stay away from him, Miz Primfield. He ain't a man for the likes o' you."

Dorie Primfield blushed becomingly. "I only asked to be introduced to him, Mr. Ross. I have no intention of pursuing him." She smiled at Zander as though they were in a conspiracy together.

"You may pursue me anytime you like," Zander said in a low voice. "I promise not to run."

Dorie giggled.

Zander smiled disarmingly. She had a dimple in one cheek. How charming. Not as charming as her heaving bosom, however. He moved closer to see if he could look down the frilly neck of her dress.

"Do you by any chance shoot, Mr.—uh, Durban?" She hesitated. Her skin was a delicate, flushed pink.

"Call me Zander." He touched his hat brim again. "At your service, Miss Primfield."

"Oh, I couldn't. Mr. Durban." Dorie Primfield smiled, and Zander's heart skipped a beat. God, her smile was sweet. Pearly white teeth, pink lips, a nose that was straight and freckled, winged brows . . . Strange. Until this moment he had never been attracted to a white woman.

She was looking at him, her head tilted to one side as though awaiting his answer.

"Uh—uh, shoot?" He stammered, feeling as awkward as a youth talking to his first maiden. He cleared his throat.

Miss Primfield giggled, and he realized suddenly that she was laughing at him. "I said, Mr. Durban, do you shoot?"

He shrugged, turning away coolly, irritated that she had flustered him. "When I have to."

"Come along, Miz Primfield," said Clifton Ross, taking her by the arm. "Your fiance wouldn't want you talkin' to Durban."

"But—but—" sputtered Dorie Primfield as Ross dragged her away, "*I* want to talk to him."

Durban smiled, his pride restored by her hasty admission. He met her last glance over the shoulder.

She smiled back.

Adora Elizabeth Primfield almost put a crick in her neck staring over her shoulder at the extremely handsome man before the crowd closed in behind her. He was tall, his long black hair hinting of something exciting about him.

His eyes, when she'd looked into them, had been the kind of deep, dark brown a woman could get lost in. He wore a fringed leather jacket over a red flannel shirt and a glistening necklet of white dentalia shells and red beads at his throat. His leather pants had long fringe on the sides and, at his waist, he carried a knife and his possibles bag, no doubt containing tobacco and dried meat and anything else he liked to have handy. Over his shoulder was slung his hunting bag containing a powder horn and shot. It was elaborately beaded in red and yellow and blue. She liked the blue-and-white floral beadwork on his jacket too.

Propelled along by Clifton Ross's hand on her arm, she had little choice but to go with him. "I wish I could have found out if he was a good shot," she huffed and unsuccessfully tried to shake her arm loose of Ross's grip.

"Now see here, Miz Primfield." Clifton Ross's voice took on the superior tone he frequently used with her. "I can't have you runnin' after every Indian buck that comes up to talk to you. Why, Mr. Biddle would—"

"I don't care what Mr. Biddle would do," snapped Dorie. "I only wanted to talk to him!"

Ross gave her a sidelong glance. "If I left you alone with that snake for five minutes, I guarantee you wouldn't be talkin'!"

"I can take care of myself, thank you!" she cried.

"No, no, you cain't, Miz Primfield. That's why Mr. Biddle hired me and Billy Bow to watch out for you." He gave her arm a painful squeeze. She winced.

"Now don't be givin' me and Billy any more trouble."

"Let go of my arm, Mr. Ross. Really! Mr. Biddle will certainly hear about how you've mistreated me!"

Clifton Ross thrust his face into hers. She gagged on his whiskey-tainted breath. "Mr. Biddle will hear nothin' but how grateful you are for the escort, *Miz* Primfield." He glared at her, something evil lurking in his black eyes. "Do you understand?"

She plucked his arm off hers. "I understand, Mr. Ross. I understand very well, thank you!"

His grizzled face was full of menace. "Good. You just remember that."

Dorie rubbed her arm and glanced away from him. She didn't like Clifton Ross. Not at all. His partner, Billy Bow, was better, though not by much. She didn't understand why her fiance would send these two rough men to escort her to the fort. Had he any idea what they were like? Evidently not. But she would let him know exactly what she thought of his choice of escorts the minute she arrived at Fort Walla Walla!

"I wish to walk along and look at the trade articles," she said stiffly.

"Very well, Miz Primfield," answered Clifton Ross, dropping back into his laconic trapper role. But Dorie was not fooled. The man was mean and she would do well to beware of him.

31

She passed an array of items set out to entice furs from the Indians. There were knives, awls, bolts of red, yellow, and black calico, and bolts of red flannels and blue silks. There were brass armbands and hawk bells, bolts of ribbon, blue trade beads, and dried raisins on the stem. There was even precious coffee. For the Indian men there was gunpowder, flints, leads, steels for fire-starting, and fragrant, carrot-shaped coils of tobacco.

She walked along, Ross meandering along behind her. They were soon joined by Billy Bow. Billy was the younger of her escorts. His strapping, sandy-haired, gangly youthfulness of four-and-twenty belied the crafty look she'd caught in his eyes. He told Dorie that he'd been trapping for ten years, but she didn't believe him. He'd told her he was a good shot, but she didn't believe that, either. Billy did almost everything Clifton Ross told him to do, unless he thought he could do something without Clifton Ross knowing about it. While sly, he wasn't especially smart, but he was big and, though she hated to admit it, there were a few times on her journey from Rochester, Missouri, when she'd been glad of his brawn.

She glanced now and then at the trade items. She really didn't give two hoots for the brass arm bands, beads, and calico cloth she saw; she'd just told Clifton Ross she did so she would have some relief from him. She already had everything she needed, including a lovely handkerchief as a gift for Prue and an absolutely delightful book of poetry for Mr. Biddle.

She walked past an Indian woman nursing her baby in front of a tepee. Dorie smiled at the woman. The Indian woman met her gaze solemnly.

It would be most fascinating to learn more about Indians, thought Dorie. Back in Rochester, Missouri, Uncle Albert and Aunt Hanna had, unfortunately, few tales to tell. There were no Indians in Rochester. The town had been settled for some time, and the farms around Rochester had long been established. When she was younger, she'd played with Barton Webster and they'd pretended to be Indians, but they really didn't know much.

She wondered how Barton was doing. If he'd improved his rifle aim. She smiled to herself.

She hadn't been surprised when Barton had declared himself, asking Uncle Albert if he might court her. But Dorie had refused; she'd known all along that Barton wasn't the man for her. Not one man in all the farms of Rochester was the right man for her. She needed a man she could admire, a man who could shoot better than she could. And Dorie could drop a squirrel at two hundred paces.

But she had agreed to marry Clarence Biddle,

33

without knowing if he was a good shot or not, and that troubled her a little. Yes it did. Her sister, Prue, had forgotten to include that information in her letters, though Dorie had asked several times.

Dorie sighed. Oh well. She would just have to hope that Mr. Biddle was a good shot. Indeed, Billy Bow had said he was. "Excellent shot," Billy Bow had said, his crafty little eyes moving back and forth. He'd added that Mr. Biddle was a good trader and very rich and made the Hudson's Bay Fur Company a bale of money. Dorie just knew that Mr. Biddle was also handsome. He must be adventurous too, she decided, since he'd chosen to live a frontier life. Her heart beat a little faster as she thought of meeting him. And Prue had assured her in letters that he was "mature and dignified to look upon."

When she'd asked Clifton Ross if Mr. Biddle was a good shot, he'd scratched his beard and looked at Billy Bow. Then he'd allowed as to how he hadn't actually seen Mr. Biddle shoot. But he'd quickly added that Mr. Biddle was real good with numbers. He could add up columns and columns of numbers quicker 'n you could blink your eye. And Mr. Biddle was real good at keeping track of trade goods; why, he could account for every single trade bead in his store, he could.

Dorie hoped Billy Bow was right about Mr.

Biddle being a good shot.

She'd actually had little choice, truth to tell. Her neighbor in Rochester, Barton Webster, had given up persuading her to marry him and gone off to England to marry his English cousin. And most of the young men on the farms were escorting more obliging girls than Dorie.

When Prue's letter had arrived, telling Dorie of this wonderful man, Mr. Clarence Biddle, who was the chief clerk at Fort Walla Walla, and of how he needed a wife and how interested he was in meeting Dorie, it had been at exactly the time when Aunt Hanna and Uncle Albert were talking about selling the farm. Dorie knew they were feeling the pinch of feeding and clothing her though they never, ever said so. Right after she had agreed to travel to Fort Walla Walla to marry Mr. Biddle, all talk of selling the farm ceased.

She was doing the correct thing, she told herself once more, as she had so many times on the journey from Rochester. She could *not* stay and be a burden on elderly Aunt Hanna and Uncle Albert. They had done enough, raising her and her sister, Prue, after Mama and Papa had died in the fire. Even Prue had begun to hint in her letters that she thought the old folks were fearful of running out of money. Dorie knew she must make her own way in the world. It was the proper thing to do.

As she wandered along, looking at the articles set out for trade, Dorie suddenly spotted a pair of broad shoulders.

"Zander Durban," she whispered. Her breath caught. He was holding a rifle and explaining something about it to an Indian man. What was it about Mr. Durban that set her heart to fluttering? she wondered as she stepped closer. She watched him talking with his customer and wondered if Mr. Biddle could possibly be as handsome. She shook off the disloyal thought.

"Good guns," she heard Zander proclaim. Then he proceeded to load the gun with powder. The Plains rifle had a heavy barrel and a chunky stock. Zander showed his rapt audience how much black powder to put down the barrel. "Use only half as much powder as the bullet weighs," he warned. "If you use too much powder, the gun recoils. And always keep your powder dry."

Next, he put the bullet down the long barrel and used the ramrod with a wad of cotton to drive the bullet home. Then he lifted the rifle and aimed at a skinny pine tree about one hundred and fifty yards away. He pulled the trigger. The flint struck the steel, the spark lit the powder, and the gun fired. The loud noise made his customer flinch.

Dorie was so caught up in staring at Zander that she failed to notice if he hit his mark. Irritated with herself, she peered glumly at the tree.

"And never," Zander was saying, "ever put anything down the barrel of a gun except for powder, a bullet, or a ramrod. Understand?"

His customer nodded solemnly.

"No gravel, no rocks. Nothing but a bullet," continued Zander. "If you use gravel or rocks, it will destroy the inside of the barrel. Then the gun is no good."

The Indian nodded thoughtfully.

The loud report of the gun brought Clifton Ross running over. His voice interrupted Dorie's thoughts. "I see you lookin' at him again."

Dorie heard the disgust in his voice and straightened her spine.

"Well, girl, I'm gonna tell you for the last time and you listen! That man is one damned 'breed who is too damned smart for his own good! I should know."

"Why should you know, Mr. Ross?" Dorie fingered some black checked calico she had absolutely no interest in trading for. But she did not want to look at smug, self-righteous Mr. Ross a second longer.

Ross spat. "Because he got me drunk and cheated me out of my best horse."

Dorie's lips quivered as she tried to keep from

laughing. "He got you drunk?" she prodded. That would not be difficult to do, she thought. Many an evening she had seen Ross staggering to his tent.

"Yeah."

Ross's disgust secretly delighted her.

"Before I knew it, I was flat on my back, lookin' at the blue sky and singin' 'My Bonny Lies Over the Ocean'. And he was leadin' away Lightnin', my best horse."

Dorie glanced at him. "Shame on you, Mr. Ross, for letting that man cheat you." She snickered to herself. "Lightning was *such* a good horse, too." She barely remembered the horse, a chestnut in Ross's train of mules and horses, but taunting him about his loss made up for her bruised arm.

"Yeah. Lightnin' was. Still is." He spat. "Anyway, you stay away from that 'breed. He ain't nothin' but trouble."

"Why, Mr. Ross," said Dorie, trying to look all wide eyed and innocent. "Of course."

She watched as Zander Durban concluded the trade with the Indian man. The Indian looked pleased and so did Zander as he carefully laid aside the five furs the trade had brought him.

She stared at his broad shoulders and lean frame. He took off his leather jacket and rolled up the sleeves of his red shirt. He wore etched brass armbands on both forearms. He was taller than most of the other men present. And certainly handsomer. Much handsomer than Barton Webster.

She took a step closer. When he bent down and stroked one of the furs, she felt herself yearning for just such a touch.

The sunlight caught his thick, blue-black hair and the strong line of his jaw. Ah, the strength of those shoulders, those arms . . .

Lordy, but she hoped that Mr. Biddle was even half as handsome.

Chapter Two

Zander smiled lazily as he studied his cards. He took a sip of whiskey, then threw a coin on the table. "I call you," he said to Dupuis.

Dupuis plunked down a coin. He spread his cards on the table. "It was a lousy hand," he muttered.

Pierre Renard smirked. "I win," he crowed. "I always win!"

"That's because you cheat," said Dupuis.

"I do not," said Renard, looking affronted. "I am verr, verr lucky!"

"Oho! So that's what it's called. I saw you palm that queen—"

"Gentlemen," interrupted Zander, "I know you both cheat. Someday, someone will no doubt shoot one of you for it, but it won't be me. I like your conversation. And your company. So shut up and play."

They played cards for a while longer, drinking whiskey and talking about where the best beaver pelts could be found. All agreed that the furs were not as plentiful as they once had been. And strangely, prices were down too. Maybe the London gents weren't wearing beaver top hats anymore.

"This is my last trading trip," observed Zander.

"What?" cried Renard. "Won't we see you anymore, *mon ami*?"

Zander laughed at his friend's disappointed expression. "I'll still pass through here once in a while," he chuckled. "But I'm heading west, to the mouth of the Columbia River."

Dupuis hooted. "*Sacre bleu*! Why would anyone go there?"

Zander answered gravely, "My people are there. My Indian people. It's time I lived among them. Settled down."

Renard slapped his knee. "Ho, ho, that is a good joke, Zander. You? Settle down? Ho, ho! You are a funny man."

Zander smiled tolerantly. He liked Renard and Dupuis.

"I've got enough now to repay Sebastian and Monvay.

"How is old Sebastian?" asked Dupuis.

Zander almost choked on his whiskey. "He's younger than you, Dupuis."

Dupuis gave a shrug, unconcerned.

"Sebastian's doing well," continued Zander. "Slowing down a bit. Monvay takes good care of him."

"Ah, Monvay," Dupuis kissed his fingers, "the Beautiful."

Zander smiled. "Still beautiful, even though she's gray now," he acknowledged. "Why, if it wasn't for her and Sebastian, I wouldn't have had the money for the rifles or the tobacco or the bolts of cloth. They started me out in trading. And now I have enough to pay them back."

"*Oui*, they are good friends to you. And to Father Ambroise, are they not?"

"Yes. Father Ambroise stays with them frequently."

"How is the old man?"

Zander smiled sadly. "Father Ambroise is very old. Every time I see him, I expect it to be the last."

"Ah," Renard wiped a tear from his eye. "He is a good priest."

"Those Jesuits, they help plenty of people," acknowledged Dupuis. "One time I was verr sick. It was over by Fort Walla Walla, what we used to call Fort Nez Perces. It was winter. Cold. I thought I was dying. I'm lying in the snow, breathing my verr last breath, and this huge man comes along. Black as the night he was. I think to myself, 'This is it, Dupuis. You going to die and you going straight to hell. Here's the demon to take you there!' " Dupuis took a swig of whiskey, enjoying his audience's attention. "That's what I think. This demon come to take me to hell. I faint. When I wake up, this black demon, he's pouring something down my throat. Tastes awful. I try to spit it out and I sit up. He laughs. Well, I never heard of anyone laughing down in hell, so I asks 'Where am I?' He tells me, then tells me he's a Jesuit. I stare. I never seen a black Jesuit before." Dupuis shook his head at the memory. "He was verr good to me. Make me drink that medicine. Tasted like beaver piss, but he make me drink it. Three times a day. And you know what? I got better!"

"Never heard of a priest like that one," observed Zander. "But I tell you, old Father Ambroise, the Jesuit, he helped me too. When my white father"—he put a sneer on the word—"kicked me out of Fort George, I was just a boy. It was the Jesuits and Father Ambroise who took me in. Educated me."

"They teach you to play cards?" asked Renard. "They teach you to drink like a fish?"

"No," laughed Zander. "I learned that from you."

"They help me too," said Dupuis. "I drink the medicine three times a day. Now I'm strong and healthy. Look!" He held up his right arm and flexed his bicep muscle.

"*Oui*, look at you," observed Renard. "So strong I can beat you at arm wrestling using only my leetle beety finger."

"You cannot!" exclaimed Dupuis.

"*Oui*, I can."

"I challenge you," cried Dupuis. "Right after this card game. We will arm wrestle!" He slapped a gold coin on the table. "We will see who is the strong and healthy one around here!"

"Verr well," agreed Renard. "You force me to take your gold. As easy as stealing furs from a drunken trapper, it is."

Dupuis cackled, "*Oui*, we will see who is the drunken trapper."

After a moment, Zander remarked, "Put the ace back on the table, Renard."

Disappointed, Renard placed the ace, face up, on the table.

"You got any more up your sleeve?"

"*Mais non!* How could you think such a thing?" Renard contrived to look hurt.

Zander laughed. "That's what I like about you, Renard. You and Dupuis. You cheat all men alike, regardless of color."

"We do," chorused Dupuis and Renard.

* * *

Dorie sat beside the fire and nibbled at her lunch: cold cornbread left over from last night's supper. In between bites, she put twigs on the fire and poked around among the embers. It was pleasant to sit and watch the trappers and Indians wandering about.

And how fortunate that she and her escorts had found a place to set up their tents, just on the outskirts of the trading area. On the other side of a small hill, she could see the pointed cones of tepees.

A man walked past her tent. Her pulse quickened. Was that Zander Durban?

Clifton Rose and Billy Bow played cards in front of their tent, set next to hers. They were arguing loudly and hadn't noticed Zander.

Dorie's eyes followed the handsome mixed-blood. He moved gracefully, she thought. She liked his broad shoulders and long legs. He wore moccasins and seemed to prowl along the trail. Why, he could easily sneak up on a deer or a bear or a—

Just then Clifton Ross chanced to glance up, and his shrewd black eyes met hers. He got up and came sauntering over. "I told you about him," he warned.

"Mr. Ross," she said with as much dignity as she could muster. "The man merely walked by. It is my understanding that we are all free to come and go as we please at the Rendezvous."

"*We* are. *You* are not," he snarled. "Mr. Biddle wants you to arrive at Fort Walla Walla all in one piece—if you get my meanin'."

She gasped. "Mr. Ross! I will not tolerate your rude talk! Your manners are deplorable, your—"

The short, stocky trapper leaned down and faced her squarely. "I don't care about manners. I don't even care about you. My job is to get you to Fort Walla Walla, and by God, I'll do it. So you can just stop lookin' at that 'breed. Now!" He barked the last word and Dorie recoiled.

"Mr. Ross," she said, her voice shaking in anger, "when we arrive at Fort Walla Walla, I assure you, no one will be happier than I!" She had a great many complaints to tell Mr. Biddle—oh yes, she did! And every single one of them was about this infernal Mr. Clifton Ross!

"That 'breed cheats at cards. He gets honest white folks drunk and steals their horses. He has a special set of Indian rifles that he trades only to Indians! He is trouble, I tell you. Nothin' but trouble!"

Dorie's mouth worked. Oh, how she wanted to answer him rudely!

"Go to your tent!" he ordered.

Furious, her face red, Dorie rose and marched to her tent, her back stiff. Then she stopped and whirled. "No, Mr. Ross, I will not." She marched back to the fire and plunked herself back down on the blanket. "I will sit here for as long as I like!" She was so angry, she was shaking, but she would defy this tyrant, yes she would!

Ross crept closer and Dorie could see the rage in his eyes. His hands were huge fists as he raised them.

"Clifton!" Billy Bow's alarmed voice halted the furious trapper. "Let her alone!" Billy hurried over. He touched his partner's arm. "We'll be at Fort Walla Walla soon. We deliver her then. No sense in makin' trouble now."

Dorie was relieved to see that his sensible words had a calming effect on Ross. The squat trapper dropped his fists. He shook himself, straightening. "You're right, Billy." He eyed Dorie balefully. "I need them furs."

"Yeah. Biddle promised us them furs for her delivery."

He led Ross back to their fire. Dorie let out her breath. Clifton Ross was a nasty man. Why, back home in Rochester, Aunt Hanna would certainly never have invited such a man into her parlor. And here, in the wilderness, Dorie had to travel with him! Aunt Hanna would burn her biscuits if she knew what Dorie was putting up with.

Dorie poked at the fire and bit into her cornbread again, but her appetite had fled. She put on her bonnet and picked up her reticule. Defiantly, she approached the trappers' fire. "I want to go for a walk and look at the trade goods," she told Billy Bow. Clifton Ross she ignored.

Billy traipsed after her, doing his duty of keeping other trappers and traders at bay.

Dorie sauntered along, wondering about the lives of the people she passed. What was it like to be an Indian? she wondered as she passed an Indian woman plodding behind her man. A trapper stopped to talk to Billy, and Dorie thought his life must be very exciting, what with living in the wilderness, fighting off bears, and trapping beaver. The trapper concluded his conversation with Billy. Dorie sauntered on.

Suddenly she saw *him*. He was standing near a bale of furs and showing a rifle to an interested trapper holding a horse.

She stopped. She shouldn't be staring, she knew she shouldn't, but it couldn't hurt just to watch him.

"Miz Primfield," came Billy's voice, "I thought Mr. Ross warned you about him."

"Oh, he did, Billy. He did." She dug in her reticule and came up with a shiny coin. "Here, Billy. Why don't you go and find something to purchase?" She smiled and batted her eyelashes at him.

But Billy's eyes had fastened on the coin. "I'll do that, Miz Primfield," he said.

She smiled as she watched him wander over to where a trader had a fancy display of beads, tobacco, and whiskey. Let Billy amuse himself, she thought. Now she was free to wander and look at the wares. No harm would come to her with so many people around.

Mr. Durban hadn't noticed her, so she moved a little closer, close enough to hear what he was saying.

"That mare is club-footed," he was saying to the trapper. "What do I want with a club-footed horse? I'd have to get new shoes made for her." He looked in the animal's mouth. "And look, this isn't some young spring filly you're trying to trade here. This horse is twenty years old if it's a day."

"That horse is my best horse," pleaded the trapper. "Traded her from the Pawnee."

"Yeah? Well, that's my best gun."

"That gun ain't worth beaver droppings."

"Then why do you want it?"

The trapper looked frustrated.

Mr. Durban turned away, blatantly looking for other customers.

"How 'bout I give you the horse and one fur?" whined the trapper. "I need a rifle."

Zander Durban glanced at him. "This rifle is made by Hawkens, one of the best rifle makers in the land. I'd be a fool to part with it for a club-footed horse and one mangy fur."

"Two furs?"

"Let me see them."

The trapper laid out the furs and Mr. Durban perused them thoughtfully.

"Three furs and it's a deal."

The trapper grinned, and rifle and horse exchanged hands. Mr. Durban tied the horse to a barrel nearby and then carefully laid the three furs on a pile of pelts beside his rifles. He looked pleased with himself.

Her heart pounding, Dorie tried to muster the courage to go approach him. Just to stand and look at him would be reward enough, she thought. She must think up something to ask him, to have a reason for approaching him. Just as she took a step, however, three hardened-looking Indian men called his name.

Her shoulders slumped as she watched him greet the men. They sauntered over, and soon all four were talking and laughing.

Disappointed, Dorie watched the Indians. One of them was tall and wore his hair in two long black braids. His leather clothes were beaded with blue and green and white bird designs. He carried a rifle slung across his back.

Another of the men had a long scar on his face that made his mouth turn down. He looked sad, thought Dorie.

The third wore unadorned leather clothes, tunic and pants, and a broad-brimmed leather hat with a black feather stuck in it. His long black hair hung loose down his back.

Dorie stared, her curiosity bubbling up. Who were they? Where did they come from? Just before her journey West, she'd read a book by the famous Professor Henry Humbert. He told of many strange things in the North American wilderness. Had these Indians seen any of the strange things Professor Humbert had mentioned in his book? Perhaps they had!

She watched Mr. Durban's white teeth flash in a grin as he joked with one of the men. Finally, her curiosity driving her, she walked over. "Oh, Mr. Durban?"

A hushed silence fell over the merry group as all four men stared at her. Dorie felt herself flush, but she forced herself to take another step. She would not be afraid—she would not!

Mr. Durban touched the brim of his leather hat and pushed it back a little. "Miss Primfield. How are you?"

"Very well, thank you," she answered brightly, pleased that the conversation was going so well. His black hair shone in the sun, and those dark eyes . . .

"Uh, Mr. Durban," she said bravely, "I have been reading Professor Humbert's noted treatise, 'Cogitations and Ruminations on the Northern American Wilderness'. Perhaps you've heard of it?" At his puzzled shake of the head, she continued, "He is a noted professor at Essexbridge College in England. Though he has never visited our vast continent, he is extremely informed about it. Why, in his article, Professor Humbert says that there are still mammoths walking around in the wilderness. I am intensely curious to know, sir, have you seen one?"

"Mammoths?" Mr. Durban drew back.

"Professor Humbert also says," continued Dorie excitedly, "that the Indian's blood is a different color from ours. I must know, sir, what color is your blood?"

One of the Indians dropped his jaw in undisguised surprise. The other two visitors stared at her impassively.

"Back home in Rochester," she fumbled, "there were no Indians, and I was just wondering—that is, Professor Humbert said no one knew—"

"You can stop wondering, Miss Primfield," answered Mr. Durban. She saw to her surprise that he looked angry. "Ross! Billy!" he roared. "Billy Bow! Get over here! Now!"

He glanced at his friends. "Where the hell are Ross and Bow?" he muttered.

"Oh, Mr. Bow is off buying whiskey," Dorie answered brightly. "But I do not believe he has read Professor Humbert's learned treatise—"

"Miss Primfield," Mr. Durban interrupted through tight lips.

Just then, Billy Bow came staggering up. Mr. Durban took Dorie by the arm and thrust her at the trapper. "Get her away from me," he ordered.

"Huh?" Billy weaved a little, trying to stand straight.

"I said, take this woman away. I don't want her near me!"

Dorie stared in open-mouthed shock. "But—but—"

"*Now*, Billy!" Mr. Durban warned.

Dorie clamped her mouth shut, then blurted out, "But all I wanted to know was the color of your blood!"

"Keep her away from me!" snorted Mr. Durban. He looked as if he'd stepped on a snake.

Billy Bow latched onto her arm and pulled. "Come on, Miz Primfield."

Dorie stood her ground. "I will not be treated like this! I—"

"Billy Bow!" yelled Mr. Durban.

"Pleeeease, Miz Primfield," begged Billy Bow.

Her cheeks burning, Dorie stared helplessly at a fuming Mr. Durban as the trapper dragged her away.

Chapter Three

Zander glared at his friends. No one dared say a word after Dorie Primfield was escorted away. What in hell was the matter with the woman?

Etienne and Charles soon bade him farewell. They had brought in two seasons' worth of furs and were anxious to get a good price from either the Hudson's Bay Company or its rival, the Pacific Fur Company. The big companies could be prodded to pay more for furs than independent traders like Zander could.

Zander's best friend, Anton Thunder Horse, swung his two braids over his shoulder and clapped Zander on the back. "You had enough trading for a while, Zander? Let us get a drink."

Zander agreed. They headed over to a tent

where a fat, balding man was pouring a steady stream of whiskey from a wooden cask directly into his customers' tin cups.

Zander and Anton got their tin cups filled and moved out of the way of the other customers. They found a place under the tent awning in the shade, for the day was warm.

Zander took a sip of the whiskey. It went down his throat smoothly.

"What color *is* your blood?" asked Anton.

Zander choked and spewed the whiskey out. "What the hell color do you think? What the hell color is *yours*?"

Anton laughed. "Last time I was stabbed it was—let's see—yeah, it was red."

Zander glared at him.

"Remember the time you saved my life, old friend?" Anton was grinning over his tin cup.

"I didn't save your life," growled Zander.

Anton laughed. "You did. That trapper at the card table was going to shoot me—right through the heart. He only winged me in the arm because you knocked his pistol aside. Said I'd cheated."

"You didn't cheat. Every man there knew that."

"Yeah, but only you spoke up. You stopped him, or I'd have been a dead man."

Zander narrowed his eyes.

"Remember?" continued Anton. "We went to

that cabin while my arm healed. Had to hide out a while. That trapper was madder 'n a grizzly bear!" Anton glanced at Zander's frown and grinned. "So maybe you're wishing that trapper *had* shot me?"

Zander laughed and slapped his friend on the back. "Naw, I'm glad you're alive, Anton. That's the God's truth."

The two had a toast to that.

"Who was the woman?" asked Anton after a while.

Zander didn't want to answer, but Anton could be a persistent man. "Dorie Primfield," Zander answered reluctantly and took a sip of whiskey so he wouldn't have to say any more.

"Good looking woman," observed Anton.

Zander shrugged. "If you like blue and yellow and bobbing feathers."

They both chuckled and Zander felt the smile linger. She *had* looked attractive in her blue dress with her yellow feather bobbing up and down.

"Her escort had a hard time dragging her away," Anton recalled. "Didn't look like she was in any hurry to leave our company, eh?"

Zander smiled. "No. She didn't."

Suddenly Anton tensed. "Zander, did you say her name was Dorie Primfield?"

"That's her name."

"Oh, beavershit!"

He had Zander's attention. "What is it?"

"Dorie Primfield," said Anton slowly, "is the woman who is traveling to Fort Walla Walla to marry Clarence Biddle."

Zander took another sip. "That so? How do you know so much?"

Anton wasn't grinning now. "My sister, Mary, has a child by him. She's pregnant with her second." He snorted. "She just happens to be Clarence Biddle's country wife!"

Zander strode through the crowd at the Rendezvous, trying to work off his anger. "That damn Biddle," he muttered aloud. "Why, he's no better than my old man!"

He headed away from the crowds and along the trail to the remuda, where the trappers' horses and mules were corralled. Two boys lounged against the rough wooden fence, guarding the animals. Though they looked young, they carried rifles. No one was going to steal a horse or mule this day.

When Anton had told him that Dorie was replacing his sister, Zander had felt his blood heat up. Zander had known Mary for as long as he'd known Anton. Why, she was a like a younger sister to him! He'd watched her grow up these past years, stopping in to visit the family on each trading trip. He'd watched her grow more beautiful with each passing season. And now she was Biddle's country wife!

He ploughed his fist into his hand. Damn, but life just wasn't fair! That a lovely girl like Mary could end up as Biddle's country wife . . . Zander shook his head, not wanting to believe it.

What the hell was a blond piece of fluff like Dorie doing taking away another woman's husband? A little child, Mary had. A girl. And another baby on the way.

Zander clenched his fists. Then Anton had told him that Mary was actually Biddle's second country wife. Biddle had already set aside his first country wife, a Nez Perce woman, to legally marry a white woman. The white wife had later died in childbirth. Anton's sister, Mary, was now Biddle's second country wife and, according to Anton, Biddle planned to set her aside for Dorie.

Neither Anton nor Mary wanted that to happen. Not Mary, because she was pregnant again and loved Biddle, and not Anton, because although he didn't like his sister's choice of mate, he didn't want to see his sister hurt. Mary was very upset that Biddle was sending for Dorie, and she had almost miscarried once.

What a fool Zander had been to see only Dorie Primfield's pretty face and blond hair. He had to laugh at himself for that one, he thought angrily. He'd been amused by her, attracted to her, while inside she was a cruel, uncaring woman. She was taking a father and husband away from an Indian woman, just like Jane Potter had taken his father away from his mother!

Zander's mouth set in a grim line as he remembered bitterly. His father had lived to regret his decision to marry Jane Potter. Over the years, Zander's brother, Willie, and his young sister, Lena, had written letters to Zander telling him how Archibald would occasionally sneak away to visit their mother. If Jane knew, she never said anything. In fact, the cur Archibald and his mother had two more children, but unfortunately both died, along with his parents, in the influenza epidemic of 1816.

And now Mary—pretty, sweet Mary—was going to be replaced by Dorie Primfield! He clenched his fists at the thought. Mary deserved better!

Dark memories of the day his father had cast his mother aside flooded Zander's mind. Anger roiled in him. His precious family had been torn apart. He'd been sent away to live with strangers. And Willie and the baby and his mother had been forced to live in a small space of the crowded family longhouse. They'd eaten others' leftovers until finally Willie was old enough to hunt and fish for food and demand a larger area to live in.

It was wrong that his friend's sister would be set aside for Primfield. Soon Mary and her innocent child would be forced to beg scraps and handouts at Fort Walla Walla! The country wife was about to be cast aside so that Miss Dorie Primfield—Miss Dorie Primfield who couldn't tell a beaver pelt from a Hudson's Bay blanket— could marry Biddle and have her lavish clothes, her three meals a day, her stupid bobbing feathers.

Zander spat in disgust.

Zander stomped back up the trail to the Rendezvous, anxious to get another drink. Damn it anyway! He was still so angry he could hardly think. Damn Anton for telling him about his sister. And damn Dorie Primfield for her reckless disregard for anyone else!

Fuming, Zander strode along. He'd almost reached the whiskey tent when he heard his name called. He swung around.

"Oh, Mr. Durban," Dorie Primfield rushed up to him breathlessly and took his hand. "I must beg your forgi—"

Zander shook her hand off. "You'll be just another trade item in Biddle's store!" he roared.

Her face drained of color, she stared up at him. Her long-lashed blue eyes looked huge in her shocked face.

"You are a useless, pampered woman— you're a luxury at the expense of other women!"

Dorie's mouth moved open and closed, but no words came out.

"The sight of you sickens me!" yelled Zander. Tears welled in Dorie's eyes, but he ignored them. "You should leave this country and go back to wherever the hell you came from!" Then he turned on his heel and stalked away.

Somehow she regained her voice because he heard her, shrill and shaking, behind him. "You, sir, are just a savage! I see I can expect no other treatment from you!"

Zander whirled and came back to her. "Is that so?" he cried. He seized her, and planted a kiss right on her lips. He lifted his head. "Savage am I? By God, I'll show you savage!" He took his time with the second kiss. His lips moved over hers. He forced her mouth open with his tongue and then he plunged into her, in a vivid act of mating. He pressed her against him so she could feel his arousal.

She squirmed. He held her to him, one hand pushing her backside so that she squirmed against him even more.

She tried to pull away from him, but he held her and soon the kiss became more than a kiss. He wanted her. God, how had this happened? He wanted her!

He pulled her closer. The kiss held and held. . . .

She went still and leaned into him. Now her

tongue was touching his, tentatively. . . .

He pulled back, gasping for air. How had this happened to him?

"There you go, Miss Dorie Primfield!" he snarled. "You've just been kissed by a savage. And," he added triumphantly, "you liked it! Now get the hell out of my sight!"

She raised her fist to her mouth as though to stem her outcry. He read humiliation and horror in her shocked blue gaze.

She whirled and ran in the direction of her tent.

He watched her go, his chest heaving. Hoots from the onlookers entered his awareness. "What the hell you looking at?" he yelled. The snickering men moved away. He was left alone.

She deserved it, he told himself. The little witch deserved it!

He glanced around and spotted his friend. "Anton!"

The younger man weaved over to him. " 'Lo, Zander," he slurred softly.

"You been drinking too much whiskey, Anton?"

Anton grinned. "It's good stuff," he said sheepishly. "Tastes real good."

"Yeah." Zander smeared his own lips with his hand, wiping off the taste of woman. "Come on, Anton. We've got plans to make. Mary needs to be protected!"

"Eh?" Anton looked bewildered.

Zander felt the surge of anger, only now it was cold. Clear. He knew what he had to do. "Anton, listen to me."

Anton swayed on his feet and Zander steadied him. "Miss Dorie Primfield is not going to marry Clarence Biddle," stated Zander.

"She's not?" Anton blinked blearily.

"No, she's not! You see, *we* are going to stop her!"

Chapter Four

Dorie sat in her tent. She'd changed into her ankle-length white chemise in readiness for sleep. But sleep wouldn't come. So she sat up and brushed her hair another one hundred strokes until her scalp tingled. Then she tied her hair into two long pigtails on either side of her head and, to amuse herself, tied big pink bows on both pigtails. She tucked the hairbrush back into her carpetbag, placing it carefully on the book of poetry she'd brought as a gift for Mr. Biddle. Under the book of poetry she'd hidden her little pistol.

Dreamily, she touched her lips. Memories of Mr. Durban's—no, Zander's—kiss came flooding back. He had given her her first real kiss.

She shivered and hugged herself.

His mouth had been bold and exciting. She remembered touching his tongue with hers, and she flushed anew. Her first kiss!

Barton Webster's kiss beneath the apple tree didn't count. He had merely pressed his closed lips to hers for three seconds—she'd counted—and then it was over.

But Zander's kiss had been something else. She tightened her arms around herself in the privacy of her tent. And oh, what feelings had enveloped her when he'd pulled her against him! She trembled again in delight at the memory.

If only he had not been so angry. She'd had no idea that her questions could anger him so. What had she said? Oh, yes. She had simply asked about mammoths. Anything else? Oh, yes, and about what color his blood was. Why, she pondered with a frown, would he take such offense? Well, she must remember not to bring up those subjects next time she talked to him. *If* there was a next time.

Her cheeks flushed as she remembered him telling her to get out of his sight. How could he say such a thing?

It looked as if there would never be a next time!

Perhaps he didn't like to be asked about mammoths. Her brow furrowed. She still didn't know what color his blood was. Yes, next time she'd stay away from those topics. Perhaps next time she'd ask him about his mother.

And his kiss. His kiss had sent shivers from the top of her head to the very tips of her toes. She lay back on her blankets, eyes shut, reliving the moment over and over. My, but that kiss had stirred her! Aunt Hanna would have been astonished.

He'd accused her of enjoying his kiss. And he was right, of course. She *had* enjoyed it. She didn't mean to, she just couldn't help herself. And she would still marry Mr. Biddle. Did Mr. Biddle kiss so well?

Dorie got to her knees and crawled over to the tent's opening and peeked outside. Should she ask someone about the kiss? About the shivery feelings she got whenever she thought of it? And who should she ask?

Billy Bow and Clifton Ross were sitting by their fire, singing and playing cards. As she watched, Billy Bow lifted his tin cup and took a long draught.

Dorie tried to picture herself asking Billy Bow about Zander's kiss. She shook her head. No. Not Billy Bow.

Clifton Ross? She was even less inclined to ask him. Oh, what should she do?

She ducked back into the tent. Should she wait until she got to the fort and ask Prue?

She imagined Prue's reaction. Prue was always so . . . so prudish. As children she had always taken the role of the proper schoolteacher or the fussy mother in their games. No, not Prue. And Aunt Hanna was so far away. . . .

Dorie wrung her hands. Oh dear, what to do? She couldn't get Zander's kiss out of her mind.

After a time of hand wringing, Dorie put her long black cape over her chemise and crept out of the tent.

It was dark, and though she could see her escorts sitting beside their fire, still she stumbled once or twice on her way to them. "Billy? Mr. Ross?"

"Over here," came Billy's voice. Then he started to sing a long, droning rendition of "Greensleeves."

Dorie waited patiently until he was done. She took courage from the fact that both her escorts looked very relaxed. Billy Bow looked so relaxed that he almost fell into the fire. Perhaps, since they were so relaxed, they would not take offense at her questions.

She sat down on a rock beside the fire. Before Billy Bow could begin another song, she interjected, "Mr. Ross, do tell me something more about Mr. Durban."

Clifton Ross glanced at her, then at the fire, and took another sip of his whiskey. "Tol' you before, Miz Primfiel'. He's trouble."

She could always tell when Clifton Ross was

drunk by how badly he mispronounced her name. From the sound of it, he was well on his way to inebriation. "Yes, yes, Mr. Ross, you've told me that. But I want to know more. I want to know what he did that you should dislike him so."

"Tol' you, he cheated me outa my horshh."

"Your horse? Oh. Yes, you told me that."

He took another gulp of his whiskey. "We sat down to drink together, me and him. He had a black mare I wanted. I had Lightnin'. Cheshhnut. Geldin'. I says, real nice-like, 'Leshh have friendly drink. Then we'll talk about your mare. Make a trade.'" Ross swayed. "So we sat down, man-to-man. I drink. He drinks. I talk. He talks."

Dorie waited while Clifton Ross refilled his mug with whiskey. When he was done, he took a long draught and stared at the fire.

"You were telling me how Mr. Durban cheated you out of your horse," she prodded.

Clifton Ross peered at her and blinked. "Yeah. I ain't forgot." He took a long sip of whiskey. "Well, I drink. He drinks. I talk. He talks. I keep waiting for him to get dru—" Clifton Ross shifted a little. "Uh, for him to offer for my horshh. I tell him Lightnin' is good horshh. But he laugh. Says my horshh is 'spavined wonder.' Them his words. Ever hear Indian talk sshho fancy?" He shook his head, baffled.

Dorie smiled to herself. That sounded like Zander.

"Next thing I 'member ish I'm laid out on my back, lookin' up at the sky. He'shh leadin' away geldin' and I'm left holdin' a rusty old rifle. Don't shoot worth a damn."

Dorie smothered a laugh. From the gaps in his story, she guessed that Ross had tried to get Zander drunk to best him in the trade—but Ross was the one who got bested.

"He'shh a wily one, Mish Primfeeeel'. Wily one. Stay away from the likeshh o' him." Clifton Ross took a great gulp of whiskey and wiped his mouth with the back of his arm. Then he stared, swaying, at the fire.

Dorie thanked him and left, stumbling only once on her way back to her tent. She removed her black cape and crawled under the blankets, feeling truly tired. Clifton Ross's warning rang in her ears. "He's right," she murmured. "He's absolutely right. Zander is wily and not to be trusted!"

Chapter Five

"Pssst, Anton! Anton, wake up!" Zander grimaced as he bent down and shook his friend. "Wake up, Anton."

"Huh?" Groggily, Anton opened his eyes. "What you want?" Then he promptly closed his eyes and snored.

"Anton," hissed Zander, "we're going to kidnap Dorie Primfield, remember? We planned it. To keep her away from your sister and Biddle and Fort Walla Walla. Anton!" Zander shook the Nez Perce man again. "Wake up, Anton!"

Anton opened his eyes and blinked several times. "I remember," he said. "The kidnapping." He glanced around, his eyes bleary in the light of the full moon. "Where is she?"

"She's not kidnapped yet!" Zander wanted to throttle his friend. "Why are you so tired?" He caught a whiff of Anton's breath. "Whiskey! That explains it."

Zander stood up. "How the hell am I going to kidnap her alone?" he muttered. "It's going to be hard enough to get her, never mind her luggage."

"The fort," murmured Anton, struggling to rise to his feet. "We're taking her to the fort . . . uh, from the fort . . ."

"Yeah, we'll take her to Fort McCraig. And that's *after* we kidnap her from here. Damn, Anton! Why'd you have to pick this time to get drunk?"

Anton weaved on his feet. "Worried," he answered, "about Mary."

"You're worried about Mary."

Anton nodded. "Feel better now. No worries." He peered at Zander. "Whatsssa matter?"

"You're a good man, Anton. But you got a little problem with the whiskey."

Anton looked surprised as he swayed back and forth. "Think so?"

"Yeah." Zander glanced around. He'd already loaded all three of his packhorses and the mule. They were ready for a quick escape. "Anton," he said, taking his friend's arm firmly. "Listen to me."

Anton weaved. "Listening," he muttered.

"You take the horses," directed Zander. "Wait with them at the head of the trail. I'll get Dorie and meet you there. Got that?"

Silence. Anton listed to one side and looked about to totter over.

"Anton?"

"Yeah?"

"Did you hear what I said?"

"Wait at head of trail," he muttered.

Zander nodded, "Good!" He clapped his friend on the back. "Be ready to ride. Fast." He looked at his friend doubtfully.

Anton laughed. "Yeah."

Zander didn't feel like laughing. His stomach clenched in a sick knot of dread. Now he had to kidnap Dorie *and* make sure Anton got the horses to the head of the trail. He glanced up the trail. "Come on, Anton."

Anton dutifully followed Zander. Zander mounted his mare, Shadow. She was a well-trained black mare with a white blaze on her forehead. Zander patted her on the neck, while he watched Anton mount his own horse. Anton made it into the saddle on the third try.

"Let's go," muttered Zander. They rode to the head of the trail. It was well screened with trees and far enough from the Rendezvous that they would have a good start ahead of any pursuers.

Zander dismounted and walked over to Anton. Anton lurched at an odd angle. Zander dragged his friend out of the saddle and put an arm around him. Together they staggered to a small creek. Zander splashed water on his friend's face.

"Hey!" sputtered Anton.

"That's better." Zander splashed him again for good measure. He stepped back.

Anton swayed, shaking his head and brushing the water from his face. "That's cold."

"Good."

They headed back to the horses. Anton approached his chestnut and mounted on the second try this time.

"Here's the lead rein." Zander handed him the reins that led the three packhorses and mule. "Be ready to ride as soon as I get here."

"Yeah." Anton sounded subdued.

Zander surveyed the horses and his friend one last time. Convinced that it was as right as it was ever going to be, he mounted his mare and patted her neck. "Let's go, Shadow." He nudged his heels into her side.

Horse and rider galloped down the trail until they reached the Rendezvous. By the light of the moon, Zander could see campfire embers burning here and there. It was about two a.m. Two traders argued with each other at one of the fires, but Zander guessed that most trappers were asleep. He certainly hoped that Clifton Ross and Billy Bow were sleeping soundly.

But just to be sure, he stopped at the tepee of his old friend, Etienne. Etienne would make sure that Billy Bow and Clifton Ross were fully occupied, should they awaken.

Zander trod softly; his moccasins kept his steps silent. He'd warned Shadow to be quiet and the mare followed behind him. He reached Dorie's tent and left the mare's reins to dangle. He took two coils of rope and a white, ragged piece of cloth off his saddle. "Stand!" he whispered, confident the big mare would obey.

He peered over at Billy Bow and Clifton's tent. Their fire was a mere orange flicker. Snores drifted from their tent.

Zander crept in under Dorie's canvas tent. It was dark inside. He waited until his eyes adjusted. Then he saw her.

She lay on her stomach, her head cushioned by one arm and a blanket drawn up to her waist. He could easily see the white blur of her chemise. He heard the soft sounds of her breathing and crept closer. Her hair was in two pigtails, tied with ribbons. God, she looked sweet, lying there.

He had to harden his heart. She was going to marry Clarence Biddle and displace Mary. That must not happen! He and Anton had made plans to take Dorie to Fort McCraig and leave her there. They must keep her away from Fort

Walla Walla and Biddle—and Mary. Zander knew he must go through with the plan; otherwise, Mary's and her children's lives would be destroyed.

Zander glanced around the tent, looking for a sack or some sign of her possessions. He spotted a lumpy carpetbag. He pushed it under the canvas tent at the rear, so that he could retrieve the carpetbag once he got Dorie on the horse.

He crept back to Dorie. Gently, he ran a finger along her cheek. Her skin was soft and warm. Hungrily, he leaned over her.

Her eyes opened. She pushed herself up on her hands. "Who are you?" she cried in sleepy bewilderment.

"Hush!" He cupped his hand over her mouth. Damn, where was the rope and the rag? He groped for them, felt the rope, found the rag.

Dorie tried to sit up. "Mmmmfff!"

He tied the rag over her mouth to silence her, then swiftly grabbed both her wrists. She tried to yank her hands out of his grip, but he held on. Her fingers turned to claws and she scratched him twice before he could tie her wrists together. By now she was out of the blanket and her chemise had hiked up.

He stared at a long expanse of thigh. Sweat broke out on his brow. This was going to be more difficult than he'd thought.

He swallowed and pulled her chemise down

to cover her long, pale legs. His hand brushed smooth flesh. "I've got to get you out of here," he muttered in her ear.

She tried to elbow him in the stomach, but he sidestepped to avoid it. He propelled her toward the rear of the tent. She dug in her feet.

"Move," he ordered.

"Mmmmmmmphhh." Whatever she'd said, he knew what it meant: "No."

"Hell," he muttered. He picked her up and carried her the little distance. She kicked and squirmed and tried to lunge out of his arms. He gripped her as tightly as he could. Her soft body pressed on his intimate parts as he carried her. He groaned.

They reached the rear canvas wall and he set her on her feet. How the hell was he going to get her to crawl under the canvas?

She kicked out at him wildly and the blow to his intimate parts caught him unawares. He grabbed himself in pain and doubled over. "Aaarrrghhh."

She darted for the front of the tent.

He lunged after her and caught her by the chemise. He dragged her back and caught the rest of her. He swung her up and over his shoulder.

She squirmed on his shoulders and he planted his feet apart to steady himself. He'd better make a run for it out the front of the tent. He poked his head out, glanced at the escorts' tent.

Billy Bow was just stepping out of his tent. Nervously, Billy surveyed the other tents and the trail.

Zander jerked back into Dorie's tent.

"I thought I heard somethin'," muttered Billy Bow. He looked around. "Guess not." A shadowy figure staggered on the trail in front of his fire. "Aah, it must've been you," he muttered.

The Indian, Etienne, flashed a jug of whiskey. "Wanta play cards and have a drink?"

With an eager grin, Billy said, "Yeah, I'll play."

Zander dashed to the back of Dorie's tent with his burden squirming on his shoulder. Her muffled grunts sounded loud to his ear.

He placed her on her feet, scooped both her feet out from under her with one swift move of his moccasined foot and she plopped to the ground. He sank down beside her and rolled her under the canvas. Snatching up the carpetbag, he lifted her by one bound arm. *Almost there*, he encouraged himself.

He gave a low whistle and Shadow trotted over. Zander looped the carpetbag handle over the saddle horn. Then he picked up Dorie and hoisted her across the horse's withers, her arms dangling, her face down. The breath went out of her, and she didn't move. Then she kicked wildly. Oh, no! He should have tied her feet, too.

Zander launched himself into the saddle. He dug his heels into Shadow's sides, exultant. The horse leapt into a gallop and they tore off down the trail.

A rough, triumphant laugh burst from Zander's throat. He had done it! He'd stolen Dorie Primfield.

Dorie grimaced as the horse's sharp backbone dug into her stomach. Each pounding step the animal took jarred her sickeningly. Her mouth was dry and chafed from the rag Zander had tied over it. Her throat felt scraped from her muffled screams.

Desperately, Dorie fought with the bindings on her wrists, but they held tight. The ground raced past her eyes in a dizzying blur. Blood coursed to her head, where it pooled and throbbed.

How had this terrible thing happened to her? Where was Zander Durban taking her?

She kicked as hard as she could. It did no good. A coil of fear settled in her aching stomach. Where were Clifton Ross and Billy Bow? They must find her!

Suddenly a heavy hand swatted down on her backside.

She flinched. This couldn't be happening to her, it just couldn't!

Then she heard Zander's wicked laugh. "By damn!" he cried, as if he'd just thought of it. "You will be *my* country wife!"

Chapter Six

They reached Anton. By the light of the moon, Zander could see that Anton was slumped over his horse's neck.

"Anton!" cried Zander. "What happened?"

Dorie started kicking and he had to grab her legs to hold her still.

"Anton!" demanded Zander.

Dorie squirmed and tried to lift herself off the mare.

"Damn!" Zander dismounted and pulled Dorie off the horse. In the moonlight, her eyes flashed; she looked as if she would yell at him, except for the gag in her mouth. He smiled. Good idea, that gag.

He took her arm and she tried to shake off his

hand. He tightened his grip and dragged her over to Anton. "Anton, what happened? Are you shot?"

Anton snored.

"He's asleep," said Zander in disgust.

Dorie stared at the sleeping man too. Zander suddenly felt like the biggest fool this side of the Mississippi. What kind of a kidnapping was this?

Gruffly he shook Anton. "Wake up, Anton. We've got to leave. Now!"

Anton snorted and tried to fall back asleep.

Zander leaned into his ear. "Wake up, Anton."

Anton shook himself and blearily opened his eyes. "Zander?"

"Yeah. Anton, I've got Dorie Primfield. We've got to get out of here!"

"Right. Fort McCraig," muttered Anton.

Zander's eyes met the narrowed blue orbs of the angry, glaring Miss Primfield. "Uh, Anton, we've got to talk."

He wanted to speak privately with his friend, but he knew that the second he let go of Dorie's arm she would run. He leaned closer to Anton and dropped his voice. "Anton. We're not taking her to Fort McCraig. Change of plans."

Anton blinked, clearly bewildered.

Zander whispered hoarsely, "We're not taking her to any fort. I've decided. I'm going to keep her for my country wife!"

"Country wife?" Anton blinked harder as though desperately trying to understand.

"We need to split up our trail," continued Zander urgently. "You head one way, I'll go another."

Anton regarded Zander solemnly. "What about Fort McCraig?"

"No. Don't go there. I'm keeping her. I'm keeping Miss Primfield with me." Zander leaned closer. "She'll make a fine country wife, don't you agree?"

Anton swayed in the saddle. "Yeah. This is a happy time." He started to sing a Nez Perce wedding song. The words slurred.

"Damn it, Anton! Listen to me. I'm taking Miss Primfield with me. You head out alone. Clifton Ross and Billy Bow will be here at—oh, about daybreak. Let them see your tracks—but just for a short distance. Then you hide. You got that?"

Anton wobbled back and forth in the saddle.

"Anton!" Zander propped his friend up. How the hell was Anton going to get safely away?

"Got it," answered Anton. "Make happy tracks. Sing wedding song. Clifton and Billy Bow come to visit."

"No, no!" Zander glanced back down the trail. Etienne would have hidden the two trappers' horses and gotten Billy Bow drunker by now, but those trappers would be here as soon as they could.

And if Clifton Ross woke before dawn, they would be here even sooner. He had to get Anton and Dorie out of here now!

"Anton. You ride back to Fort Walla Walla. Got that?"

Anton nodded. "Fort Walla Walla," he mumbled.

"Good. Cover your tracks. Walk up to that big tree," Zander pointed to a wide tree trunk leaning out over the river. "Then walk your horse through the creek and follow the trail on the other side."

Anton nodded and started singing the wedding song again.

"Hush!" cried Zander, gripping his friend's arm and giving him a shake. "You have got to wake up. You hear me?" He gave Anton another shake.

The wedding song ended on a sharp 'yip'. Anton's bleary eyes focused on Dorie. "Where you taking her?"

He seemed to be a little more aware, and relief swept through Zander.

"I'm taking her to the cabin."

"The cabin where my arm healed," mused Anton.

"That one," agreed Zander. "No one knows where it is."

Anton nodded, almost wisely. "Good." He glanced back up the river. "I'll leave now. Make the trail to confuse them."

Relieved that Anton had seemed to shake off some of the whiskey's ill effects, Zander slapped his friend's horse on the rump and hoped for the best. He watched as Anton rode away, his back momentarily straight in the saddle. Zander shook his head and muttered to himself.

When he glanced at Dorie, she glared at him. He met her angry gaze. "Uh, we should have planned this better," he said apologetically. Then he laughed. What was he apologizing to her for? "Get back on the horse," he added tersely.

She refused to budge, so he had to drag her over to Shadow. He lifted her up on the horse and put her in the big saddle. She gripped the saddle horn, though her wrists were bound. Then Zander mounted behind her, encircling her body with his arms as he held the reins. He tried to ignore the close proximity of their bodies.

He guided the mare along the trail, the packhorses and mule following. Their hoofprints mixed with Anton's horse's on the trail. Satisfied that the prints would confuse any followers, Zander headed for the creek and splashed into the water.

When he had gone some distance, he guided

the mare out of the water and onto a trail leading through the sagebrush. "They won't find us," he chuckled aloud.

Dorie squirmed and turned around to glare at him. Her warm body, clothed only in the thin night shift, pressed up against him. Every movement she made, his anatomy answered.

She must have felt something because she straightened her back suddenly and tried to separate herself from him. He gave up trying to ignore her and began to enjoy her awkward attempts to squirm away from him.

He tightened his arms ever so slightly until he was pressing against her sides. He liked the way she fit in his arms. He leaned forward and sniffed the nape of her neck. She smelled like spring flowers. He let out his breath slowly on the back of her neck. She shivered, and he chuckled low in his throat.

He began placing tiny kisses on the nape of her neck, working his way up the warm, slender column. He tickled her skin with his tongue and was rewarded with a strangled cry of rage. He smiled and tickled her again.

Her breasts were thrust forward in a futile attempt to get away from him. He passed the reins to one hand and slid his other hand up to cup her. God, she felt good!

He pulled her gently back to him and, as the mare walked, the rhythm of the horse's steps set a rocking motion. He leaned into Dorie, fondling her breasts with one hand and kissing her neck. She struggled to get away from him, but her movements soon slowed. He smiled to himself.

But soon, kissing her and pressing her to him wasn't enough. He wanted more and shifted so that he was more comfortable in the saddle. He was just wondering if he could take her, right there on the horse, when she elbowed him in the stomach.

He winced and glanced around. Dawn's light was creeping into the east. "We'll stop here," he said gruffly. He dismounted and reached up for her. Though her hands were bound, she refused to come into his arms so he grasped her and pulled her toward him. She slid down his length, squirming and struggling all the way, causing him great sensation in his loins. He groaned. What was he going to do with her? And how soon could he do it?

He glanced around, looking for a place to take her, but the hard rocks were not tempting. He settled for undoing the rag that encircled her lower face.

"How dare you?" she sputtered, once he'd removed the rag. "How dare you kidnap me? How dare you touch me like that?"

He thought about replacing the rag again to silence her, but she looked so sweet, sputtering in her outrage, that he had little inclination to retie her. One of her pink beribboned pigtails was askew; the other pigtail, ribbonless, bobbed with each infuriated movement of her head. She looked so vulnerable and helpless in the thin white chemise with the tiny pink bows tied at the neck. He reached out and untied one of the bows, his fingers deliberately brushing her collarbone. He grinned as she clumsily tried to dodge his hands but couldn't.

Leisurely, he slowly explored the soft skin at the base of her throat, his steady hand belying the thick, heavy pounding in his blood. God, he wanted her!

She was staring at him, her eyes wide, breath held. He leaned into her and pressed her up against the horse so that he was touching her in all the intimate places. Her head fell back, exposing her vulnerable throat. He kissed his way up her neck and then he took her mouth. Dear God, she was sweet! He held the kiss because he could not let her soft lips go.

She was the first to break the kiss, her eyes huge. "Are you quite finished, sir?" Her shaking voice took all the power out of the demand. "For if you are, I would ask that you let me go."

"No," he said softly, shaking his head. "I cannot do that. You see, I've captured you."

"I will not be your wife," she hissed. "Ever!"

He laughed and the sound was cruel even to

his own ears. "That is well and truly said. You will be my *country* wife!"

He glanced around, his ardor cooled somewhat by her shaking desperation. Clifton Ross and Billy Bow might have picked up their trail. "Get back on the horse," he said brusquely.

She gasped as he picked her up and hoisted her alongside the horse. Both her plump buttocks filled his hands. Slowly, excruciatingly, torturing himself with her, he lifted her onto the horse. She scrambled onto the saddle and leaned away from him. He laughed, pleased to have her at his mercy.

They rode for a long time. They passed round clumps of sagebrush; they passed rocky columns of black basalt. Dorie's straight back slumped; the mare's jarring trot pounded Zander's flesh hard against the saddle. But he knew they must keep going. Clifton Ross and Billy Bow must not catch him.

"I want my clothes," Dorie demanded suddenly. Her voice pierced through Zander's plodding concentration on the winding trail.

"No," he answered. "I'm not giving you your clothes." If he kept her clothes, he'd be able to keep her nearby. If he gave her her clothes, she would surely run. Besides, it amused him to keep her humble.

"I want to go to Fort Walla Walla," she continued doggedly. "My sister is there. She will help me."

Zander didn't answer, but he had no intention of letting her go to Fort Walla Walla.

"My sister will be worried," prodded Dorie. Zander wanted to laugh at the hopeful note in her voice. She thought she could convince him, did she?

"My sister is expecting me. She will worry when I do not arrive in time."

Still he kept silent.

"My sister will pay for my release," Dorie added. "She will pay gold for me." After a while she concluded, "And she will pay furs."

If he wanted gold or furs, he would get them himself, thought Zander. He did not have to kidnap a woman to get them.

"Mr. Biddle will shoot you," exploded Dorie, obviously angered by his silence.

Zander grinned to himself.

"Mr. Biddle is an excellent shot," she continued confidently. "He will find you and shoot you and I will go free!"

Zander thought about that. "Biddle," he answered, "can't shoot worth a damn."

She squirmed and peered at him over her left shoulder. "Can't shoot?" she squeaked.

Enjoying himself hugely, Zander said, "Nope. Biddle can't shoot. Everyone knows that." They didn't. He didn't, but she didn't know *that*.

Dorie's silence spoke of her disillusionment.

"He's fat, too," continued Zander blithely, adding a few more questionable facts to his list. "Big and fat. For breakfast alone, he eats half a deer. And a whole batch of cornbread."

Dorie shifted uncomfortably in the saddle. Zander leaned forward and said, "He's balding, too. Bald as that rock over there. Not a hair on his head."

Dorie's spine straightened and she heaved herself forward as though to get away from his words.

"Have you seen Biddle?" asked Zander conversationally. "No? Well, let me tell you, he is old. Oldest man at Fort Walla Walla. Easy to spot. Yeah. Biddle's old enough to be your grandfather."

Dorie groaned. She frowned as clumps of sage blurred past the trotting mare. Prue's letters took on new meaning for Dorie now as she considered Zander's words. "Mature', Prue had described Biddle. Dorie thought Prue had meant wise and solemn. Not—not fat and bald.

"Responsible', Prue had written. She hadn't said "old'. Dorie swallowed. Oh, how could Prue have deceived her so? Or had Dorie *wanted* to be deceived?

She was still pondering Prue and Biddle when Zander halted the black mare. "Here's a creek," he observed. "We'll drink and then move on."

Dorie swallowed. Her mouth was dry. She needed water, assuredly. When he lifted her off the horse, she didn't struggle. Perhaps if he thought she was docile and obedient, he would untie her hands and arms. "Please," she whispered. "Please untie me so I can drink."

It worked. His deep brown eyes met hers and then he strode over to cut the ties binding her hands. She flexed her fingers as the blood rushed painfully into her hands and wrists.

Zander pulled a tin cup off one of the packhorses. "Here," he said, coming up beside her. "You can drink from this."

She took the cup, unwilling to glance at him now that he had done what she wanted and untied her. Lips tight, she bent and scooped the cup through the trickling clear liquid. She raised the cup to her lips and drank; cool water slid down her parched throat. Water dripped down her chin but she did not care. It tasted too good, too refreshing.

Suddenly she threw the cup down and dashed off. She ran as fast as she could, the gravel hard beneath her feet. If she could just get over that next sage-covered rise of hill, she could hide from Zander Durban and find her way to Fort Walla Walla. She could!

Her feet pounded. The gravel cut her feet, but

she kept running. Her breath came short, yet still she ran. She had to get away!

Suddenly strong arms wrapped around her and lifted her off her feet and swung her around.

"No, you don't!" he exclaimed. "You're not getting away from me!"

"Put me down," she cried, beating ineffectually at his broad chest with her fists.

But he only laughed and carried her back toward the horses. When they reached the pack train, he set her on her feet, retaining a firm grip on her arm. "Come along, Miss Primfield," he said.

"Let me go!" she cried. "I'll only run from you, every chance I get!"

"Thank you for alerting me to your plans," he said dryly.

She glared at him, her fists clenched, her heart pounding. "How dare you kidnap me!" she cried. "How dare you!"

He smiled. "I dare. There's no one to stop me."

His arrogance enraged her. "Oh!" she cried. "You won't be so smug when Mr. Biddle gets his hands on you!"

"He won't," answered Zander with maddening calm.

She clenched her teeth. "He will, I tell you! Mr. Ross and Billy Bow will find me. Mr. Biddle is a rich man, and he will pay them well for my return!" Even as she said the words, she prayed they were true. She bluffed, "Why, Mr. Ross and Billy Bow are searching for me this very minute!"

He laughed, showing strong white teeth. "You think so?" Then he pulled her hands together and tied them.

"What are you doing?" she cried, staring down at her bound hands in disbelief.

"Readying you for our journey," he said. "Get on the horse."

Dazed, she felt him lead her to the black mare. Once again, she was squeezed into the saddle. "Oh, no," she moaned, wondering when this nightmare would end.

Zander nudged his mare and jerked the lead on the packtrain and they started off. Dorie stared helplessly at the sagebrush-studded horizon. "Why has this happened to me?" she murmured dismally. "Why, oh why?"

Zander squeezed her waist and pulled her closer to him. She felt his warm body behind her and squirmed, trying to get away from him. When she turned to demand that he stop touching her, he winced.

"On second thought," he said, his eyes narrowed on her chemise, "it's time for you to get dressed!"

Chapter Seven

Dorie smiled to herself. Now she could get her pistol! It was hidden in her carpetbag, with her clothes.

Zander helped her off the horse once again, and she held up her bound hands. "You'll have to undo these," she said demurely, "so I can get dressed." She wouldn't meet his eyes, afraid he would read her excitement. The pistol!

She could feel him watching her as he slowly sliced through the bindings. She walked over to the mule, Zander right behind her. Nervous, she turned and demanded, "I suppose you are going to watch me dress too!" She needed such a little time to get her pistol.

"No," he said gruffly, "what I'm going to do is

find you a dress. We need to travel."

"But I—" she cried.

"I'll find something," he muttered, pushing her aside and rummaging through her carpet-bag.

"Please—"

He waved her away.

She held her breath as she watched his hands plough through her clothes. The pistol! He'd find the pistol!

"Here," he exclaimed, tossing out a red and white pin-striped day dress. "What the hell is this?" He held up the book of poetry she was going to give to Mr. Biddle.

She reached to take it, but he jerked it out of her reach.

"George Gordon, Lord Byron?" Zander lifted a brow, then opened the first page. "A romantic sort, are you, Miss Primfield? And what is this? 'To my husband-to-be, Clarence Biddle,' " he read in a high, mimicking voice. " 'In happy anticipation, Adora Primfield.' "

He snapped the book shut. "*Is* it happy anticipation, Miss Adora Primfield?" he sneered. "Marriage to a fat, bald old man?"

She flushed.

"I can see that it is. How sweet."

"Please," she said, reaching for the slim volume. "Give it to me."

"Oh, no," he answered, and tossed it back in her carpetbag.

She bit her lips nervously. "I need a petticoat to go with this dress," she protested. She inched closer to her valise. "Just let me find s-something—"

"Here." He tossed her a pale green petticoat. "And here's a shawl." He crumpled it up and threw it at her.

The shawl was mauve brocade lined with ice blue satin. She'd sewn it especially to match her best mauve dress. "Oh, no!" she wailed, wrinkling her nose. "This doesn't match my red pinstriped dress!"

He glared at her. "Wear it." He yanked out her only pair of high-buttoned boots. "Put these on," he snorted. He closed the carpetbag and hooked it back on the mule's pack. Then he glanced at her. "Still standing there? Get dressed. We've got to keep moving."

When she glared at him, he explained, "Your good friends, Clifton Ross and Billy Bow. Remember?"

"I hope they find me soon!" she exclaimed and stomped off to change. She glanced around at the dismal landscape. Nothing but hills and sagebrush and the occasional rock. There was nowhere for her to hide.

"I'm going to change over here," she called to

him from the other side of the last packhorse. "And don't watch."

She thought she heard a snicker, but mercifully he kept his back to her. Quickly she stripped off her chemise and put on the green slip, then the pin-striped dress.

She glanced down at herself and winced. The red and white dress clashed hideously with the mauve and blue shawl. She sat down and pulled on the black high-buttoned boots. At least her feet were in the very height of Rochester, Missouri, fashion. Then she forgot fashion. Zander's broad back was still turned to her. As quietly as she could, she tiptoed over to the mule. She reached for the carpetbag.

"Ready? Let's go," Zander said, coming up behind her. "Forgive me if I don't sit and chat about how lovely you look, as no doubt Lord Byron would do. But Clifton Ross and Billy Bow will soon be on our trail. You said so yourself." He clamped a large hand on her arm and dragged her toward his mare.

She sighed and gazed longingly at the carpetbag. Then he hoisted her onto the mare. Tears of frustration welled in her eyes. How she wanted her pistol!

They rode for hours, a grueling ride. Her legs felt numb, and her buttocks had lost all feeling a long time ago. "Please," she murmured at last, "can't we stop?"

He glanced at her dusty face. She knew she looked like yesterday's porridge, with huge sodden spots darkening her dress under the arms, but she was too tired to care. The day was extremely warm and they'd ridden forever.

"All right," he said gruffly. He dismounted and helped her down. He gave her a drink of water from a small metal flask he carried.

She drank the water, glad of the reprieve.

She glanced over to see Zander Durban taking kettles and furs off a short, stocky chestnut gelding. He walked over and piled the trading goods on the mule. Next, he put a bridle on the stocky gelding. The horse looked vaguely familiar to her.

"Here. You can ride him." Zander handed Dorie the reins. She stared at the horse, then at Zander.

"What's his name?" she asked at last.

"Lightning."

Dorie blinked. Was this the gelding Zander had traded away from Clifton Ross? Her heart beat excitedly. Perhaps the gelding was so named because he could run swiftly. She remembered that Clifton Ross had claimed it was his best horse. She brightened for the first time. "Thank you," she murmured, her hopes rising.

She mounted Lightning and watched Zander mount his black mare. A niggling little idea ate at her. Now that she had a horse, and a fast one, why not flee?

She stared at Zander's broad back as the niggling little idea bloomed into a full-blown thought. He hadn't even bothered to take her horse's lead rein; Dorie was holding the reins herself. Did Zander think her so cowed that she would not flee?

Lips tight, she watched the packhorses and mule ahead of her as they plodded along behind Zander. He hadn't even bothered to glance back at her even once since they'd started. He must truly believe her to be cowed, she thought in sudden irritation.

Zander rode up a small hill, the packhorses and mule dutifully following.

Dorie seized her chance. She wheeled the stocky chestnut around and headed him back along the way they'd come.

Dorie laughed to herself and tossed her head in delight. She was free! She nudged the chestnut faster.

But something was wrong. The gelding, instead of racing across the sage-filled plains as Dorie expected, was trotting at a very bumpy, but slow pace.

"Faster!" she yelled to him. The horse bumped along. Dorie leaned forward, her weight over the gelding's withers, and cried into his twitching right ear, "Faster!"

She dug her heels into Lightning's sides. "Faster!" she urged.

But no amount of heel digging, no amount of yelling, could get the stocky horse to run. A trot was as fast as he would go.

Bouncing along, her teeth rattling, Dorie wondered if perhaps she had badly misjudged Lightning.

"Enjoying the ride?" came a deep voice from just behind her. She craned her neck to look. Zander smiled and nodded as he pulled up easily alongside her. His black mare was not even winded.

Dorie refused to look at him; she stared straight ahead. How had her life come to this?

She thought of them trotting along the trail, her staring straight ahead, Zander laughing at her. While she was wondering what to do, he reached for the bridle and gave a gentle tug. The traitorous chestnut halted. Dorie glared at Zander.

"Are you quite done with your little ride?" he asked politely.

"Yes," she snarled, "I am."

"Good. We'll continue on our way then," and he pulled her horse's head around until they were facing the other direction.

"I should mention," he said, "that Lightning has to be treated carefully, or he'll go lame. His previous owner did not take good care of the

101

horse's hooves and so he can only trot. Slowly."

Dorie wanted to sink into a good sulk as they trotted back along the trail to where the packhorses stood patiently waiting. That's what she would have done if she were at home in Rochester, Missouri. But she was not at home in Rochester, Missouri. She was here, in the wilderness, with this maddening man and no help in sight. "I hope," she finally bit out, "that Clifton Ross and Billy Bow find us soon."

Riding alongside her, Zander did not reply. Perversely, she felt like goading him. "Where are you taking me?"

His only answer was a clenched jaw.

"It doesn't matter where you're taking me," she bluffed. "Mr. Ross and Billy Bow will find me."

He shifted a little in the saddle, but he did not glance at her.

"And I will not be your wife!"

His profile could have been carved of stone.

"Do you hear me? I refuse, utterly and completely refuse, to be your wife!"

He nudged his horse ahead, and she found herself staring at his broad back. His silence was even more provoking than his words. He wanted her to give up, that was it. He wanted her to give up hope that she'd ever be rescued, and this was his way of weakening her resolve. By ignoring her. Well, it would not work. It took more than a man's silence to cow Dorie Primfield! She was made of sterner stuff. Why, Clifton Ross and Billy Bow were no doubt following after her this very minute. They would find her and save her!

And there was something else in her favor, something very important: she could shoot a squirrel at two hundred paces. She was, no doubt, a better shot than Zander was!

Her glance strayed to her carpetbag. She still had her pistol. Oh, yes she did.

Wearily, Zander slumped in the saddle. They had been riding for what seemed to be days but was actually only part of a day. But keeping one eye out for pursuers, and the other on Miss Dorie Primfield, tended to exhaust him.

They were perched on the top of a low hill. Below and ahead of them the trail ended at a river, wide and slow. The silver water sparkled in the clear afternoon light.

He turned back to Dorie. "Give me your reins," he ordered.

Meekly, she handed the reins over to him. He was not fooled. The woman was a little hellion, and she would run off the first chance she got.

They forded the river; the water was shallow, reaching only to the horses' knees. The packhorses willingly followed, and the crossing was made without mishap.

Once on the other side, he handed the reins back to Dorie. She took them, her almond-shaped blue eyes holding his for an instant.

She was beautiful, he had to admit. A woman this beautiful would cause trouble anywhere on the frontier—or in a fort. Men would fight over her. Zander was probably doing Biddle a favor by taking her off his hands.

He eyed her possessively. And she was his; all his. He smiled slowly at the thought, savoring it.

He liked it that she traveled without complaint. Though the ride had been arduous, she had not cried or wept or lagged behind or begged him to halt their escape.

However, she *was* a problem. She was always trying to run off—at every opportunity. And Zander was becoming too exhausted to keep watch over her.

He glanced back across the wide river. There was also the little problem of pursuit by Clifton Ross and Billy Bow. Damn, he wished that Anton had been able to stay and help him. Anton could have watched Dorie while Zander rested and slept, and he would have been an ally if the two trappers found their trail.

But Anton was not here to help.

Zander glanced at Dorie. Her dress was hiked up to her thighs so that she could ride astride the saddle. He stared. Come to think of it, she wasn't that much of a problem. In fact, just to look at her gave him a new feeling of life. He grinned at her. How wise of him to steal her away. And how pleased his mother would have been to know that he did so for such a good cause. Mary's position as Biddle's country wife would be unchallenged. Mary need not fear losing her husband. This woman, this Dorie Primfield, with her skirts hiked up her legs, would never take Biddle away from Anton's sister. Never!

"Let's stop. We'll make camp." The words sounded terse, even to his own ears. He ignored the look of fear that crossed her lovely face.

Billy Bow bent over the muddied horse tracks by the river. "Cain't tell which way they went. Or how many of them there are," he said. He stood up, his expression baffled.

"Cain't you do nothin'?" demanded Clifton Ross from his vantage point in the saddle of his gray mount. "What the hell good are you anyway?"

"Well, you get down here and look-see fer yerself, then," said Billy Bow.

"I'd get down and help you, only my haid don't feel so good," responded Ross.

"Your haid? What about my haid?" answered Bow. "I'm down here lookin' for whoever done took Miz Primfield, and I got a haid that aches worse 'n yourn!"

Clifton Ross looked disgusted. "Quit your complainin'. That's all I get from you. Goddamn complainin'."

"Yeah? Well think what you'll get from Mr. Biddle when you come back to Fort Walla Walla and you ain't got no Miz Primfield!" Billy Bow looked triumphant. "Old Mr. Biddle gonna skin you and tan you and hang you up to dry in the wind, boy. Jest like a ol' beaver pelt."

"Biddle ain't gonna do nothin' to me," snarled Ross.

"When he finds out they got a day's start on us, he's gonna be real mad."

"Yeah? Well, ain't no one gonna tell him now, is there?" Ross glared fiercely at his partner. "Took you too damn long to find the horses in the first place!" He snorted in contempt. "Cain't even remember where the hell you bed horses at night!"

"Me?" exclaimed Billy Bow. "I ain't the one what tied 'em on the other side of the Rendezvous."

"Shut up," snarled Ross.

Billy Bow squatted and stared at the ground. "Here's some more tracks," he said. "They leadin' off this way. One set. Mebbe it's Miz Primfield or whoever took her."

Ross walked the gray over and glared down

at the ground through red-rimmed eyes. "Mebbe."

They followed the tracks, but the prints disappeared at the river's edge.

"Dang!" said Billy Bow. "We done lost him."

Clifton Ross rubbed his gray-stubbled chin consideringly. "You sure?"

Bow spat. "Yeah." He squinted up at Ross. "Say, mebbe we should just keep headin' south. Away from the Fort, like." He glanced around uneasily. "Mr. Biddle ain't gonna like it that we lost his fiancée."

"Naw," answered Ross, "he ain't gonna like it, true. But he's holdin' a season's worth of my furs. Yourn too, in case you forgot. We cain't just walk away from them pelts."

Billy Bow stared at the muddied tracks and shook his head mournfully. "Naw. I guess we cain't." He looked longingly to the south. "Sure would like to, though."

Ross swung his horse's head to the north. "Yeah? Well, to hell with that. Mount up. We'll go to Fort Walla Walla and tell Biddle his precious fiancée's done gone."

Chapter Eight

Dorie lifted the saddle off Lightning and staggered over to place it near a large brown boulder. Zander was taking the packload off the white packhorse. Seeing that he was busy with the skittish horse, she sauntered over to the mule. She reached for her carpetbag.

"You can gather wood for the fire," Zander interrupted. "I'll unload the packhorses."

"I just—"

"I'll unload the mule." He carefully placed a long wooden box on the ground. "You get the wood." He jerked his thumb at a spindly grove of pines. "Move."

She dropped her trembling hand. Her pistol was so close!

While she gathered the skinny pine branches and twigs, she kept one wary eye on Zander. What should she do? Her mouth was so dry from thirst that she could barely swallow. Her stomach rumbled as she gathered the wretched wood. Her backside ached from the long ride.

She tottered along the gravelly ground in her high-buttoned boots. When she had an armful of wood, she tottered back to where Zander was. He used a wicked-looking knife to make a pile of wood shavings off a dry branch.

He glanced at her. "Decided not to run?" he asked.

She eyed the knife, then threw her armload of sticks on the ground and glared at him. "What do you plan to do with me?"

He grimaced and went back to shaving the twig. His silence filled her with foreboding. What plans did he have for her? Was he going to force himself upon her? Was he going to leave her, helpless and abandoned and naked, lying in the gravel as he rode off? She shivered in fear.

Glancing over at his horse, she gauged the distance between herself and the horse. Maybe she should ride off on his horse—it was a faster mount than Lightning.

But he was watching her. "There's a rabbit," he pointed to a dead hare. "Clean it."

"Clean—?" Her mouth dropped open in

astonishment. How dare he force her to clean the evening's meat! Her stomach revolted at the very thought. "No!" she cried. "I will not!"

He stared at her grimly. "If you're going to eat, you're going to help."

She stared at the dead hare. It looked unappetizing to her. "I'll eat anything but that," she said in a huff.

"Suit yourself."

That night, at dinner, she choked down dried-out cornbread that he handed her from his saddlebag. *He* smacked his lips over a roasted rabbit. Her stomach rumbled again. She pretended not to notice when he set a roasted rabbit haunch on a tin plate. When he left the plate there, she realized he'd put it out for her.

Her mouth watered as she stared at the brown haunch. The herbs he'd put on the meat smelled delicious.

Dark descended. A coyote howled. She peered this way and that, out into the night, trying to locate the animal.

"Afraid?" Zander's voice sounded mocking. She glanced across the fire at him. He was watching her, his piercing dark eyes boring into her. The orange flames flickered, showing his high cheekbones and highlighting his raven hair.

She straightened. "No."

"Liar," he said softly.

Her eyes narrowed. "I have no reason to be afraid," she answered. "Clifton Ross and Billy Bow will be here at any time to rescue me. Mr. Biddle pays them well to be my escorts and they will soon arrive." Let him answer *that*!

He sighed. "They will be delayed," he said at last. "Clifton Ross and Billy Bow will take quite a long time to find you."

"How do you know that?" she demanded.

"My friend, Etienne, hid their horses."

She was silent, pondering.

"And after they find their horses, they'll still have to find our tracks," he added.

"They'll find our tracks," she said confidently. "They are expert mountain men."

"Do you think so?" asked Zander interestedly.

He sounded decidedly too cocky, she thought. And the news that Ross's and Bow's horses had been deliberately hidden to delay them was most disconcerting.

Reluctantly, Dorie picked up the tin plate with the rabbit haunch and stared at it. She lifted the haunch to her lips and nibbled. Oh, it was delicious. She strived to take small bites of the luscious meat, but her mouth was watering. She ended by wolfing it down in a most unlady-like manner.

She caught him staring and felt vaguely guilty, as if she had somehow betrayed herself.

"I need food to survive this ordeal," she pointed out.

He nodded. "You do," he answered gravely.

She was relieved he didn't mock her. "Where are you taking me?"

His dark eyes were thoughtful in the flickering orange firelight. She watched his face, his strong jaw, his straight nose. Odd, in other circumstances she might have been drawn to him. But not now. Not when she was his captive.

"I'm taking you to Fort George," he answered at last.

She remembered poring over maps before she'd left Rochester, Missouri. "Fort George?" she asked, surprised. "Why, that is far away. At the mouth of the Columbia River. On the Pacific Ocean."

"Yes, it is," he agreed. "Far away. My people are there."

"But I don't want to go there!" she wailed. "I want to go to Fort Walla Walla."

"You have no choice." His curt tone was dismissive. He rose, picked up her tin plate, and put some more rabbit meat on it. Then he handed it to her. "Eat. You are going to need your strength."

She had refused Zander's second offer of food, but he saw how upset she was. Upset or no, he knew she'd try to run away if she could.

Better to tie her to him while they slept. That way she couldn't escape.

He left her by the fire and wandered over to the saddlebags. He rummaged through them until he found the long piece of leather he was looking for.

"Zander?"

He swung around.

In her trembling hands, she held a pistol—pointed right at his chest.

Chapter Nine

"I've shot many squirrels in my life," said Dorie steadily. "This is the first time I've shot a rat."

Zander regarded her shaking hands, the pistol she held, and then her fierce gaze. Beads of sweat popped out on his brow. He raised his own hands as though to stop her. "Let's not act in haste now," he warned.

She cocked a winged brow. "Like you did in kidnapping me, Zander?"

He waved a hand dismissively. The pistol jumped and he froze. "Don't shoot."

She peered down the short barrel as if to get a fix on his heart. The gun's point made a little circle as she concentrated.

Sweat dribbled into his eyes and he blinked.

Rivulets of sweat ran down his back. "Miss Primfield," he said, striving to keep his voice calm, "if you shoot me, you'll be left all alone. Out here. Just you and the packhorses. Alone."

"I like being alone," she observed coolly.

"There are wolves out here. And trappers. Indians, too," he said desperately.

The smile vanished from her face. She frowned at him.

"You don't know where we are," he continued. "You'll get lost. You'll wander around in circles. You'll run out of food. Not much cornbread left now. You'll run out of water, too. Why, you'll be dead in a matter of days!"

She was silent, her eyes narrowed as she glared at him. "I've got my pistol."

He eyed the old flintlock pistol. "So you do, but like all single-barreled flintlocks, it only shoots one bullet at a time."

"Only takes one bullet to shoot a rat," she answered.

He ground his teeth. "You wound me and I'll be mighty angry."

She smiled sweetly. "I'm a dead shot."

Shivers ran down his spine. There was a distinct chill in the warm evening air.

"Miss Primfield . . ." God, he hated pleading with her. Thank God Anton couldn't hear him begging. "Miss Primfield, if you shoot me, you'll die too. Just a little later."

"Pack up the horses, Zander," she answered.

He met her eyes. Those almond-shaped blue eyes were serious, deadly serious. And she had the gun. Damn, why hadn't he checked her carpetbag for a weapon?

He shrugged and went to pack up the horses. He finished packing the white one and the chestnut.

"The mule too," she said, waving the pistol.

He didn't believe she was a dead shot. Probably had never fired a pistol in her life. Which made her *very* dangerous. He'd better keep her calm.

He packed up the mule.

She approached him cautiously. "Now your mare," she instructed.

"You're going to take my mare?"

"That's right. She's a fast horse, as we both know."

"Are you going to leave me Lightning?" Damn! There was that pleading note in his voice again.

"No."

He bit back the angry torrent of words that rushed to his tongue.

He saddled Shadow. When he was done, he patted the mare's white blaze on her nose and whispered in her ear.

"Step away from the horse, Zander."

Damn, but he hated the tight control she had.

117

Her eyes were as cold as blue ice—and as beautiful.

"If you leave me Lightning," he said, moving slowly away from the mare, "I'll tell you which direction Fort Walla Walla is in." He crossed his arms and glared at her, waiting for her to bargain.

When she was mounted on Shadow, she eyed him. The pistol still pointed his way. Zander clenched his jaw.

"I know where the fort is," she answered.

He didn't think she did. How could she? He tightened his lips. Well, he'd be damned if he'd tell her!

"Give me the reins to the packhorses," she said.

He gathered each lead rein and presented them to her.

She took the reins, her pistol steady. "Now"— she smiled—"take off your clothes."

"What?" Utter shock coursed through Zander. What the fool hell—!

"Take off your clothes, Zander." Her voice was even, her blue eyes steady.

She couldn't mean it! He glared up at her, arms across his chest. "No." No one, and no little pistol, was going to make him strip off his clothes!

She leaned forward, the hand holding the pistol as steady as a rock. "Take off your clothes,

Zander, or I swear I will shoot you right through your cold heart!"

He didn't like the tone of her voice. It sounded like she meant it. He stood still.

She waved the gun menacingly.

"No," he gritted.

"The trigger is half cocked," she warned.

His eyes narrowed. The fool woman who didn't know what the hell she was doing with a loaded gun now had the trigger halfway pulled! A cold sweat broke out on his forehead. "Don't shoot."

He saw her ease her finger off the trigger. A shiver of relief went through him. He had to keep her from going for the trigger again. With a grunt, he removed his possibles bag and his hunting bag. Then he took off his leather jacket. He started to unbutton his red flannel shirt. Her eyes followed every move of his fingers. Her pink tongue came out and delicately licked her lips.

So she liked it, did she? Deliberately, he took his time undoing the buttons. Then slowly, he peeled back the shirt, showing the left half of his broad chest. She leaned forward in the saddle expectantly.

He glared at her, then shrugged half out of the shirt. It still covered the right half of his chest and he lazily drew that back, taking his

119

time, suddenly amused by the hungry look in her eyes.

He tossed the shirt to the ground. "Seen enough?" he asked indifferently.

"All your clothes, Zander." Was that breath-lessness in her voice?

To taunt her, he sat down and took off one of his moccasins. Instead of looking irritated, however, she watched him avidly. He pulled off the other moccasin and cast it aside. He wiggled his toes. Still she stared.

He got to his feet and shook his shoulder-length black hair back from his face. He turned to the side a little, to see the effect on her.

She'd stopped breathing.

He untied the leather belt he wore at his waist. He set the belt and knife holster aside. "Well, that's it," he said. He crossed his arms and met her eyes.

"No," she said hoarsely. She waved the pistol at him. He knew what she wanted. He glared at her.

"All your clothes," she whispered, her eyes wide. He took a breath and let it out.

The pistol held steady.

Slowly, he untied the top laces that held up his leather pants. The small action bared him just below his navel.

Her eyes followed his fingers. He unlaced all the way down; she never took her eyes off him.

Angry now, not caring what she thought, he yanked the pants off and kicked them aside. Her eyes flew to his manhood, and he saw her cheeks flush red. He was glad she had *some* shame!

He stood there, arms crossed, jaw clenched. "Seen enough?" he demanded.

She gave a little cry, then swallowed. Her pistol faltered. She blinked several times and her mouth fell open.

He raised a brow.

Still staring helplessly at him, she wheeled Shadow's head around. She kicked the mare's sides and they dashed off, packhorses and mule galloping behind.

Zander watched in disgust as they raced back along the trail towards the river. When they'd disappeared, he picked up his leather pants and yanked them back on.

His thoughts were grim as he laced himself back up. Miss Dorie Primfield would pay for that little trick. And pay dearly.

Chapter Ten

Dorie squeezed her eyes shut as the black mare carried her farther and farther away from Zander Durban. The wind cooled her hot cheeks; her blood pounded. She'd had to do it—to slow him down. She simply had to; she had no other choice. But even now, she squirmed in the saddle as she thought of him standing there. Naked.

Lordy, he'd looked magnificent, standing there as natural as could be. At first she'd been merely practical. She knew he'd follow, so she had to find some way to slow him down. But then she'd become curious, wanting to see what he looked like. She'd had no idea whatsoever when she'd ordered him to undress that the

sight of him would unnerve her so. He was so
. . . so big!

Mortified, she held on to the reins and pistol
and yelled at the mare to go faster. She glanced
back over her shoulder. It was ridiculous to
think he could pursue her. How could he? He
was naked and on foot. She had the horses and a
head start. Shivers coiled up and down her spine
as she thought of him. Naked—and menacing.

The mare raced along the trail, and Dorie
bounced with each step. This mare was fast!

It was getting dark now; soon she'd be unable
to see. She must put as much distance between
herself and Zander as she could before she
stopped for the night.

She squeezed her eyes shut again. In her
mind rose the image of Zander. Naked. Lordy,
what had she done? Of course, she'd had no
choice. He was dangerous. She had to slow him.
She had to! If Prue knew her deepest thoughts
right then, why, she'd be appalled. Aunt Hanna
would be shocked.

Oh, what was happening to her? One look at
his body and she was . . . She was a lustful
wreck, was what she was.

She had to get away from Zander! She had to.
She could never, ever look that man in the eye
again!

The racing mare finally slowed, and with
shaking hands Dorie pulled her to a stop. She

glanced around and saw the dark shapes of several pine trees and a big rock. It was more hidden here than on the open trail. Dismounting, her legs shaking, Dorie tottered away from the mare. It was late dusk now, and she could barely see the packhorses and mule. Oh, what should she do?

Striving to calm her pounding heart, she patted Lightning. Zander had loaded him with a saddle and two lumpy sacks. The stocky chestnut was solid and familiar. She kissed his brown forehead. "Next time I'll ride you, Lightning. Zander's mare is too spirited for my taste."

Lightning bobbed his head as if in hearty acknowledgment.

Dorie chuckled and glanced around at where they'd stopped. She could hear a river, though it was too dark to see it.

"We'll stay here for the night," she told Lightning. "At least we're close to water." She patted him again. "You and the other horses will have to wait until morning for a drink, though. Sorry, old horse."

It was pitch black now. She shivered a little; it was colder in the evenings. But she couldn't risk a fire. A fire would guide Zander right to her. If he looked for her.

Then she shook her head. Of course he'd look for her. She had his horses and all his trade goods.

She led Lightning over to the black mare and had to set the pistol on the ground while she pulled the reins over the black mare's head. Then she tied the mare's reins in with the pack-horses' and tied them all, in one knotty clump, to the saddle horn of Lightning's saddle. She picked up the pistol again and led the stocky gelding, the others following, over to where she'd seen the rock.

"Ouch." She stubbed her toe on the rock. With careful fingers she felt along its rough, hard surface. Then she lowered herself to a sitting position on it. "We'll wait out the night here," she informed the horses and immediately felt less alone.

She would have to stay awake through the night, of course.

She sat on the rock and drew her knees up. Her pistol pointed out into the night, ready. Oh yes, if Zander came, she was ready for him.

A tug on the reins told her that Lightning had lowered his head and was sniffing around for grass. He found some and munched, stepping slowly away from the rock. His search for grass almost caused him to tug her off the rock. "Lightning!" she cautioned and gave a yank on the rein to bring him back.

She could hear the other horses' restive movements. She felt surrounded by the dark. All that seemed real to her was the pistol, Lightning's rein, and his occasional tug on it.

Lordy, she hoped morning came soon.

She snapped her head up, suddenly awake. How could she have fallen asleep? She glanced around in the utter blackness, eyes straining. What had awakened her?

She shivered in the cold. Her pin-striped dress was too thin to provide any warmth. Not even her lovely shawl of mauve and ice blue had kept her warm. And her feet were cramped in her ridiculous, fashionable black boots.

She yawned and straightened. She heard a creaking sound. Was that what had awakened her?

"Zander," she yelled, her head swiveling. "Zander, if you're out there, I've got my pistol!"

Silence.

The fear coursing through her wakened her further. She tightened her lips in determination.

Another creaking sound.

"Zander! I'm warning you. I'll shoot!"

Silence.

She waited. A long time passed. Her head nodded, but she brought herself awake. Nodded again, but she woke herself. Nodded again . . .

She awoke at dawn. Her pistol had fallen onto the rock beside her though she still clutched

Lightning's rein. She jumped to her feet. "Where—?"

The packhorses and mule were gone. So was the black mare.

She peered around, rubbed her eyes, peered again.

Everything was gone! Even the two lumpy packs on Lightning's saddle were gone.

"How—?" She caught a movement out of the corner of her eye and whirled. It was only a blue jay. He flew to a branch of pine.

Dorie grabbed her pistol and swung around, glaring at the pine trees and rocks as if she expected them to jump at her. "How did Zander do that?" she wondered aloud. She'd heard nothing in the night. Nothing!

Lightning snorted and nosed a clump of bunchgrass.

Then Dorie's shoulders slumped. She was safe. Zander had taken his trade goods and horses and left. He would not be coming after her.

Thank the heavens, she still had Lightning. She could find her way to the fort much easier on horseback.

She glanced around. What should she do now? She didn't know in which direction the fort lay, though she'd told Zander otherwise.

She stared at the trail she'd ridden over yesterday. No, not that way. She glanced around;

she could hear the river, but she still couldn't see it.

"Come on, Lightning," she said, holding the pistol firmly and leading the chestnut along. "Let's find breakfast."

Lightning found his breakfast easily; grass and weeds satisfied him. Dorie spied a bush with fat red berries. "Are these good to eat?"

Still holding the pistol, she picked a berry and peeled the flesh apart. Sniffed the orange insides. A tangy, musky odor. She backed away. No, these were not familiar berries. If she ate one, she might get sick.

She wandered afoot for a distance, her stomach grumbling. She looked for berries or seeds or something to eat, but there was nothing, at least nothing she recognized as edible.

Her feet hurt, too, from walking on gravel in the tight little boots. She wished now that she had brought more practical shoes. Like moccasins.

"Well, Lightning," she sighed at last. "There's nothing for me to eat here. Let's ride down the trail."

She reached up to the saddle horn and lifted one foot into the stirrup. Just as she gave herself a little boost off the ground, she was suddenly grabbed from behind and dragged off the horse. The pistol was torn from her grip.

A loud shot rang out, frightening her. "Zan-

129

der!" She struggled to break free of his hold. "Damn you!" she cried. "You shot off my only bullet! Give me back my pistol!"

"No." He laughed, tucking the smoking pistol at his waist. "I've waited too long for this."

She gritted her teeth and elbowed him in the stomach.

He groaned and bent over. She raced along the trail, the sound of the river guiding her.

She ran past some large boulders and clumps of pine and burst into the open. There it was— the river!

She plunged into the muddied, swirling water. Strong hands grabbed her shoulders and dragged her back to the shore.

"You fool!" yelled Zander. "That current's swift. You could have drowned!"

Dorie glared at him. "That river is calm," she cried. "I know there's a current, but I'm a strong swimmer! I would have made it to the other side. And escaped!"

He glared back at her. "Get out of the water," he bit out at last, dragging her along. "We're leaving."

Dorie, exhausted, had no choice but to be propelled along.

Her feet squished in her squeaking wet boots; her sodden dress clung to her legs. Her shawl was the only dry piece of clothing she had left. She'd been chased and dragged along. But she would not cry. No, she would not!

He boosted her onto Lightning, his touch swift and impersonal. She sat in the saddle and met his hooded eyes. Suddenly she remembered how he'd looked when naked. Her cheeks grew hot.

His black eyes flashed angrily, as if he knew what she was thinking. "We're not done yet, you and I," he snarled, "not by a long shot."

Then he turned on his heel and led Lightning along a trail that followed the river.

Dorie heard a sound like thunder. At first she thought it echoed the sadness in her heart. Then she realized that it was coming from outside her. She surveyed the sky, but there were no black clouds of an approaching storm, only blue sky.

They soon came to the clearing where Zander had hidden the packhorses. The pounding, thundering sound grew louder with each step. Still holding the chestnut's reins, Zander mounted his black mare. The pack train started off. They rode toward the thundering sound and turned a corner of the trail.

There Dorie saw the cause of the loud, pounding thunder. Rapids!

They reached a long, narrow, water-filled canyon. White water churned and crashed against the red-brown rocks. The thunder obliterated any possibility of speech.

Muddy, swirling water broke over a rock thrust up in the middle of the river and then tumbled through high, narrow walls of stone.

Dorie peered at the leaping water and shivered. The sound made her want to cover her ears.

Mercifully, they headed away from the rapids and the sound gradually diminished, but Dorie realized one thing. Zander had told the truth. If she had escaped into that river, the current would have caught her and carried her to the rapids where she would have been dashed to certain death upon the rocks.

The man had saved her life.

Chapter Eleven

They had been on the trail for four days. Dorie slumped in the saddle, scarcely moving despite each jolting step that Lightning took. Her once lovely red-and-white pin-striped dress was wrinkled and smelly and torn. Her blond hair hung down in limp, greasy strands; her feet were bare. Days ago, in a fit of pique, she had torn off the foolish, fashionable high-buttoned boots and flung them away. Now she had calluses on her feet and, she thought ruefully, she probably had calluses on her buttocks from bouncing along on Lightning.

Wearily, she wiped the sweat from her eyes and sighed. How much longer until they reached wherever they were going?

Just then her stomach rumbled with hunger. Over the past few days she'd eaten rabbit, turtle, fish, and Indian bannock. What she wouldn't give for a piece of cornbread just now!

They rode up a rise and came to a small blue lake. The shimmering water looked inviting, and she was hot and dusty. "Oh!" she groaned, staring at the sparkling blue water. If only she could swim in it! She pulled at her dusty dress to keep it off her sweat-coated skin. She stole a glance at Zander Durban, wondering if she should ask him to stop and rest. Lordy, but she hated to ask anything of the man. He was so uncaring.

Finally, she threw caution aside. "I wish to cleanse and refresh myself. I want to swim."

A slow grin curved Zander Durban's firm lips. "Certainly, Miss Primfield. Let us stop." He gestured at the lake. "Swim to your heart's content."

She smiled grimly, surprised at his easy acquiescence. Then she shrugged and climbed off her horse. Lightning limped up to the edge of the lake and began slurping the fresh, clear water. Dorie eyed him enviously. She would have to wait for *her* drink. She tied him to a small cottonwood tree.

Zander Durban crossed his arms lazily and rested them on the saddle horn as he watched her.

"Of course, you will have to turn your back. . . . " she encouraged him.

He grinned at her. "I'll do better than that, Miss Primfield. I will leave you to your privacy while you swim." His grin was distinctly wolf-ish, but she ignored the warning bells going off in her mind.

He rode the black mare back over the rise and disappeared from view.

She gave a huge sigh of relief. *Perhaps I should run*, she thought. *But if I run, he'll no doubt catch me. Besides, the water looks soooo enticing. . . .*

Without another thought, she peeled off her sticky dress. She rubbed her poor, aching feet; then, wearing only her pantaloons and green cotton petticoat, she waded into the water.

Sinking into the cool depths, she gave a lux-urious sigh. The water soothed her skin and re-laxed her tired muscles. She kicked and splashed. Many a summer day she had spent at Aunt Hanna and Uncle Albert's farm, swim-ming in the river near their house. She loved swimming.

She swam back and forth; the water was waist-deep. She stood up and glanced across the lake, wondering if she could swim that dis-tance. It was farther than she usually swam at home in Rochester, but she thought she could make it.

She struck out for the opposite shore, the water's coolness feeling good on her sore muscles.

She reached the shore and scrubbed her hair in the shallows, dipping her long blond locks now and then to wash out the dust. That done, she waded onto the small beach. As she sat panting, waiting to regain her breath, she glanced across to where Lightning was tied.

Zander was standing, arms crossed, grinning at her. At his feet were her clothes.

Dismayed, she hurried back into the water and swam back across the lake. She paused offshore, the water up to her shoulders. "What are you doing?" she demanded. "You said you'd give me some privacy."

He shrugged and reached down for her dress. He picked it up and held it. "I thought I'd help you."

"I don't need any help from *you*," she answered, raising her chin.

"Yes, you do." He held out the dress, his eyes laughing at her.

She glared at him. If she walked out of the water in her wet underthings, she might as well be naked. The thin cotton of the wet petticoat stuck to her skin and made her garments almost transparent. It would look as if she was not wearing a stitch! she thought angrily.

He shook her pin-striped dress tauntingly.

She shrugged and lazily floated on her back,

watching him and pondering. What was he up to?

He sat down on the bank to wait for her.

She decided she could outwait him. She continued splashing and swimming, pretending he wasn't there. But he was. And she was conscious of him watching her. The water, once so cool and refreshing, was becoming cold. And her skin was wrinkling up like one of Aunt Hanna's breakfast prunes.

"I want my dress," she said at last, standing, arms crossed over her breasts and glaring at him.

He nudged her dress. The implication was clear. Come and get the dress. But if she did that, he'd see her—almost naked, she thought morosely. Oh, why had she trusted him, the rat!

"Your lips are turning blue," he said.

She tightened them mutinously. Then she started to shiver.

"Better get your dress," he said, as if he were truly concerned. But she knew better. The skunk was laughing at her!

"Why are you doing this?" she demanded.

He grinned. "A little matter of someone holding a pistol on me"—the grin disappeared—"and forcing me to strip!"

"Oh." She flushed. Whatever his reasons, she certainly did not deserve this treatment!

She moved closer, until the water was waist-

137

deep. She held out one hand, still keeping an arm across her breasts. "Give me my dress."

He languidly rose to his feet and yawned as if he couldn't care less about her and her dress. But she wasn't fooled. He picked it up and displayed it. "Come and get it."

Her nostrils flared in anger. The water was cold and he was irritating her more with each passing minute!

She stood there, wondering what to do. Should she continue to stay in what was now freezing water? Or should she wade out, snatch the dress, and run and hide behind those cottonwood trees growing near the water? That would be the sensible thing to do, she decided, as she shivered. Her teeth were chattering now.

"Your dress," he said softly, encouragingly, as he dangled the garment in front of her.

At last, irritated and afraid, she marched out of the water, arms across her breasts, and strode up to him. She reached for the dress.

He snatched it out of her way. "Oh, no, not so fast," he warned with a laughing glint in his black eyes. "You have to give me a kiss for it."

"A kiss!" she shrieked. "How dare you?"

He laughed. "Believe me, lady, I dare. After what you and your little pistol did to me and my clothes and my vanity, you're getting off lightly."

She considered his reasons. He *had* looked

rather upset standing stark naked like that. Yes, indeed . . .

So be it. She reached for the dress and grabbed it and leaned into him at the same time. She gave him a quick peck on the cheek. "There."

He pulled the dress out of her grasp and shook his head. "No."

"No? What do you mean, no? I gave you a kiss!"

"I want a real kiss."

She reddened. "I suppose you mean on the lips." Her heart was pounding rapidly at the thought.

"Yes."

She closed her eyes and stood on her tip-toes. Slowly she placed her lips against his. He pulled her to him, and his lips moved on hers. She heard him groan. He smelled like woodsmoke, and his lips were firm. Then he gripped her closer. She broke away. "Please may I have my dress?" she demanded, not quite meeting his eyes.

His eyes, dark and intense, searched her out. He lifted her chin until she met their obsidian depths. "Another kiss?"

"No! I want my dress."

He chuckled and handed her the garment. She stared down at it. It was dusty and sweat-stained and she couldn't imagine putting it next to her clean skin.

"I should have rummaged through my carpetbag for a dress," she said in irritation. Devil take the man! He clouded her thinking.

"But this was so much better," he said, eyeing her in amusement.

Her lips twitched. She would not be amused—she would not!

She turned away. "I have to get dressed," she said gruffly and headed for Lightning. Taking her carpetbag, she stumbled behind some cottonwoods. She emerged wearing a blue calico dress.

His dark eyes admired her, but he said nothing.

They mounted the horses and continued on their way.

Later in the day, she noticed that they'd gradually been climbing higher, first into foothills, then into low mountains. When she turned in the saddle, behind her she could see, far below, a long shining ribbon of river winding through the brown, dusty sagebrush-dotted land. They were passing pine trees regularly now. She liked the smell of the pines; it revived her.

"How much farther?" she asked Zander.

He turned and glanced at her, his handsome, rugged face relaxed. During the past days, she'd come to see a different side of her abductor.

He'd cooked the game he shot for them, he'd fed and curried and cared for the horses well, and he'd packed and unpacked his trade items carefully each day. In spite of his glaring faults, she judged him to be a man who took good care of what he had.

She set her jaw. She did not want to pay heed to his good qualities. No. He was ruthless. He'd kidnapped her and he would not let her go. She needed nothing else to prove he was evil.

"How much farther?" she asked again, the words escaping through her gritted teeth.

"Soon," he answered.

She groaned. He'd answered the same way every time she asked him. What he thought to be "soon" and what she thought it to be, were proving quite different.

She gazed ahead, first at Zander's broad back, then at the ground slowly passing under her horse. Suddenly, Zander shifted direction and headed for where the pine trees grew thickly.

She stared. What was that ahead? It looked like a cabin.

As it proved to be. Half-hidden by large boulders, the gray log cabin perched on the side of the mountain, surrounded by pine trees. A small creek ran a little distance away. Two cords of neatly cut wood were stacked under the trees. A small corral was situated to one side.

Zander dismounted and walked over to her.

141

"We're here." He lifted a hand to help her off her horse.

She stared at the cabin. She bit her lip uncertainly. How was anyone ever going to find her now?

She peered around at the mountainside, ignoring Zander's outstretched hand. She'd given up days ago hoping for any help from Clifton Ross and Billy Bow. Now, seeing the cabin's location, she feared that even if Mr. Biddle or Prue hired someone to search for her, they would never find her. Not on this mountainside.

Zander smiled at her. Her eyes fell from the triumph on his face to her pistol, still tucked at his narrow waist.

She dismounted, ignoring his outstretched hand. He chuckled.

She winced as her bare feet struck the ground. She still wasn't accustomed to going without shoes. "Is this your . . . yours?" she asked.

He shrugged. "I use it. It belongs to Old Man Sheridan. He's away trapping right now. We can use it as long as we replace any food or wood we use."

She lifted a brow. "Do many people use this cabin?" she asked hopefully. Perhaps when someone stopped by, she could ask him to help her escape.

"No," he answered cheerfully, "very few people know of it at all." He smiled.

She sighed in frustration. How was she going to escape this man? He was most determined. Every time she ran away, he dragged her back, she thought dispiritedly, ignoring the glint of amusement in his dark eyes.

"Help me unload the animals," he said.

With another sigh, she began taking the saddle off Lightning.

When the animals had been unloaded, watered, and led to the small corral, Zander picked up her carpetbag and said, "Come. I'll show you the cabin."

"I don't want to see it," she answered, stubbornly keeping her eyes on the horses.

He took her hand and pulled her along. She went grudgingly.

They walked up the two wooden steps and onto the small porch. Zander pushed open the door and stepped inside.

Curious now, Dorie followed him in.

The cabin was one large room. A mud-and-stone fireplace stood in the wall opposite the door. Along one wall was a window, shuttered now. A table was pushed against the wall and there was a low counter along the same wall. Above the counter were some empty shelves. A bucket sat on the counter. Across the room, a large black bear fur was nailed on the wall. Beneath it, tucked in the corner, was a single wide bed.

Only one bed. Dorie's heart sank.

There were no chairs, no curtains, or any of the other amenities that Dorie considered necessary in a house either.

She took a breath and forced a smile. "It will do for now," she said with false heartiness, "because I won't be staying long."

"That so?" he asked interestedly and gave a soft chuckle.

She grimaced. "I intend to go to Fort Walla Walla, Mr. Durban," she said determinedly. "And I *will* go."

He said nothing to that, only pulled her to him and touched her lips with his. He kissed her, and it was a long kiss. When his tongue demanded entrance to her mouth, she gasped in surprise and then he was in. She struggled against the complete possession she felt overtaking her.

Her body felt heavy, not her own. He rubbed his chest against her breasts and she gasped again. His tongue was the complete invader and she the invaded. Her limbs felt heavy; her eyes fluttered closed. She moaned and tried to lift her hands. He loosed them, and she used her freedom to pull his head closer.

He groaned. "I've got to have you. I can't go on any longer, seeing you, watching you, wanting to touch you, wondering what your skin feels like. I've got to know."

"What?" she asked, a strange bodily lethargy consuming her.

"I want you," he breathed, his warm breath feathering her lips.

"You can't do this, Zander," she protested weakly, trying to pull away.

"I can," he whispered back. "I want you, Dorie. And I will have you."

"But I—"

"Hush," he said, and he kissed her mouth to still her protests. "I will not hurt you. It will be good for you, you'll see."

"No!" She tore free, her breath coming in quick pants.

"You'll see," he said softly, reluctantly letting her go. Then he turned on his heel and left the cabin. She stared at the closed door, her heart pounding. She touched her lips and a shiver went through her. When at last her heart resumed its normal pace, she peeked through the open door and saw that he had picked up a saddlebag and a lumpy sack of what was probably trade items and was bringing them back to the cabin.

Hastily she crossed the room and plunked herself and her carpetbag on the bed. The bed was a lattice of rope tied to a wooden frame. Her hands were shaking. What had he done to her? Those kisses of his were heady. She glanced around the cabin, wondering how she could keep him away from her. *Maybe if I claim the bed first, he will be a gentleman and sleep on the floor!*

Just then Zander entered and placed the saddlebag on the table. He grinned wickedly when he saw her sitting on the bed. "I see you've made yourself at home."

She flushed and wanted to jump up, but instead she stayed put and glared at him. She would not give up the bed! He could have the floor.

He rummaged through the saddlebag and took out two small sacks. He caught her watching him. "Bullets," he explained. "And black powder." He tucked the small sacks inside his jacket and carried the saddlebag and big lumpy sack to a corner of the room and dumped them there.

"There's some dried meat left in the sack," he said. He patted her pistol, still at his waist. "I'm heading out."

With that, he strode out the door.

Mystified, her jaw dropped. She wanted to run after him and ask him to explain. Was he leaving her? Here? All alone?

She wanted to cry out and ask him to stay with her. She didn't want to be left alone in this cabin on this mountainside. What would she do? She had no gun. No protection.

She ran to the lumpy sack and stared at the contents. At least she had food. And water was outside.

She raced to the door and peeked out. Zander was striding down the hill with his rifle. Puzzled, she watched him walk away. He was leaving the horses—even his black mare. Wouldn't he at least take his mare?

Not knowing what to think, Dorie sat down on the step and watched him go. When he disappeared behind some trees, she heaved herself to her feet and scurried back into the cabin. She pulled the door closed behind her.

The bearskin caught her eye. There were bears in the mountains. Wolves, too. Trappers. Indians. Cougars.

There might be mammoths, too, she thought, remembering Professor Humbert's learned treatise on the wildlife of Northern America. Professor Humbert should meet Zander, she thought ruefully.

She sat on the bed for a time, her knees up to her chin and hugging herself. At last she decided she could not sit on the bed forever. If she was going to survive, she needed water.

She got off the bed and took the bucket off the counter. Then she slowly opened the door and peered out. Looking in every direction, she was relieved to see that all appeared well. The horses munched dried grass in the corral and seemed calm.

Tentatively, she crept out the door onto the porch. She stood poised, ready to run back into the cabin should anything—*anything*—move or flutter or shake or growl at her.

Nothing did.

She stepped down the first step and scanned the mountainside. All looked well.

She glanced at the creek. It was about a hundred yards from the cabin. Not far. Unless there was a bear around. Or a wolf. Or a . . .

Stop it! she ordered herself. *Walk over to that creek and get that water, girl. Then you walk back to that cabin and close the door! You'll be safe.*

She wished she could believe her own promise.

She stepped down the second step. Now her feet were on the hard gravel.

Taking a breath, she took a few steps, then a few more. Soon she was walking swiftly to the creek. She reached it, bent, filled the bucket, and hurried back to the cabin, water sloshing on her dress and bare feet in her haste.

She climbed the steps. Pushed open the door. Stepped inside. Slammed it. Safe!

She let out a loud sigh and glanced down at the brimming bucket. She'd try to make this water last as long as she could.

Relieved now, she found an old ladle and a

148

tin cup. She scooped out a drink for herself and retrieved a piece of dry meat. She must remember not to leave the meat in the corner like that. Mice would get it. She glanced around and saw the shelves. She placed the remaining meat from the lumpy sack on the shelves.

After she'd eaten her simple meal, she glanced around, wondering what to do. She wandered over and sat on the bed. Was Zander going to return? Or had he abandoned her?

The next day, Dorie opened the cabin door and stepped out onto the porch. She was sick of sitting in the cabin. It was hot in the one-room cabin and there was nothing to do.

She scanned the pines and rocks below her. Nothing. And worse, no one.

Where was Zander? When was he going to return? *Was* he going to return? She had spent a wretched night, tossing and turning and listening for animal sounds in the night.

Now she sat in the hot sun, staring out at the pines and sun-drenched brown rocks. Had she been kidnapped and taken to this forsaken little cabin only to be abandoned? Would she ever see Prue again? Tears welled in her eyes as she thought about never seeing her sister. She loved Prue. She loved Aunt Hanna and Uncle Albert. When she'd come West, she'd thought she would see them all again. Now, sitting on this step, it appeared most unlikely. What had happened to her? Her life was destroyed!

She put her face in her hands, and her body shook with sobs. Alone. Abandoned. Never to see her family again.

At last she swiped at her eyes to dry the tears.

"Why are you crying?"

She jumped at Zander's voice. "When—where—?" she stuttered. He'd come up behind the cabin. A fat doe was slung around his neck.

"I thought you weren't coming back," she muttered.

He set the doe down and met her gaze, his own unreadable. "I was hunting."

She thought she heard remorse in his voice, but could not be sure. She rose to her feet and wiped her face. "Do you want me to help you with the deer?"

"I'll skin it and butcher it," he answered. "You can cook it."

Embarrassed now that he'd seen her tears, she nodded, and with as much dignity as she could muster, she rose and entered the hot little cabin.

Dorie sat on one corner of the bed, at the foot, and chewed her lip nervously. Out of the corner of her eye, she watched Zander move restlessly around the room.

Night had descended, and the large room was

cooler; the dishes from the evening meal had been washed and put away. She picked up a corner of one of the two heavy wool eight-point Hudson's Bay blankets that Zander had earlier taken from his saddlebags and placed on the bed so that the webbing of rope was covered. The blankets were a creamy color, with wide stripes of green, red, yellow, and black.

Dorie fidgeted with the blanket absently, the dim light of the oil lamp dulling the bright colors. Her mind whirled. Was Zander going to sleep on the floor? Or would he demand the bed for himself? She shivered as she remembered his kiss. Would he demand that she stay in the bed and that he sleep there too?

She bunched the blanket tightly at the thought.

Zander left the cabin and walked out into the darkness. She heard him go down the steps.

She glanced up. Was he going to sleep outside? Relief swept through her. What a wonderful solution to her dilemma!

But her hopes dashed when he came back through the door and strode over to the bed. He was naked to the waist, and his hair was wet. He'd been to the creek to wash up, she realized.

She glanced down at her dirt-streaked blue calico dress, and then she picked up a lank curl of blond hair and wound it around one finger. Suddenly she wished that *she* too could go to

151

the creek and cleanse herself.

But he seemed not to notice. He sat down on the bed, and she stared at him—at his wet, black hair that brushed his shoulders, at his massive bare chest. "What—?" she croaked, backing away. She cleared her throat, "What are you doing here?"

"I'm going to sleep here," he said simply and lay down.

She stared at his feet, mere inches from her. If she moved out of the way, he could straighten his legs. But she wouldn't do so—oh no, not until she knew what was going on.

"Where am I supposed to sleep then?" she demanded and heard the trembling in her voice. She hoped he did not.

He put his head in his hands, elbows askew, and stared at the ceiling. "You can sleep right here on the bed," he answered coolly.

She stared at him, wondering what he meant. When he said nothing further, she thought perhaps she could lie beside him on the bed as long as she was close to the wall and not one part of her body touched him. Could she fall asleep that way? Yes, she decided, yawning. She could.

She edged across the bed and settled into the slight depression her body made on the rope. She kept her back to Zander and stared at the large shadows on the wall. A few minutes later, he blew out the oil lamp.

Then there was only darkness. And the sound of crickets chirping outside the cabin. And Zander's even breathing. And her own pounding heart.

She lay there like that for a long time, fighting sleep, wondering if he was going to touch her.

When he didn't, she yawned again and began to relax.

"Dorie?"

She tensed, her stiff back protecting her from him. "What?"

"I wouldn't go off and leave you. I intended to return. Had to hunt."

Whatever she had expected him to say, it was not this. She kept silent, wondering what to answer. Should she even let him know it had bothered her that he'd left? Then she remembered: her tears. He already knew it had bothered her. The man probably thought she'd missed him and was crying with longing for him! He didn't understand that she was crying from the fear of not seeing her family again and the loneliness of staying on the mountainside.

While she was trying to decide how to answer, she felt him put an arm over her, and then he started to plant soft kisses on the back of her neck.

"Zander!" she hissed. "Stop that!"

He kept kissing her. "You smell so good."

She thought of her hair and dirty dress and

153

giggled. "Here I am, wearing the same dress for two straight days. I haven't had a change of clothes and only one swim a few days ago, and you say I smell good."

"You do, to me."

She peeked over her shoulder. "You have no sense of smell then, Zander," she dared.

He sniffed the air above her. "Think not?" She heard the smile in his voice. "In the morning I'll take you to the creek so that you can bathe."

She thought about his offer. "Very well," she accepted agreeably.

She thought then he'd take his arm away from her. But he kept it there, warming her. And when she woke in the morning, his arm was still around her.

In the morning, he kept his word and walked her to the creek. When they reached the water, he handed her a piece of lye soap. She accepted it, pleased. She wondered what other luxuries he had in his trading packs.

She waded into the water and he politely kept his back to her, his rifle held loosely in his arms as he kept watch on the hillside. She didn't feel like such a fool today, when she saw that even Zander was wary of animals and possibly humans, enough so that he carried a rifle.

She peeled off her dress and washed as much of her skin as she could. Then she washed her hair, shivering in the chill liquid of the stream. When she was done, she dried her hair with a piece of cloth and put on the green morning dress she'd removed from her carpetbag. She felt so much better!

They ambled back to the cabin. She shook out her long, tangled wet hair and combed it slowly to let the air dry it. She felt better, and cleaner, than she had in days. Perhaps it was the mouth-watering smell of the deer meat Zander was frying for breakfast over a small outdoor fire. Whatever it was, the bath or her newly awakened appetite, she felt better.

After breakfast, Zander showed her how to start tanning the deer hide. She watched his strong hands as he made the round wooden frame to lace the hide on to keep it from curling once the fat was scraped off. When he took the deer brains and smeared them on the fat side of the hide, she thought she would lose her breakfast. But she didn't. She used a knife, as he taught her, to carefully scrape the fat away. When he complimented her on her handiwork, she glowed inside.

Later in the day, she watched as he made bullets. First, he built up the fire so that it was hot enough to melt the lead. He took a lead bar out of a saddle pack and placed the bar in an iron pot. He set the pot on the flames and waited.

Dorie drew a little away from the heat. Her

eyes followed his every move.

Once the lead was melted, he walked over to the saddle bag to get the bullet mold. When he returned, he also had a pair of thick leather gloves to protect his hands. He ladled out some liquid lead into the eight-hole bullet mold. When the bullets had cooled and hardened, he put them on a piece of leather. Then he ladled more hot lead into the mold. Soon he had a small pile of bullets.

"When will you free me?" Dorie asked.

He gave a start, and hot lead spilled onto his left glove. He tore it off before the lead could burn through to his skin.

He picked up the glove and peered at the hole in it. When he met her eyes, he said coolly, "I am not going to free you. You are going to be my country wife." He bared his white teeth in a feral grin. "But I am a patient man."

Then he went back to pouring lead into the bullet molds, and each movement of the ladle bespoke his caution.

Dorie pondered his answer while she watched him ladle out hot lead. He had finished making the bullets and was heading back to the cabin when she finally shook herself from her reverie. Slowly she moved to follow him. *His wife*, she mused. *He wants me for his wife.*

Their days settled into a routine, Zander fishing or hunting during the day and bringing the fish or game back to her. She cooked the meat and worked on tanning the hides of the game he killed. Together they gathered grass for the horses, walked them to the creek, and brushed them down. Lightning's hooves, injured as a result of Clifton Ross's careless neglect, looked much better because of the several days' rest the horse was enjoying.

Sometimes she and Zander would stroll on one of the deer trails that led through the pines. Once they wandered for a long time, following Kicking Horse Creek to its source, a bubbling pool. Zander swam in the icy water, but she was content to dip her feet only.

Her time with him was becoming quite pleasant, she realized. He had not forced himself upon her, although at night he continued to enfold her in his arms and they slept together that way. And she had accepted it. It was simply for warmth in the night, she convinced herself each day. But each evening a hungry anticipation grew inside her whenever she thought of the bed they would share later that night.

In the daytime, he exerted himself to be the perfect host and she almost came to believe that she was on an extended holiday in the mountains. Almost.

One day he led the mule out of the corral and began saddling him.

Dorie stepped out of the cabin and walked

over to see what he was up to. "We're leaving," he announced.

She glanced at him, bewildered. Then she put her hands on her hips. "If you expect me to be your wife," she protested, "then you must have the courtesy to tell me where we're going."

As she stood there glaring at him, his dark eyes met hers and he grinned rakishly. Her heart skipped a beat.

Then he slowly unsaddled the mule.

Dorie dropped her hands from her hips, her anger fleeing as shadows flee the sun. She watched him warily. She didn't trust that rakish smile. Had she just won a battle against him? Or had she lost one?

Zander grinned to himself as he uncinched the mule. So, she was accepting the idea of being his wife, was she? He started to whistle softly to himself. Suddenly the day seemed brighter, the birds' songs clearer. Elation shot through him.

He pondered what her acceptance meant as he lifted the saddle off the mule. He wanted her—and he wanted her willing. She was watching him; he could feel her eyes on him. Good.

He took a deep breath. Now was not the time to drag her off to another place to hide. Now was the time to bed her!

Chapter Twelve

Clifton Ross marched through the gate into Fort Walla Walla and past the six-inch-thick, eighteen-foot-high wooden plank palisade that protected the fort. Billy Bow plodded after him, leading the packhorses.

Clifton Ross did not see the walkway that encircled the walls so that the stout fort could be defended by riflemen firing from the upper story. He was oblivious, too, to the ten swivel guns and the four cannons housed in each of the four corner bastions. Each bastion also held huge water containers, needed if the fort caught fire.

Clifton Ross ignored these features because he had seen them all before. He muttered under his breath, practicing the bad news he must deliver to Clarence Biddle.

Then Ross and Billy Bow passed through a second, twelve-foot-high plank stockade that surrounded the dwellings and storehouses within the fort. Indians were only allowed in the second enclosure with permission of the factor. Fort Walla Walla, the strongest fort west of the Rockies, was not called the "Gibraltar of the Columbia" for nothing.

As they walked along, Ross muttering, Bow leading weary horses, a trapper hailed them. Ross waved back absently and stayed on his dogged course for the chief trader's house.

They reached the largest wooden structure in the fort. It was the chief trader's residence; the only other house, a smaller dwelling, belonged to Mr. Leland Pomeroy, the fort's clerk.

Clifton Ross marched up to the front door of the chief trader's home. Billy Bow halted the packhorses and watched nervously as Clifton Ross knocked. A pregnant, weary-looking young Indian woman thrust her head out.

Clifton Ross demanded, "Tell Mr. Clarence Biddle we got business with him."

The woman closed the door.

"Not good enough to invite in, am I?" muttered Clifton Ross to himself as he stood shifting from foot to foot, waiting for Biddle. "Good enough to do all your dirty work—trap beavers, escort little sluts—but not good enough to darken your doorway, am I?"

In a short time, Clarence Biddle himself opened the door. He was a tall man with a partially bald head and an owlish look to his blinking eyes behind round glasses. He seemed to be a comfortable, well-fed man with a plump, soft stomach that added padding under his leather jacket.

"Ross," he acknowledged curtly. "About time you got here." He stepped onto the porch, leaving the door partially open. From inside the house came the faint sounds of a child crying. The Indian woman crept to the doorway. He saw her and pulled it closed, then turned to glare at Ross. "Where is Miss Primfield?"

Clifton Ross dangled a single pink ribbon from his fingers. "This is all we have left of her, sir."

"What?" cried Biddle. "What?" He turned on his heel and reopened the door. "Mary, go and fetch Mrs. Pomeroy. Now!"

The young Indian woman shuffled out the door and headed in the direction of the clerk's house. She gave Ross and Billy Bow an impassive glance as she passed them.

The men waited. Biddle took off his glasses and polished them with a thin piece of calico. "What happened to Miss Primfield, Ross?" Biddle held up the glasses and peered through them.

"Somebody done stole her. We don't know who, sir, but somebody did."

Biddle rubbed the bridge of his nose. "Well, then somebody had better find her!"

"We done looked," protested Billy Bow. "The tracks—they was muddied. We couldn't find her nowhere!"

A white woman, carefully holding the front of her long brown-and-white calico dress off the ground, walked sedately toward them. As she reached them, the Indian woman slipped into the house and silently closed the door.

"Good day, Mr. Biddle," said the white woman graciously. Her brown hair was fashioned into a neat knot at the back of her head, and she appeared to be a matron of some thirty years.

"Good day, Mrs. Pomeroy," answered Biddle. His voice was tight with suppressed anger.

The woman glanced questioningly at Ross and Billy Bow and waited. "Why have you summoned me?" she asked at last.

"Tell her," said Biddle curtly to Ross.

"*You* tell her. Sir." Ross wasn't going to deliver the bad news a second time.

Clarence Biddle put on his glasses and cleared his throat. He peered at the woman.

162

"Prudence," he said, "I'm afraid I have some terrible news."

Alarm crossed Prudence's face at these words and she paled. She clasped her hands together.

"I hired these two—uh, trappers to escort your sister to our fort," continued Biddle. "They tell me that she has been stolen."

"Stolen?" gasped Prudence. Her hand flew to her throat.

"Stolen," confirmed Ross sullenly.

Her jaw dropped. "What? How? Who?"

"It's true, ma'am," said Billy Bow earnestly. "She was stolen from us at the Rendezvous."

"My sister!" cried Prudence. "My poor, poor sister! Oh, where is she?" Her voice rose on a scream. Her fists flew to her chest as though her heart pounded so hard she feared it would jump out of her chest.

She glanced wildly at the packhorses, at Billy Bow, then at Clifton Ross. "What do you mean she's stolen? Who stole her?"

With a disdainful grimace at Biddle, Ross took a step backward and glared at her. "She got herself stolen at the Rendezvous and we had to search for her. Couldn't find her, or who did it. Trail disappeared."

Biddle, the glasses distorting his eyes so that they looked round and huge, glared at Ross. "Did you *look*, Ross?" he demanded.

" 'Course I looked," answered Ross. "You got

my furs. I did everythin' I could to find that woman."

"Yes, I do have your furs, and I will be keeping them."

"You cain't do that, Mr. Biddle!" exclaimed Ross. "Me and Billy Bow traveled all the way from Missouri with that woman. We only lost her at the Rendezvous. We deserve to be paid for our troubles! You cain't keep our furs!"

"I can and I will," snapped Biddle. "And I'm not paying you a penny until Miss Primfield turns up!"

"She ain't gonna turn up," wailed Billy Bow. "We done looked for her, I tell ya! She's gone!"

"My sister," cried Prudence, lifting the skirt of her dress to dab at her eyes. "My poor, poor sister." Her muffled sobs brought a look of irritation to Biddle's face.

"Yes, yes, Mrs. Pomeroy," he muttered, "we'll do something to find your sister."

"I should hope so," she snapped angrily, lifting her tear-streaked face, mottled red from her crying.

Before she could say anything else, Biddle said, "I am offering a reward of twenty furs for the safe return of your sister, Mrs. Pomeroy. Twenty furs!"

She dabbed at her eyes. "That is very generous of you, Mr. Biddle, but my poor sister . . .

Alone, out there, somewhere . . . Oh, how terrible!" she wailed.

"I will offer twenty furs for any information whatsoever about your sister!" cried Biddle. "Just stop crying, Mrs. Pomeroy."

"I can't," she cried, sobbing into the hem of her dress.

Irritated and angry, Biddle whirled on Ross. "Get out of here! I have seen enough of you for one day!"

Ross shrugged. "Come on, Billy," he said. "Let's go unload the horses. We don't get no decent treatment around here, anyway." He stomped off, angry at not receiving his payment or the furs that Biddle still held. Billy Bow followed glumly after him.

"Oh, my poor sister," wailed Prudence. "Who knows what horrible things are happening to her!"

Chapter Thirteen

The Sheridan Cabin

It was evening. The autumn nights were cooler now, the days still warm. Zander had wandered off in the direction of the creek. Dorie squinted her eyes in the waning light, the better to see him as he walked. What, she wondered, had caused him to change his mind about the trip?

He was whistling when he left, and she knew something had warmed his mood and caused the change of plans. Indeed, he had been most . . . most pleasant. It had started when he took the saddle off the mule earlier in the day and announced they were not leaving after all. Why? Why weren't they leaving?

It had seemed to her, too, that every time she glanced at him, their eyes met. Oh, not obvious stares, just little glances that warmed her somehow and made her feel all trembly inside. And then there was that jaunty whistling.

What could it mean? she wondered as she stirred the rich deer stew over the open fire Zander had made. It was easier to cook outside on the open fire rather than inside the cabin using the fireplace. So Zander obligingly made the fires outside.

She checked the pan of Indian bannock that was frying in the embers. Several times she had watched Zander make the thick, unleavened bread of flour and water, baking powder and grease, and decided to try making it herself this time. The combined smell of the stew and the bannock made her mouth water.

She heard him whistling to himself. The man was impossible to figure out. First he'd kidnapped her, then he'd treated her . . . Actually, he treated her very well.

He returned from the creek, sauntering along with his red shirt thrown carelessly over one broad shoulder. Her breath caught in her throat. His broad chest glistened with drops of water, and his long black hair was slicked back from bathing in the creek. His long legs, encased in leather trousers, took ground-eating strides smoothly.

On his feet he wore the moccasins that kept his footsteps so silent. He could sneak up on anyone and they'd never know he was there, she thought ruefully. Like the night he'd taken the packhorses and trade goods and secreted them away, leaving her holding only Lightning's reins.

He met her eyes, his dark ones crinkling at the corners as he grinned at her. He sniffed the air. "Smells good," he said, his deep voice warming her. Blushing, she stirred the stew, striving to keep her traitorous eyes from staring at him.

He knew it, too; she could tell. He seemed to know about this strange, intense desire she had to watch him, but he didn't know about the strange, curling sensation in her stomach. Or that her heart pounded faster when she looked into his eyes. Or that her hands trembled so that she needed both of them to stir the stew. No, he didn't know that.

She glanced up to tell him that their meal was ready, but the words died in her throat. He met her eyes, and she saw possessiveness flash in them; she clenched the spoon tightly. His nostrils flared ever so slightly, and he leaned toward her. He wanted her, she realized suddenly. Excitement darted through her. And confusion.

"Our meal is ready," she managed to croak.

Then, without looking at him and knowing her cheeks were aflame, she picked up a tin plate and ladled out the deer stew. Carefully she used a metal spoon to retrieve a chunk of bannock bread. "Here," she said, handing the plate to him. "I—I've fixed the cabin. We can eat inside."

His hand brushed hers as he took the plate, and she snatched her hand back. She fumbled for the second tin plate and began to dish out her own food. He waited until she was done, and then they walked the short distance to the cabin. Her heart was pounding. Every step brought them closer, closer . . . to what?

Something was different between them, something new. She could feel it. But what was it?

She followed him up the two steps, and they entered the cabin.

The cabin was freshly swept; she'd used a bushy pine branch until the floor was uncluttered. On the table a candle burned. A little apart from it was a bouquet of yellow cottonwood leaves she'd found. The shutters on the window were wide open, and the cabin had a clean smell to it. Now and then a cricket could be heard.

Dorie moved toward the table, which she'd pushed next to the bed since there were no chairs in the dwelling.

She sat down on the bed; the table was at just

the right height to eat at. He saw her sit and squeezed in next to her. She stared at her food plate, her stomach a queasy knot. Oh, what was the matter with her?

He took a bite of bannock; oh, why was she so aware of him? Of his every move? She could feel the length of his thigh pressed against her own leg, her thin calico dress no protection from his bodily heat.

They ate in silence, Dorie barely able to choke the delicious stew down. The bannock must have tasted acceptable, but somehow she couldn't think about bannock. Not with him sitting so close to her.

When they were done eating, she picked up the tin plates and fled out the door. *Coward*, she berated herself as she ran towards the creek with the dishes. *Coward. Oh, what a fool he must think you!*

But evidently he did not, for he sauntered after her, a flintlock rifle in the crook of his arm as he watched for bears and wolves.

She thrust the plates in the cold water and swirled sand over them to remove the food, but her mind was on the man accompanying her. Oh, why was she so aware of his every move?

Realizing that she could no longer put off walking back to the cabin, she rose and carried the plates. Zander scooped up the empty stew pot and utensils as they passed the dying fire.

"No sense in calling the bears," he said amiably. They returned to the cabin.

She entered slowly and the burning candle stub caught her eye. She placed the tin plates on the counter against one wall and stood there, staring at the wooden wall. She bit her lip. *What do I do now?* she wondered.

For tonight seemed different, not like the other evenings they shared. Different . . .

She turned to stare at the bed, wondering how she could possibly cross the room to get there with legs that trembled as much as hers did. She met his eyes. She saw the naked desire he had for her in them. Did he see desire in *her* eyes?

"Come," he said, gently taking her hand. She felt his warm touch on her cold fingers and let him lead her to the bed.

He sank down on the thick blankets and pulled her down on top of him. She tried to pull away, but he held on to her hand and then brought her head down for his kiss.

When his lips touched hers, Dorie tried to pull away. But he would not let her, and his lips convinced her to stay. The warmth of his breath, the firmness of his lips on hers, his hands roving her back and holding her gently in place—all of him convinced her to stay. She settled on top of him, her breasts pressed against his hard chest. He smiled and reached up to touch her hair. "You are very beautiful," he whispered. "I've wanted to touch you for a long time."

She sighed, feeling the deep purr of his voice against her breasts. "I've wanted to touch you too," she confessed in a whisper, startled at the truth in her words.

He spread out his arms in a simple invitation for her to touch him. "Oh, Dorie . . ."

But she buried her face in his neck, embarrassed by her own wanton desires. "I can't," she said, muffled.

He put his arms around her. "I can," he assured her.

She felt the cool air on her back suddenly and realized he was peeling off her dress. She lay there for a moment, her face still pressed to his neck, her heart pounding in excitement.

Then he stroked her back gently and murmured reassuringly to her.

Taking courage, she sat up and helped him take off her dress. Once that was done, he removed his leather breeches and moccasins. Then he pulled her to him and there were no barriers between them. Only her skin and his. Warm, smooth, hard. All of him.

He held her to him, stroking her back and sides and speaking softly to her as she lay atop him. She kissed the skin of his neck and found he tasted salty. Bolder now, she kissed her way

173

to his lips and claimed them for her own. He groaned, and his hands circled her naked buttocks and pushed her into the swell of his manhood. She squirmed around on him, trying to adjust to this new sensation. He groaned again and lifted her gently and entered her.

She liked what he was doing and she liked moving against him. She wanted to touch him, she wanted to move inside him, she wanted, she wanted . . . she didn't know what she wanted. Only to be a part of him.

He wanted the same, she realized, trembling, as he moved under her. She felt powerful, having him under her like that, moving with her as she commanded. It was a power she'd not felt before, this power over a man. But it was a gentle power, a giving power, and she thought it just might please her to keep him under her like this for the rest of her life!

But just as she thought it, he reared up a little and rolled her over so that now he was on top of her.

Now she could feel his strength, feel his power as he thrust into her. She glanced down at their joined bodies and a thrill went through her. He was strong, he was gentle, and he was hers!

A growing excitement in her loins had her straining ever closer to him. Then she felt a sweet sensation, a sensation she wanted to hold on to forever and ever. . . .

Suddenly he stiffened and cried out, and she held him to her. Then he relaxed on top of her.

Lazily she opened her eyes and met his dark ones regarding her solemnly. Then he smiled into her eyes and kissed her on the nose.

She stretched and squirmed happily. Well-being flooded through every part of her body, and she kissed him back.

He had claimed her, she thought drowsily, claimed her thoroughly—and she, him.

Zander rolled off her but continued to hold her. Close. Possessively. She felt warm and happy in his embrace. Married, she thought in awe. It was as if they were married. And she was his wife. After all, hadn't Zander called her his *country wife*?

Yes, he had. But what was a country wife?

She wanted to ask him but his eyes were closed. She wouldn't disturb him. A country wife, she reasoned to herself, must be a woman who had a binding promise to be wed as soon as a minister of the church was in the vicinity. Yes, that was it. How lovely. It was no doubt a very practical custom on the frontier and completely understandable too, she thought. After all, ministers and priests were very scarce in the wilderness.

Happy with her reasoning, she sighed luxuriously. "Ah, Zander," she murmured. "Now I am your country wife."

Chapter Fourteen

Dorie moved shyly around the cabin, her eyes on the empty shelves, her mind on her body and on what had happened last night. Right now, she was supposed to be preparing breakfast, a task she'd set herself.

"What would you like for breakfast, Zander?" she asked brightly. "Dried meat and water? Or perhaps you'd like our other great favorite, water and dried meat?"

She smiled as she watched him stretch lazily in the bed. Her cheeks warmed as he cast the blanket aside and stepped onto the cold wooden floor. His naked body reminded her of what they'd done together. She turned away quickly, before he could see her embarrassment and—yes, her excitement.

He chuckled and pulled on his leather breeches and shook back his hair, running his fingers through it. "I'll go to the creek for the water," he answered. "Want to come?"

She nodded. He took the bucket and together they walked, hand in hand, to the creek. Once there, they parted and she washed her hands and face. She'd forgotten to bring her comb. It was back in the cabin, in her carpetbag.

Her eyes dropped from his broad chest to where her pistol sat, tucked at his waist. She reached for it, her fingers curling around the handle of her weapon and brushing his warm stomach. He placed a hand on the gun to stop her. She smoothed out her hand and ran her fingers over his flesh, forgetting the pistol.

He watched her for a moment. Then he pulled the weapon out and handed it to her. "I can return this to you now."

"Are you so certain I won't shoot you?" She giggled as she took the pistol from him. Then she raised it and pointed it at his chest to tease him.

He pushed the gun aside. "It is loaded," he said evenly. "And primed. Ready to fire."

She frowned and pointed it at the ground. "You know," she said casually, "I have never seen you shoot. Do you shoot well, Zander?"

He shrugged his broad shoulders. "Well enough to get game when I need it."

She smiled. "Well enough to get game when you need it," she repeated thoughtfully. She glanced over at a small, almost bare aspen tree that grew about one hundred yards away. "See that yellow leaf?" She pointed at a quivering leaf on one branch of the aspen.

"I see it."

"Watch," she said confidently. Aiming carefully, she pulled the trigger on her pistol. The flint struck against the iron and the gun fired, the report loud in the quiet morning air.

The leaf disappeared.

"Good shot," he said. She was pleased to hear the surprise in his voice.

She handed the pistol back to him. "I am a *very* good shot," she answered.

He looked at her with new respect. "I see I was in danger of my life every minute I was with you."

She frowned at the laughing tone she heard in his voice. "You were," she acknowledged.

He eyed her, thoughtful. "I will remember that. I would not want to cross you."

"No," she answered coolly. "Not a wise thing to do."

He grinned, his teeth white and predatory in the sunshine. "Let's go and have that breakfast you promised me."

179

"What do you choose for breakfast?"

"Water and dried meat."

"Ah. Our great favorite," she answered.

It was mid-afternoon when two strangers approached the cabin. One rode a white gelding, the other a weary-looking chestnut mare. Behind them plodded a heavily loaded gray mule. Zander's packhorses in the corral whinnied in welcome and curiosity to the arriving animals.

Dorie peered out the door of the cabin. Zander was chopping wood, his shirt off as usual. Her glance skidded from admiring his muscles to glaring at the newcomers.

Both men were older, one a little stooped with lank red hair, the other stocky and sporting tangled gray hair dangling from under his leather hat. They both wore typical mountain man garb—brown leather breeches and jackets with leather fringe across the chest—and both carried hunting bags and possibles bags. Rifles bristled from one side of the mule's pack. On the other side was a large wooden cask.

They greeted Zander, and it was obvious from his manner that he recognized them. Dorie watched their approach warily.

"Afternoon, Durban," said the gray-haired man. He spat on the ground as he rocked back and forth on his booted feet. "See ye holed up here in the Sheridan cabin, eh? We were kinda hopin' to stay here a few days ourselves, were we no', Campbell?"

The man with the stringy red hair bobbed his head in dutiful agreement.

" 'Course, we didna know ye was here."

Zander straightened from chopping the wood. "You're welcome to camp here a day or two, Burke. It's Old Man Sheridan's cabin, not mine." He glanced at the cabin and spotted Dorie. He frowned and mouthed something at her.

Thinking he wanted her to come forward and be introduced, she stepped outside. From the frown on Zander's face, she guessed, too late, that he'd wanted her to stay inside.

Ignoring their uncouth stares, she walked towards the newcomers. "Good afternoon," she said, greeting them as graciously as she could. After all, they were friends of Zander's. "Welcome." She smiled at them and said proudly, "I am Zander's country wife."

"Huh?" Burke, the foremost of the two, looked from her to Zander and back again. Then he pushed his leather-brimmed hat back and scratched his head. Campbell, his partner, stared at her, his eyes almost popping out of his head. "Ye're a bonny lass," he breathed.

She smiled tightly. "Thank you."

"Country wife, eh?" said Burke, his head still swiveling between her and Zander. "Well, I'll be . . ." He grinned at Zander and held up his hands as if to ward off Zander's glare. "Makes no mind to me, Durban," Burke added. "It's yer business. . . ."

Dorie wondered what he was talking about. She wanted to ask Zander, but he didn't meet her eyes, keeping his own instead on the two trappers.

"Och, Campbell, go get the whiskey," chortled Burke. "Let's have a wee droppie to celebrate Durban's good fortune here." He paused. "It *is* good fortune, is it no'?"

Campbell eagerly ran over to the mule and lifted off the large wooden cask with a small tap on one side. He plucked two tin cups out of the mule's saddlebags and hurried back to where the others waited. He plunked down the cask beside the wood Zander had been chopping, narrowly missing Dorie's toe.

Each of the trappers filled his cups and sat down on a log. Dorie thought they would have "celebrated" whether she and Zander were there or not. Burke lifted his cup and crowed, "Get your own cups, lads and lassies!" Then he threw back his head and drank noisily.

Zander did not appear interested in "celebrating" and went back to his chopping. Dorie stood there, wondering what to do.

The two trappers soon finished their cupfuls. Campbell leapt to his feet and filled both cups once more with a golden stream of whiskey from the cask. After one more drink, he started singing. Off key.

Dorie hurried back to the cabin. She did not want to "celebrate." She wanted them to leave.

After sitting in the cabin by herself for a while and listening to the garbled singing and the steady chopping of Zander's axe, she decided to go back out and see if she could persuade him to go for a walk with her. He'd been out there a long time. She hadn't realized there was so much wood to chop.

She walked up to him and stared in puzzlement at the growing pile of wood. And all the wood was in small, fine pieces. Evidently, he'd chopped and chopped.

Zander's face was flushed, his lips a tight seam, as he concentrated on placing the axe just so.

". . . ooowhee," chortled Burke, interrupting himself with a hearty swig from his tin cup, "and then there was the time when we got this one Indian so drunk he fell asleep in the middle of a trade, he did! Helped myself to all his furs, to his horse *and* his rifle, I did, and we was on our way 'afore he even waked up!"

"I remember that," chuckled Campbell, slapping his knee in amusement. "That's happened a time or two. Nothing like a wee droppie to grease the wheels of trade!"

183

Whack! whack! went the steady chop of Zander's axe.

Maybe, thought Dorie, these men were *not* friends of Zander's.

"Zander," she urged, "let us go for a walk. There's enough wood to replace what we've used. Surely Mr. Sheridan will be satisfied."

He threw down the axe, picked up his shirt, wiped his brow and followed her. Behind them, Burke and Campbell burst into song.

"What awful men," she said, trying to keep pace with Zander's long strides. "Where do you know them from?"

He shook his head. "Wish I didn't know them," he answered. "They're trappers. I've met them a time or two. At the Rendezvous and at some of the forts."

"Well," she sniffed, "they remind me of Mr. Ross and Billy Bow."

He glanced at her.

"And we both know what fine gentlemen they are!" she observed frostily.

He burst out laughing. Then he dropped one arm over her shoulder and hugged her to him.

She kissed him.

They walked along until they were far from the cabin and surrounded by stunted pines.

Zander sank to the ground and pulled her down beside him.

She kissed him then, wrapping her arms

around him and bringing him to her. Their lips clung, and she felt warm and cherished. He held her to him, and she felt as though he would never let her go.

Forgetting the men, they kissed, and he murmured, "Dorie. We must take this dress off you."

"Only if we take your red shirt and leather pants off you, Zander."

Quickly, they shed their clothes and pressed against each other. His body felt smooth and hard, and she clutched him to her. The hair on his chest felt bristly and tickled her skin. "Mmmmm, Zander," she murmured. She giggled and sighed luxuriously. "Ah, Zander. Do you know how happy I am?"

"How happy?" He was kissing one of her breasts.

"Very, very happy. I am under the wonderfully smelling pine trees. I am held by a warm, caring man . . . Ah, do that again. . . . "

He kissed her other breast. Her skin felt warm, and she glanced down to see herself rosy. A languid sweetness filled her limbs. "Oh, Zander," she sighed.

God, how he wanted her. It was all Zander could do to hold himself back. Would he ever get enough of her? No, he thought. He wanted her now, and he wanted her forever. She was sweetness itself. As gently as he could, he kissed her, but he could feel his body urging him on.

She felt soft, yielding . . . He moved his hand down her stomach and she squirmed. He wondered if he'd tickled her, but no, her eyes were closed, her face intense; she liked what he was doing!

The realization forced him onward. He had to do something soon or . . . "Dorie," he whispered as he hovered over her, "I need to . . . I need to have you now or I'll burst."

"Oh, yes, Zander," she moaned. She gripped him tighter about the shoulders and he followed her urging. He parted her legs with his hand and positioned himself for what he wanted to do. "Ah, but you're so warm and wet," he murmured. Then he put the tip of his manhood against her warm femininity. "Aaaah, God," he sighed. His shaft slid down, down, and he moved gently against her, searching for the welcoming place he knew was there. He found it and drove into her with all his might.

"Zander!" Dorie held onto his shoulders. "Oh, Zander." She had frozen in his arms.

He kissed her forehead frantically. "Are you all right, Dorie? God, I hope I haven't hurt you."

"No, no, it is just that, aaaahhhhhh . . ."

He was moving back and forth in her now, trying desperately to hold back the powerful urge that drove him on. Finally, he could no longer control himself. He plunged once more into her. "Ohhhhh, God," he cried. "Dorie!"

Her fingers tightened, and he felt her nails dig into his flesh. "Zander!" she cried. "Something is happening to me!"

He caressed her intimately then, his hand between them.

"Oh, it is beautiful!" she cried.

He clutched her to him, hoping she was not hurting. If she hadn't told him it was beautiful, he would have thought she was in terrible pain.

Dorie gave herself up to the sweet spiraling sensation that filled her head and body. Waves of sweetness washed over her and then broke in one big, cresting burst of liquid honey. She screamed her delight.

Later, panting and spent, she lay under him.

"Zander?" she asked, her voice low and lazy.

"Hmmmmmmm?" He sounded as if he wanted to fall asleep.

She did too. A delicious warmth and satedness had overtaken her.

"You are heavy, Zander."

"Oh." He groaned and moved off her.

She smiled into his black eyes. Such a thing had never happened before. "Oh, Zander. Again!"

He glanced down at himself. "I am not ready yet, Dorie. These things take time."

"Not too much time, I hope."

He chuckled and kissed her. Soon they were making love again.

* * *

It was dusk. Dorie and Zander stood at the creek, not far from the cabin.

Dorie ran her fingers through her long hair. "Do you see any more pine needles, Zander?" she asked.

He examined her critically. "None," he pronounced.

She smiled up at him and pulled a handful of dried pine needles out of his black hair. "There. They'll never know what we've been doing," she giggled.

"Don't be too sure," he warned. They approached the cabin.

"Zander, I didn't leave the oil lamp lit when I left," cried Dorie in dismay. "Did you?"

He halted and stared at the yellow light shining out of the cabin window. "No."

"Oh no," she moaned. "Those awful men are in our cabin!"

They hurried up to the cabin. Zander strode onto the porch. Dorie ran behind him.

Inside the cabin, Burke was asleep on the bed and snoring loudly. Campbell was sitting on the floor, waving his cup in the air and singing "Scotland the Brave."

"Come on in," he called with a happy grin when he saw them. Pieces of Zander's dried meat were scattered over the table, and only white crumbs remained of the bannock Dorie

188

had cooked at the morning meal. "Come on in."

Dorie shot a look of disgust at Zander. He shrugged.

"Thought we'd settle in," said Campbell. "Old Man Sheridan is right hospitable, don't ye agree?" Then he burst into a full-throated rendition of "Danny Boy."

Zander started collecting the meat off the table.

Dorie reached for the pine branch she'd been using to sweep the floor clean. Sweeping the floor vigorously gave her time to rein in her temper, which was racing ahead of her as fast as Zander's mare.

Lips tight, face pale, with a shaking hand, Dorie pointed at the door. "Out," she cried. "Get out and stay out!"

"Aw lassie," complained Campbell, making no move to obey her. "Ye canna kick two old Scotsmen out into the cold." He took a long sip from his tin cup. "Och," he observed, "ye're a bonny one." He gave her a broad wink.

Dorie felt ill. "Get out, Mr. Campbell." She bit each word out. When he continued to sit there and swing the cup in the air, she turned to Zander. "Will you help me get this *gentleman*"—her teeth were so clenched, she could barely get the word out—"up and through the door?"

"Be happy to," he responded. He picked Campbell up under the arms and helped him to his feet. Then he gave him a push in the general direction of the door. Campbell staggered out into the night, waving his cup and singing loudly.

"Now this one," ordered Dorie, pointing to the snoring Burke.

Zander woke Burke too and escorted him out the door.

Burke and Campbell stumbled around outside. Then they planted themselves down beside the whiskey cask.

"No man," said Burke wisely, "and I mean no man, comes between me and my whiskey."

"Right ye are, laddie," agreed Campbell with a chuckle and a wink.

"Yep," Burke sighed expansively. "No man crosses Ian Burke."

"No man crosses William Campbell either," said Campbell. He gave a loud burp and peered owlishly around. "Who said that?"

Both men laughed.

When Zander returned, Dorie was pushing the table towards the door.

"What are you doing?" he asked.

"Help me," she panted. "I want to barricade the door. I don't trust those men. They are rude, greedy, insensitive louts!"

Zander grinned, and with his help, Dorie soon had the table moved into place. She sagged against him. "Thank you for your help," she whispered.

He kissed her. "You're welcome."

"Now," she said, taking his hand and leading him toward the bed. "Let us get some rest."

"Is that what you have in mind?" he asked.

"Oh, yes," she said. "I do. Most definitely."

The next morning, Dorie rose while Zander was still abed. She rummaged through the dried meat and picked out the best pieces. Then she climbed back into bed. He lunged for her, dragged her under him, and had his way with her. Afterwards, glowing and happy, she sat next to him in bed and fed him the choicest morsels, one by one.

When they were done eating, they got up and got dressed. Then she picked up the bucket and opened the door. "Come with me, Zander," she urged. "I know Burke and Campbell are out there. I shouldn't have to face them alone."

He chuckled. "I'll face them with you. Lassie."

She elbowed him in the stomach for that remark.

They stepped outside, and Dorie saw to her surprise that the two trappers were running to the corral.

"What's the matter?" called Zander.

"A horse has been stolen!" cried Burke.

"Which horse?" demanded Zander, hurrying down the steps.

"A white mare."

Zander ran to the corral.

"Looked like a Nez Perce," cried Burke after him. "He got on the horse and rode off! Campbell and I tried to catch him."

The horses were restive; Shadow trotted over, tossing her head and whinnying. Dorie patted Lightning and whispered into his twitching ears.

"Easy, Shadow, easy girl," crooned Zander.

"It's fortunate that the thief didn't steal your black mare," said Dorie.

"Yeah. But the white mare is a loss, too."

Burke ran up, panting heavily from his exertions.

"How did a Nez Perce get so close to the horses?" demanded Zander. "And in broad daylight?"

"Dinna know," answered Burke. "Me and Campbell, we was just sittin' by the fire, drinkin' our breakfast—"

"We didna hear a thing," said Campbell, "until he galloped off. Then we jumped up—"

"But we were too late," finished Burke. "Far too late, laddie." He shook his head regretfully.

Zander glared at him. "Well, we won't find him if we stand around here talking."

"He's long gone now, Durban," said Burke.

"Yep," agreed Campbell.

Sebastian surveyed the hillside, looking out over the creek and pine trees. "Did you see any others? Might have been a whole Nez Perce horse-stealing party."

Burke and Campbell shook their heads. "Nope. Just the one Injun," answered Burke.

Zander stared off into the direction where the Indian had disappeared. Then he glanced at the two Scotsmen. "Time for you and Campbell to move on," said Zander briskly.

Burke reluctantly agreed. "Sure had a good time celebrating with you and the missus though," he chortled. "Your country wife, eh?" Then he shook his head and muttered, "Never thought I'd meet a woman who'd put up with such a thing so willingly! And her a white woman, too."

"Zander?" asked Dorie curiously. "What is he talking about?"

But Zander shook his head and stared at the corral.

Dorie went back to the cabin. She wanted Burke and Campbell to leave as soon as possible.

Zander followed her to the cabin. "They're leaving," he said.

"Good."

"Come out and tell them farewell," he said. "Then we'll try and follow the trail of the thief.

The horses could use some exercise. They're getting fat."

Reluctantly, she went back out to face her unwanted guests.

"Zander," she gasped, seeing something flutter in Burke's hand. "What has he got? It looks like my—"

"Wait here," ordered Zander.

He strode over to the two trappers. "Where are you going with that pink ribbon? That belongs to Dorie."

"Oh. This one?" Burke held up the pink ribbon Dorie had worn the night Zander captured her.

"That one," confirmed Zander.

"Heh, heh, not to be getting upset about this now," said Burke, acting jovial.

"Zander, he stole it!" said Dorie, appalled.

"Give it back to her," ordered Zander.

"We were going to trade her for it, laddie," protested Campbell.

"Give it back." Zander's face was implacable.

Reluctantly Burke handed the scrap of ribbon to Dorie. She took the ribbon from him and an idea formed in her mind. "If you wish to trade for this ribbon, I will oblige," she informed Burke.

He brightened and pointed at the heavily laden mule. "We got plenty to trade for it," he said genially. He grinned at her, then nodded at

Zander, as if trying to mollify them both.

Dorie decided to use the situation to her advantage. She walked over to the mule. "I want to see what you have to trade for it," she said.

Burke dug into saddlebags and boxes and baskets and soon had a small array of bells, beads, handkerchiefs, rings, and armbands for her to look at.

She picked up a little bell and shook it, listening to the tinkling sound.

"Oh, lass," said Burke, "ye'll need more'n one ribbon to trade for that. Them bells donna come cheap." He shook his head. "No sir, they donna."

"I do not want the bell," answered Dorie frostily.

She put down the bell and picked up a linen handkerchief. The work was delicate, and she wondered how such an uncouth man as Burke had such a fine item to trade. Probably stole it, too, she decided.

"That will cost ye, lass," said the irrepressible Burke. "Ye got anything else to trade besides that skinny ribbon?"

"*If* I wanted this handkerchief," stated Dorie, "I could add something to the ribbon. A book of poetry perhaps."

"Well now, depends on the poet," said Burke. "We don't take the books of just any old poet ye know."

"Does Lord Byron meet with your tastes?" demanded Dorie. Really, this man was exasperating!

He jumped back a step. "Oh, yes, lass. Lord Byron, why, he's a fine poet, lass."

"Glad you approve," said Dorie through clenched teeth. "Show me your rings."

"Oh, our rings are all very expensive," said Burke.

"Show me your rings," gritted Dorie.

Burke pointed out the rings. " 'Course, they's kinda expensive," he repeated.

"Mr. Burke," snarled Dorie, "all your trade items are expensive, are they not?"

"Well, yes, lass, they are."

"Very well. Since that fact is now well established, please allow me to examine the rings in silence."

"Yes, lass." He rolled his eyes at Campbell.

Really! These trappers were the most uncouth—suddenly a pretty ring that looked like carved, entwined grape leaves caught her eye. The ring was solid and well-made and the leaves looked realistic. She picked it up and admired it; it was the very thing she wanted.

"How much for this ring, Mr. Burke?"

He eyed the ring, then Dorie's rising color. "I expect the ring is worth the ribbon o'course and the book o' poetry and something else."

"What else?" Dorie tapped her foot impatiently. She did *not* enjoy haggling with this man!

"Ohh," mused Burke, examining her. "Maybe a wee kiss . . ."

"The ribbon and the book of poetry will suffice, Burke," broke in Zander's deep voice.

Burke sighed and nodded. "Very well, I accept yer offer, lass." He held out the ring. "Take it."

"Thank you," she said, pleased, and slipped it on her middle finger. The ring was too big. She smiled and turned away from Zander so that he could not see it. He would learn of her plans for it later.

Burke and Campbell put away their remaining trade goods and mounted up. As they started to leave, Burke pulled abreast of Zander and said casually, "No need to mention to anyone that ye saw us here, now is there, Durban?"

"You hiding out from someone?" asked Zander in amusement.

Burke chuckled. Campbell squirmed in embarrassment. "Ye might say as much," Burke acknowledged. "Got into a wee bit of trouble a time back."

Dorie would have bet her best mauve dress that it was more than "a wee bit of trouble" those two got into.

Zander nodded and gave a wave. "Farewell," he said to the trappers, and at last Burke and Campbell departed.

Dorie watched them move slowly down the mountainside and disappear into the pine trees. She said to Zander, "I'm certainly glad we've seen the last of those two!"

That night, after Dorie and Zander made love, they lay in bed and listened to the crickets singing. "Ah," sighed Dorie. "This is a happy time for me, Zander."

"Is it?" he asked drowsily.

Her eyes fastened on his handsome face, all that she could see of him by the light of the candle on the table. "Yes," she answered. She snuggled closer to him. "Oh yes, Zander."

Then she pushed off the blanket and climbed over him. "Where are you going?" he complained. "Come back and warm me, woman!"

She giggled and, by the light of the single candle, found her way carefully to the table. On top of the table was her carpetbag. She fumbled inside it and finally found what she sought. Then she shuffled back across the wooden floor to the bed and climbed over Zander.

"Ouch," he moaned.

"Sorry," she replied, not at all repentant. She could tell he wasn't hurt.

She settled under the blanket again. "Zander?"

"Mmmm? You have cold feet," he observed.

"You have warm thighs," she answered,

plunking her feet on his limbs.

When he groaned, she said, "Zander, open your eyes. I have something for you."

She felt him stir next to her. "What is it?"

She waited until he opened his eyes. She smiled into those dark, dark eyes. "Here, my love," she said gently, taking his left hand. Then she slid the brass ring gently over the knuckles of his fourth finger. "For you, my husband."

Chapter Fifteen

One month later
Fort Walla Walla

Early one evening, Clifton Ross and Anton Thunder Horse sat playing cards at a plank table in the men's quarters.

Ross reached for his tin cup of whiskey and took a drink. "I'm about done," he said. "You cleaned me outta coins tonight."

"Aw," answered Anton, his speech slow, "no need to go yet. Let us have another game."

"Don't want to," answered Ross, getting to his feet.

Anton reached out a hand and plunked him roughly back onto the wooden bench. "Sit."

Clifton Ross sat down. He glared at the Indian, who met his eyes with a dark, unblinking stare.

"You been drinkin' too much of that whiskey," observed Ross.

"No." Anton dealt out another hand of cards. "You play," he ordered.

Clifton Ross sighed. "Oh, all right. One game of poker. That's all. Then I'm going."

Anton said nothing, but kept dealing.

Clifton Ross filled his tin cup with whiskey again, hesitated, then poured some into Anton's cup. "Here. And that's the last of the whiskey for you."

Anton growled at him. They began to play cards.

As he stared at his hand of cards, Ross said, "That Biddle sure is angry these days. You notice?"

"I noticed," slurred Anton.

"Yeah, well, I know why he's so mad. He's mad 'cause he had to increase the reward for findin' Dorie Primfiel' to fifty furs. Fifty!"

Anton took a slurp of his drink.

"Sure wish I had them fifty furs," said Ross, laying down a card. "I could use them." He glanced at Anton. "What the beaverdam are you smiling about?"

Anton's smile disappeared. "The game."

"Oh. Am I losing?" Clifton Ross studied his

TO THE RETAILER:

You must be authorized by the Department of Agriculture to participate in the Food Stamp Program before you may accept food coupons for eligible items.

CERTIFICATION OF PERSON TO WHOM ISSUED:

I certify that I applied for and was issued this coupon book. I agree to show this book to the retailer at the time of each purchase and to provide identification if requested.

_____
City and State

_____
Signature of Person to Whom Issued

DO NOT REMOVE COUPONS UNTIL TIME OF PURCHASE!

FINDER: PLEASE RETURN THIS BOOK TO THE NEAREST WELFARE OFFICE

A61555869U

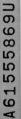

cards. "Fool Injun. I'm not losing." He shook his head. "You know, Biddle ordered me and Billy Bow to look everywhere for that dang woman."

"Who?" smiled Anton.

"Miz Primfiel'. The slut."

Anton frowned at his cards.

"Me and Billy looked everywhere, and we still cain't find her," whined Ross. "We looked along every river we found and done checked every trapper's cabin we knowed was there. Even found two more cabins we didn't know about. Even asked at the Injun villages. But no dang Dorie Primfiel'.

"So then we went into the Blue Mountains," continued Ross. "Me and Billy wasted a whole week wanderin' through them hills and checkin' around."

"Ah, you won't find her there," slurred Anton.

Ross froze. "What'd you say?"

"Your turn," said Anton hastily. He reached for his tin cup and tipped it up, drinking until it was empty.

Ross threw a coin on the table and laid down his cards, eyeing Anton suspiciously. "I see you and I call you."

The game ended and Anton pocketed the small pile of coins on the table. "I won," he chortled.

"Yeah," agreed Ross slyly, getting up from the table. "You won, all right."

*   *   *

A little later that evening, Clarence Biddle sauntered into the men's quarters and scanned the smoky room. He passed by men asleep on their narrow bunks. Others were drinking or playing cards, and these, too, he ignored.

His eyes finally fixed on one person and he strode over to where his quarry sat, snoring, still seated at the table.

"Wake up, Anton," ordered Biddle, shaking the Nez Perce man.

"Huh?" Anton's eyes flew open, and he blinked several times when he saw Biddle. He sat up, his eyes bleary. "What do you want, Biddle?"

Biddle smiled down at him with an oily grin, his eyes owlish behind the round glasses. "Why, Anton," he said, "Mary misses you. You haven't been by to visit your dear sister for some time. She's been asking about you."

Anton said nothing to that, only watched Biddle warily.

Biddle clapped him on the back. "Come on, Anton," he said heartily. "Come on over to my house and we'll have a friendly drink. Just like brother-in-laws do. What do you say?"

He waved casually at a man he recognized while waiting for Anton's answer.

At last, Anton rose shakily from the bench. "Need . . . a drink."

"Ross was right," Biddle said under his breath, helping Anton as he staggered across the floor. "You can have that drink. Then you'll tell me everything I want to know."

Chapter Sixteen

Dorie stood rubbing her eyes in disbelief. "Zander, what are you doing?" she demanded as he led the mule out of the corral. The packhorses already stood loaded with goods.

Dorie glanced around, bewildered. Because she'd been feeling so tired, she had taken a nap late that morning. Odd, how she was taking naps the last few days and feeling tired and sick. But at least her stomach felt better now than it had earlier this morning.

Still dazed from her nap, she'd tottered outside to look for Zander.

"What are you doing?" she asked him again.

"Get your things," said Zander.

"What? Why?" she mumbled. "Where are we going?"

"Get your things."

She whirled and stomped back to the cabin. "How am I supposed to pack when I don't even know where we're going? You'd think that Mr. High-and-Mighty Durban would at least have the courtesy to tell me where we're going, but no. Just *get your things*," she mimicked. She scrunched her dresses into her carpetbag and rattled around the cabin, looking for any item she'd missed and still muttering to herself. At last, satisfied that she had everything, she headed out the door.

"Now what?" she exclaimed, exasperated. Zander held the reins of Lightning and his black mare, both already saddled. "Will you please tell me where we are going?"

He handed her the reins to Lightning and took her carpetbag from her. He strode back to the mule and hooked the carpetbag to the mule's large load.

Then he mounted the black mare and sat calmly waiting for her to mount Lightning.

With a last cry of exasperation, Dorie put her moccasined foot in the stirrup and swung up onto the chestnut gelding's back. "Do you think Lightning's rested his lame hooves long enough?" she asked anxiously, secretly hoping Zander would reconsider leaving the cabin.

"His hooves looked fine to me," answered Zander. "He will not give us any trouble."

Disappointment swooped through her. She didn't want to leave the cabin. She liked it there and they'd already spent over a month on the mountainside, by her reckoning.

But Zander looked most determined. She took a breath. "Zander," she said, as patiently as she could, "I want to know where we are going."

No answer.

"If you will not tell me," she snarled, "then we have little to say to one another."

He shrugged and nudged the black mare forward.

Dorie shook Lightning's reins and they started off. While he bumped along, she turned in the saddle for one last look at the cabin.

She would miss this place, she thought. The place where she and Zander first made love, first became husband and wife. She sighed. If only he would tell her where they were going. Sometimes the man was so exasperating!

Dorie bumped along, lost in her thoughts, until she noticed that the black mare was some distance ahead. The packhorses were strung in a line between Zander and herself. "Come on, Lightning," she clucked. "Move faster. Giddap!"

The horse obligingly increased his pace— from bumpy to bumpier. Her stomach felt queasy again. Dorie sighed. It was going to be a very long ride—to wherever it was they were going.

Zander rode in thoughtful silence. He had decided not to tell Dorie why they were leaving the cabin. It was because he feared it was only a matter of time before they'd be discovered.

They'd already spent as much time as he dared on the mountainside, and now it was time to move on. Burke or Campbell might let it slip that he and Dorie were hiding out at the cabin. Or someone might be searching for them on Biddle's orders. Or even Old Man Sheridan might return and get suspicious. No, it was best they move on now, before word got around that they were hiding out at the cabin.

But where should they go? he wondered as Shadow trotted along.

His original plan to trade his way out to Fort George still sounded like a good one. But would his people accept Dorie once he got there?

He caught himself up short. What was he thinking? She was his country wife, not his true wife. His people would accept her. But some of the trappers and traders, especially those higher in the fur companies' hierarchies who looked down on any unsanctioned unions, would not. They would condemn her.

A guilty feeling stirred in his gut. What did it

matter what a few traders thought? Actually more than a few . . .

He couldn't live his life based on the opinions of men who would be all too happy to condemn an innocent woman.

Then what about Mary? She was a country wife, with no protection for herself or her children. No one gave a damn what happened to her! Why should Dorie Primfield be coddled and protected? His gut was hurting now.

He surveyed the barren country as he pondered. Dorie was very quiet, he realized after a while. Was she still angry at him because he had not told her where they were going?

He turned in the saddle and tried to catch her eye. Her face was pale and stony. She stared straight ahead, ignoring him.

Let her, he thought angrily as he settled himself in the saddle again. If she wanted to ignore him, let her! Two could play at that game.

They had reached the bottom of the mountain trail, and the ground was still rocky. He turned once more in the saddle to make certain the packhorses plodded steadily.

Suddenly, to his horror, he saw Lightning stumble. Those damn hooves! he thought, and then he was racing the black mare as fast as he could to reach Dorie.

But he was too late. The gelding toppled and Dorie crumpled to the ground. Her head hit a rock and she lay there, unmoving.

Chapter Seventeen

Thunk, thunk, thunk, thunk.

The loud pounding sound woke Anton. He held his head. The blood in his brain seemed to pound in time to the terrible sound. His stomach roiled with last night's drink. Lord, he felt awful.

He glanced around. He was lying on the ground outside the chief trader's house. Biddle must have kicked him out after the drinking last night, Anton realized slowly.

He sat up, trying desperately to remember what had happened last night. He could remember playing cards with Clifton Ross, and winning. He could remember Biddle coming along and taking him over to his house for a

213

drink. He remembered seeing Mary and the child. And the drinks. Many drinks. But after that, he couldn't remember a thing. Not a thing.

Wait. There *was* something . . . Something tickling at the back of his mind . . . It was Biddle. He'd asked about Zander. And Dorie Primfield. But what had he asked? And worse, what had Anton answered?

Shaking his head in the struggle to remember, Anton slowly got to his feet. He felt like vomiting right there on the path. His body shook as though with fever, and his stomach heaved. He swayed; every muscle of his body screamed in pain.

No more whiskey, he vowed to himself. *No more whiskey! Never again. It is poison to me. And no brandy either,* he warned himself. *That's what Biddle gave me to drink. Brandy. Sweet, thick brandy.*

He leaned against the chief trader's house. The building lurched and the pounding rang in his ears. "Stop," he mumbled.

Still the pounding continued. A trapper finished hammering a nail into a log on the side of the building and walked away.

Through bleary eyes, Anton stared at the fluttering piece of paper nailed to the wall. Then he turned away, unable to read.

Mary. Maybe his sister could tell him what had happened last night.

He staggered to the back door of the chief trader's house. Mary let him in and helped him to sit at the table. She ladled out a cup of water and shuffled over to give it to him, her belly heavy with her growing babe.

Anton took a sip of water. "What—" He swallowed. "What happened last night?"

Mary shrugged. She looked so young. She was only a kid, this little sister of his. "I do not know, Anton," she said. "I went to bed." She sat down on a chair and eyed him, growing concern in her lovely dark eyes. She brushed a lock of hair from her thin, high-cheekboned face. "Clarence is in a good mood this morning," she finally said. "He has been very difficult to live with. For many, many days he has been gruff. He yells at me. At our daughter." She shrugged. "This morning he was singing." She smiled at Anton. "Maybe you told him some good jokes, brother."

Anton shook his head, his stomach lurching. Dread seeped into him. "I do not think so." He took another sip of water. "Where is Clarence now?"

"He and some of the men are out pounding nails and fixing the fort." Her daughter called to her fretfully from the bedroom. Mary rose and shuffled into the bedroom. While she was gone, Anton staggered to his feet and slunk out the back door. His head hurt.

He shuffled across the yard to the men's quarters. He was just about to enter when he spotted Billy Bow nailing a piece of paper to the log wall. "What is that?" asked Anton.

Billy Bow stepped back from his handiwork and read proudly, "Ree-ward. One hunnerd furs. For the return of Miz Dorie Primfield of Rochester, Missoura. Miz Primfield has been missin' since August. Last seen near Kicking Horse Creek with Zander Durban, half-breed. Report any news you have to Mr. Clarence Biddle, Esquire, Chief Trader, Fort Walla Walla."

Anton's head reeled. "Dorie Primfield and Zander?" he whispered. "At Kicking Horse Creek? How—how does Biddle know?"

A firm hand clapped him on the shoulder. "Ho, ho," boomed Biddle. "Anton, old boy! I see young Billy's just informed you of our new information on Miss Primfield. One hundred furs, eh, Billy?"

Billy nodded happily. "I aim to get me them furs."

Clarence Biddle grinned at the trapper. "Good, good," he said, waving Billy away. Then Biddle lowered his voice in Anton's ear. His grip tightened on Anton's shoulder. "You've earned thirty of those furs, Anton." He laughed. "Or would you prefer thirty pieces of silver?"

Chapter Eighteen

Zander leaped from his saddle and raced to Dorie's side. He knelt beside her and peered into her deathly pale face. His stomach clenched into a cold, frozen knot. "Dorie," he cried. "Wake up!"

He almost shook her to wake her, but something stopped him. With sensitive fingers, he ran his hands along her limbs, searching for broken bones. There were none that he could detect. He couldn't feel her backbone because she was lying on her back and he dared not move her just yet.

She moaned and her eyelids fluttered. He held his breath, hoping she would awaken, but she did not. His heart sank.

"Dorie," he groaned, "what has happened to you?"

He glanced around, frantic, wondering what to do. Then he leaned closer and peered at her head where it touched the rock. Blood seeped through her blond hair. He closed his eyes. Oh, God, she was hurt. Bad.

He ran to the mule and dug through the saddlebags. He raced back with a piece of cloth and lifted her head, placing the cloth against the back of her head. He had to stop the bleeding!

When he was satisfied that the bleeding was stanched, he stood up and glanced around.

He had to get her to some kind of help. But who? Where?

Wait! There was an Indian village not far away. One he'd visited a few times during his years in trade. Perhaps they could help.

He leaped to his feet and ran to the chestnut packhorse. Heedless, he tore off trade goods and threw them on the ground, uncaring about their value.

Lightning nibbled at a bunch of dried-up grass, obviously recovered from his fall. But Zander dared not use Lightning to carry Dorie—not after that stumble—even though his hooves looked fine.

He finished unloading the chestnut, then led it over to Dorie's still form. Taking a deep breath, he lifted her. Her head fell back; she was like a limp rag in his arms.

He stumbled over to the horse, hoisted Dorie onto the mare and tied her to the saddle. He saw with a sickening jolt that the back of her head was coated in dried blood. At least the bleeding had stopped.

He jumped onto Shadow. The packtrain headed along a little-used trail that Zander hoped led to the Indian village. It had been two years since he'd traded with them, he remembered now. And it was about this same time of year. But would the Indians still be there? Most Indian groups moved around frequently, following the seasons and the animals.

He glanced back at Dorie's unmoving body draped over the saddle. He halted Shadow, dismounted, and ran to check Dorie. Her face was red. Her feet felt very warm. Her blood, he realized, was pooling in her head and her feet. She couldn't ride a horse very long that way. He cast around, anxiety straining at him. What should he do?

He lifted her off the chestnut and laid her gently on the stony ground. He stared at her pale face. Oh, God. How had this happened? What if she was going to die? Here, on this deserted mountainside with only him for a companion? Him. The man who had stolen her. Taken her virginity. Oh, God.

He put his head in his hands. He'd never

meant that this should happen. Never. But it had. Wearily, he wiped at his face. What should he do?

A litter! He could make a litter for her and drag it behind the horse.

He cut two long, strong, pine poles and tied a heavy Hudson's Bay blanket between them. Then he tied the poles of the litter to his black mare.

Carefully, he lifted Dorie onto the litter and placed her as comfortably as he could. He put another blanket over her. He mounted the mare and they set off.

Dragging the litter slowed him down. He had trouble keeping the mule and Lightning and the other packhorse away from it too. They were always bumping into it, trying to take their usual place right behind Shadow.

After a time he came to a stream and halted. While the horses drank, he filled a tin cup with fresh water and walked over to Dorie. She was still unconscious. He knelt beside her and put the cup to her lips. He managed to get some water into her mouth, and she swallowed reflexively. He wiped his brow. It was hot, this autumn weather. He had to make certain she had enough water.

He got back on the black mare and they set off once again. He could see faint traces of the trail and he hoped it was the one he should follow.

He kept riding until night descended, forcing him to halt. Dorie was still unconscious, though she accepted a little more water. He clenched his fists and sucked in a sob. She had to live. She had to!

At dawn, he rose and dressed swiftly. Thank God she had lived through the night.

He was walking back to his mare when suddenly she made a small sound. He turned. Her face twisted; she gagged and spat foam. She was convulsing! He grabbed a stick off the ground and put it in her mouth to keep her from biting her tongue. Her arms and legs shook spasmodically. All he could do was hold the stick and wait. "There, there," he said despairingly, trying to soothe her. And himself.

At last her convulsions stopped. Relief crept through him when he felt her grow still again, but she was still unconscious. He tucked the blanket around her, then trudged back to his mare. They started on the trail once more.

His days with the Jesuits had taught him few things that he could use in this world. But one thing they *had* taught him was to pray. He did so now, harder than he'd ever prayed in his life.

Zander woke up in a tepee and stared at the conical hides above him. He blinked in the early evening light. It took him a moment to remember where he was. Ah, now he remembered. He had finally reached the Indian village.

He remembered pointing to Dorie before he'd collapsed to the ground, exhausted. It had taken two days to find this village—two nightmarish days during which Dorie had not awakened.

"Dorie . . ." he murmured hoarsely, tossing a Hudson's Bay blanket off himself and standing up. He must get to Dorie. A surge of fear shook him. Was she still alive?

Yanking on his shirt and trousers, he staggered out of the tepee. It was early evening, and a blue, smoky haze hovered among the tepees. Women stirred big pots at the fires, cooking the evening meal. Dogs and children ran around the dwellings. "Where is she?" he muttered, fear gripping him still.

He began to search frantically. Where was she? He searched for any sign of her, of his horses. As he hurried past a tepee decorated with several red lines and the picture of a hawk, a handsome Indian man emerged and greeted him. Zander halted. He was just about to ask the man if he'd seen Dorie when the man pointed to a tepee and said, "Come."

"I need to find Dorie," protested Zander, but the man beckoned him firmly.

Shrugging, Zander followed him to a tepee

set at some distance. "Inside this lodge. Your woman."

Zander heard a woman's voice, singing. It did not sound like Dorie. He slowed his pace and gathered his courage for what he would see. He pushed the flap aside. "Dorie?"

"You go in," said the man, in halting English. He waited for Zander to enter the tepee, then followed him inside.

Two Indian women sat inside. The man spoke to the younger woman with a papoose on her back. She smiled at him as she answered. No doubt she was his wife, thought Zander, as he watched her tend the small fire in the center of the tepee. On the other side of the fire, several furs were spread out, and Dorie lay upon them. Sitting next to her was an old woman; it was she who was singing. The pungent odor of burned herbs hung in the air. Zander coughed and sat down beside Dorie.

"Gentle Fawn," said the man. "Get visitor food. He sleep for two days."

Gentle Fawn rose to her feet; the baby on her back stared at Zander with alert brown eyes. The man's eyes lovingly followed the baby and the woman as they left the tent. Zander watched the little family, sensing the strong love between them. *That's what I want with Dorie,* he thought wistfully. Then the thought was gone as swiftly as it had come. He was left alone with the man, the old woman, and Dorie.

"Do—do you think she will live?" croaked Zander. The Indian man did not answer; Zander turned to the old woman and waited as patiently as he could for her answer.

"She live if Great Spirit wills it," said the medicine woman finally.

Zander's eyes fastened on Dorie. Deep within him something stirred, wanting wholeheartedly for her to live. "If the Great Spirit wills it," he muttered, turning the words into a prayer.

Gentle Fawn returned then, bearing a bowl of stew. She handed it to Zander and he ate. The stew tasted delicious. He closed his eyes. Deer. With roots. And herbs. He opened his eyes. Would Dorie ever eat again? Or would she die?

"If the Great Spirit wills it," the old woman had said.

After he had eaten, Zander thanked the man and the women and staggered from the tepee. Was life really so simple? he asked himself. *Was* Dorie's life truly in the Great Spirit's hands?

Yes, he answered himself. It was.

Could he trust the Great Spirit to know what was best for Dorie? Did the Great Spirit know that the best thing for her was to live?

No, he answered himself. He didn't think the Great Spirit knew that. The Great Spirit had to be convinced. With prayers. Zander's prayers.

Zander wandered blindly along a short trail

Thrill to the most sensual, adventure-filled Historical Romances on the market today...

FROM ⎣⎦ LEISURE BOOKS

As a home subscriber to Leisure Romance Book Club, you'll enjoy the best in today's BRAND-NEW Historical Romance fiction. For over twenty-five years, Leisure Books has brought you the award-winning, high-quality authors you know and love to read. Each Leisure Historical Romance will sweep you away to a world of high adventure...and intimate romance. Discover for yourself all the passion and excitement millions of readers thrill to each and every month.

Save $5.⁰⁰ Each Time You Buy!

Each month, the Leisure Romance Book Club brings you four brand-new titles from Leisure Books, America's foremost publisher of Historical Romances. EACH PACKAGE WILL SAVE YOU $5.00 FROM THE BOOKSTORE PRICE! And you'll never miss a new title with our convenient home delivery service.

Here's how we do it. Each package will carry a FREE 10-DAY EXAMINATION privilege. At the end of that time, if you decide to keep your books, simply pay the low invoice price of $16.96, no shipping or handling charges added. HOME DELIVERY IS ALWAYS FREE. With today's top Historical Romance novels selling for $5.99 and higher, our price SAVES YOU $5.00 with each shipment.

AND YOUR FIRST FOUR-BOOK SHIPMENT IS TOTALLY FREE!

IT'S A BARGAIN YOU CAN'T BEAT! A Super $21.96 Value!

⎣⎦ LEISURE BOOKS   A Division of Dorchester Publishing Co., Inc.

GET YOUR 4 FREE BOOKS
NOW—A $21.96 Value!

Mail the Free Book Certificate Today!

Get Four Books Totally FREE – A $21.96 Value!

PLEASE RUSH
MY FOUR FREE
BOOKS TO ME
RIGHT AWAY!

Leisure Romance Book Club
65 Commerce Road
Stamford CT 06902-4563

AFFIX
STAMP
HERE

that led to the river. He threw himself down on the grass that grew along the stream and stared at the water. Frogs croaked a merry chorus at him. Crickets sang. All around him was life. But back in that tepee, he thought starkly, was death. Dorie's death.

He picked at a blade of grass and stuck it in his mouth. He chewed on it while he thought about her. He should tell the Great Spirit what to do. Tell Him to save Dorie's life.

For what? came a tiny voice in his mind. *So that you can use her and discard her and humiliate her?*

His conscience writhed under that question.

No! I would have married her, he thought at last. *I would have loved her and married her.*

No, you would not, answered that terrible, honest voice from deep inside him. *You would have destroyed her. Like your father destroyed your mother. Do you still plan to?*

Zander kept silent. Damn his Jesuit education, he thought at last. Why had he been taught to do what was right? What was honorable? Why couldn't he have been taught to satisfy his needs, with no regard for anyone else? Other people did it. He saw it often, especially in trading. People stole, people cheated, people lied; sometimes they killed one another.

Why did *he* have to have this terrible, honest little voice inside him?

Everyone has the truth inside him, came the voice. *You only need heed it.*

Zander squirmed. He did not like the conversation he was having with himself on this riverbank. Or rather, he did not like what he was learning about himself.

He stared pensively at the water. He could not bring himself to pray. He could not ask the Great Spirit or the Christian God or whoever the hell was in charge of the universe to spare Dorie's life. Not when there was this confusion within him.

What was true, he realized at last, was that though he had not planned to use Dorie and cast her aside, that could be a possible outcome of the events he had set in motion. She had no protection, no promises from him, no approval from society. She had only her trust in him. She had given generously of herself and her body. He had seen her love for him in her eyes, heard it in her voice, felt it in her touch. Yet the situation was ripe to humiliate her. And for what?

So that Mary, vulnerable Mary with her children, could be saved from the exact same fate he'd visited upon Dorie! Zander squirmed.

How did humiliating Dorie help Mary or avenge Zander's mother? How?

It didn't.

He rose, unable to continue this terrible, horrible honesty any further. "Enough," he cried. "Enough!"

Zander glared at the water. If Dorie died, he'd be left alone. Just as he'd been when the Jesuits took him in. Loneliness he could understand. He did not want to be alone like that, ever again. Dorie was his. He'd stolen her. She belonged to him.

He could not pray for her to live for her sake, he realized. He could only pray for her to live for *his* sake. *What a selfish bastard I am*, he thought, even as his lips moved and formed a prayer.

"Lord, please spare her. Let her live. For my sake," he prayed.

Then he grew crafty. "If you let her live," he prayed, "I will marry her." There! That would be acting honorably toward her. If the Great Spirit willed it and Dorie lived, then he, Zander, would marry her.

He smiled to himself, pleased with his bargain. Now all God had to do was meet His side.

"That's the deal," whispered Zander. "You let her live, and I'll marry her. I'll be happy to marry her. I want to marry her. Only let her live. Do you hear me, God? That way we are both satisfied. You and me. It's a good deal for both of us," he added persuasively.

And what about Dorie? came the little voice deep inside him.

"It's a good deal for Dorie too," he prayed. "She gets someone who loves her. Stands by her. Marries her. Of course, she doesn't get a choice in the deal, but then choice is a small thing anyway. Just a luxury."

What would Dorie choose if she ever got a choice?

"Well, she wouldn't choose me if she knew what I'd done, that's for certain!" Zander answered himself. "I know that. No, if Dorie ever learns what a country wife is, I'm in deep trouble!"

Sadly, he realized that he almost wished she had known. At least then she'd be alive. Not teetering on the brink of death.

Slowly he retraced his steps along the trail back to the tepees. His mood was glum. He entered the tepee where she lay. The singing had stopped.

Dorie lay in the same position. Deep despair gripped Zander's heart. This was no game. He had it all wrong. This was no contest with God to see who could outwit the other. This was life and death. Dorie's life and death.

He knelt beside her and took her hand. A burst of love and caring for her, every positive feeling he'd been tamping down, rose spontaneously within him. "Please spare her, God," he prayed, the words forming easily in his heart. "Please spare her and I will marry her. I will love her and cherish her until the day of my death. This I promise."

He squeezed her hand, wanting to give her some of his life—yes, even his love. She had to live. She had to!

Then he sank back beside her to wait, his heart full of the love he had just discovered he had for her. He brushed a finger across her forehead, moving a blond lock of hair gently aside. Her breast rose and fell with each breath. At least she still lived, he thought. Perhaps his prayers had helped.

"You love her?" croaked the old medicine woman.

Zander glanced up. He had forgotten she was there.

She was sprinkling a pinch of dried leaves in a cup of warm water.

"Yes," he answered slowly.

"Love very strong," said the old woman. "Sometimes heals."

Zander stared at Dorie, the feeling of love for her strong within him. He took on new hope from the medicine woman's words. Something about her reminded him of his Jesuit teachers.

"But sometimes not," the old woman added. She crumpled some more dried herbs into Dorie's drink. "Only Great Spirit knows."

"He may know," answered Zander, "but He's not telling us, is he?"

She shook her head and gave a cackle. "No." She watched him. Then she poured a little of the tea into Dorie's mouth. Dorie swallowed.

At last the old medicine woman said, "Will be a surprise. Great Spirit always like give surprises."

Chapter Nineteen

Dorie's eyes fluttered, trying to open. They felt heavy, very heavy, too heavy to open. But she knew she was lying under a thick feather quilt in Aunt Hanna's parlor. That would explain why she felt so extremely warm. She shifted restlessly under the hot quilt. A pungent smell drifted past her nose. Someone was putting warm tea in her mouth. How kind of Aunt Hanna to make her a cup of tea. But Dorie wanted lemonade—a cold cup of lemonade, that was what she truly wanted. Tea was too hot. The quilt was too hot. She must tell Aunt Hanna. . . .

Dorie's breathing quickened; she struggled to wake up. It felt as though she was dragging herself to the surface of the river back home on the farm. Yes, that was it. She'd dived into the river and was swimming underwater and now she must swim to the surface. But the surface was so far away, so far away . . .

Dorie shifted restlessly on the bed, trying to throw off the quilt. She must get up. There was something she must do, someone she must see, but she could not quite remember what she must do or whom she must see. Someone important, someone she loved . . .

A hand touched her brow. She had to have more quilts now. "Aunt Hanna, more quilts," she mumbled. "I feel so cold." Her feet were cold, and her whole body trembled in the chilly air. It was winter, that cold, cold winter they had on the farm in the blizzard of 1818. And Aunt Hanna had just gone to fetch another quilt. "Hurry, Aunt Hanna," Dorie muttered. "Hurry back. I'm so desperately cold." Her teeth chattered from the chill.

Another quilt was laid atop her, and Dorie's chills subsided. The last thing she remembered was the soothing touch on her brow.

Dorie opened her eyes. She blinked. Where was she? She stared at a cone-shaped ceiling. What had happened to Aunt Hanna's parlor? Dorie squeezed her eyes shut, then opened them again. It was still there, blue smoke drifting lazily through the smoke-blackened top. Where was she?

She turned her head and dizziness stabbed through her. A man slept beside her. She frowned. He looked familiar. She'd seen him before. What was he doing in Aunt Hanna's parlor? But she wasn't in Aunt Hanna's parlor. No. She was in a . . . strange house. That was it.

And someone was singing. Quietly, the way a person might sing if he didn't want to disturb someone else. Dorie moved her head cautiously. A shadowed, hunched shape sat by the fire on the floor. What a strange place to have the fire. On the floor. And the person was rocking gently and singing. It was an old woman. Aunt Hanna? No, Aunt Hanna did not have long gray braids.

Who then? But before she could answer herself, she fell back to sleep.

When she awoke again, her thoughts cleared swiftly. She saw the cone-shaped ceiling. And the man. It was Zander.

"Zander?"

Instantly his eyes opened and met hers. He sat up and took her hand. "You are awake!"

"Yes?" she asked uncertainly. "Of course I am awake. Did I sleep so long, then?"

He held her hand tightly and bent and kissed her fingers. "You slept very long. Too long."

She didn't understand his words, or the intense way he said them. She yawned. "Where is Aunt Hanna?"

He frowned. "Aunt Hanna?"

"Yes. I want to thank her for the tea."

"Oh, you mean the old medicine woman. She is not here. She went to visit her niece and baby."

Dorie murmured, "She has a kind touch. I thought it was Aunt Hanna." She smiled ruefully. "I—I feel confused, Zander."

He touched her forehead and she remembered that touch too. "It was you," she breathed. "It was you. While I slept."

Zander snatched his hand away. "You fell off Lightning and hit your head. You've been unconscious for four days. Four long days." His voice was matter-of-fact, and the intensity was gone.

"Oh." She thought about that. Her limbs felt heavy; she still felt drowsy. And hungry.

"Zander." She tried to sit up. "Is there something to eat? I'm very hungry."

He pushed her gently back down. "I'll get you some food," he said and slipped out of the tepee.

She slept until he returned. He carried a bowl of steaming broth. He helped her sit up so she could eat.

She ate a little, then set the bowl aside listlessly. "I am so tired," she said. "I want to sleep." And she fell over to the side, already asleep.

When she awoke again, she was able to sit up. No one was in the tepee, though she heard voices outside. After a little while, Zander entered.

"You are awake?" He seemed surprised.

"I want to get up," she answered.

"No, no. Wait. Stay and rest. I do not want you to get sick again. . . . "

"Pshaw, Zander," she said, pushing the heavy blanket off herself. "I'm feeling much better. I do not need to be lollygagging around here. That's what Aunt Hanna would call it. Lollygagging."

He seemed unimpressed with Aunt Hanna's wisdom. "Dorie," he said. She glanced up at the strained note she heard in his voice. "I did not drag you halfway across the country and bring you to this medicine woman only to have you jump out of bed the first time you feel better."

"Oh?" She sat up straighter and glanced around the tepee. The sudden movement made her wince. "Ohhh, my head," she moaned. She touched the back of her head. She looked at the dried blood on her fingers.

"What happened?" she asked, staring dazedly at him.

"When you fell off Lightning, you hit your head. On a rock."

"Oh."

"Yes." He sighed. "It has been a long journey,

Dorie," he mumbled. "I am glad you are awake." He met her eyes and she stared into his. Incredulity filled her. There was love in his eyes. For her. She saw it. She smiled and reached for his hand. He took her fingers in his. "Thank you, Zander," she said shyly. "Thank you for helping me."

He sank down beside her and hugged her to him. "I thought I'd lost you, Dorie," he said, and the words sounded choked out. "I thought I'd lost you."

He held her to him for a long time. Dorie wondered what had happened to Zander. He was so . . . so changed.

It was late evening. The village had grown quiet.

"Zander?" said Dorie. "I'm cold. Would you get me another blanket?"

He brought her another blanket, an eight-point Hudson's Bay blanket with wide green, red, yellow, and black stripes. The eight-point blankets were made of the heaviest, thickest wool.

He kneeled down and leaned across her to spread out the blanket.

She grabbed him around the waist and pulled him down on top of her. "Aha!" she cried. "I have you now!"

He toppled onto her. "Oh no," he said,

sprawled all over her. "What will you do with me?"

"Have my wicked way with you, of course. But—uh, not too wicked. I *am* your wife."

He met her eyes and she saw a flash of sadness.

"Zander, what is it?" He shook his head, refusing to tell her.

"Dorie, are you sure? Can you—that is—" He paused delicately. "That is, you are just healing from an injury. . . . "

"Oh, pshaw!" she exclaimed. "Get in under these blankets with me and I'll show you what I can do."

"You will?" He threw off his red shirt and peeled off his leather pants. Then he was scrambling under the covers with her.

She had her wicked way with him.

The next morning, she awoke with his arms around her. She sighed happily. Her head felt better and she was in the arms of the man she loved. Loved. She loved him, she thought in awe, as she watched him sleep.

He awoke then. His smile set her heart to thumping in her chest. Was ever a woman happier than she?

Dorie walked out of the tepee on shaking legs. "There is something I must find," she told Zander as he put his hand under her elbow to steady her. She pushed his hand away, determined to walk on her own. "I feel better," she said stoutly.

He followed her carefully. She glanced around. "Where are they?"

"Where are who?" he asked.

"The packhorses."

"In the corral where the Indians keep their horses."

"Is it far?"

"Some distance."

"Zander," she said thoughtfully. "What I wanted was to give a gift to the medicine woman who helped me. She saved my life."

He nodded. "She did," he agreed. "What gift did you want to give?"

"Help me find my carpetbag. My thinking is still muddled. I thought it would be on the packhorses."

"No. I unloaded the packhorses days ago. I wrapped your things in oilcloth and hid them. Shall I show you?"

"Please do."

She hobbled after him across the gravel. He halted when they came to a small rock overhang. He reached under the overhang and dragged out a long parcel. "Here is your carpetbag, and some of my things also."

She opened her carpetbag, looking for something she could give to the old woman.

"No, not that. She'd never wear it," she muttered, setting aside a lacy yellow petticoat. "Not that. It's too small." She pushed aside a wooden comb. "Oh, what can I give her? I've already traded away my poetry book. She might have liked that." She stared at him, worried.

"You would have given her your poetry book?"

She shrugged. "It is valuable. And precious. And pretty. And I like the poems."

"Dorie, she can't read."

"Oh." She stared thoughtfully into the distance. "What can I give her?" she mused. Then she dug through the carpetbag again. "A dress?" she asked helplessly, holding up her best mauve dress. "It looks too big for her." She threw the dress down and put her face in her hands. "I so wanted to give her a gift. She's been so kind to me. . . ."

He patted her shoulder awkwardly. "There, there, Dorie."

She drew herself up, trying to compose herself once again.

"I've found," ventured Zander, "that Indian women often like to trade for kettles."

"Kettles?"

"Mmmm. Copper kettles are lightweight and easy to carry from place to place. And they're big, for cooking large stews in. Would you like to give her a copper kettle?"

"Oh, yes," said Dorie. Then her face fell. "I don't *have* a copper kettle."

"Ah, but I do. I have several of them, in fact." He smiled. "Would you like to give her one of mine?"

"No, I would not. Because then it's you giving the gift. Not me."

"Dorie. I am grateful that she helped you, too. Let me give the gift."

"No," she answered. "It is my life she saved. Not yours."

She met his dark eyes, and she could see the stubbornness in them. "I tell you what," she said.

"What?" he asked cautiously.

"You like to trade, do you not?"

He nodded.

"I'll trade you something for the copper kettle, then it will be mine and I can give it to her."

He chuckled uncomfortably. "Why won't you just accept the copper kettle?" He glanced around. "I'll *give* it to you, but don't tell anyone. You would ruin my reputation as the shrewdest trader this side of the Mississippi."

She snorted and held up her mauve dress. "This," she announced, "is my best dress. Take it."

"Dorie," he pleaded, "does it have to be your best dress? Why not your second-best dress? Or your third best?" He picked up a yellow-and-white checked gingham dress. "This will do fine."

She snatched it out of his hand. "That is my second-best dress."

"I'll take it," he said, snatching it back.

"No! It was my life she saved, and I will give her the best gift I can!" Dorie grabbed the gingham dress with both hands.

"Have it your way," he sighed wearily, picking up the mauve dress. He held it up.

A pang of regret tore through Dorie. She looked at the thick mauve brocade with lace at the collar—lace she'd had to send to St. Louis for. The dress hung in long, soft folds. It was truly a beautiful dress, and she'd spent many hours sewing it. She steeled herself. The medicine woman had saved her life. Dorie would repay the debt.

"I have never," said Zander, "in my life as a trader, ever descended to such depths."

"Good," she chuckled. "Now give me the copper kettle."

They rewrapped the goods in oilcloth and stashed them under the overhang. They wandered back to the tepee and Zander pulled out a kettle from among his trade goods. The copper was shiny, the kettle sturdily made. Dorie hoped the old woman would like it.

They took the kettle to the old woman's tepee. She invited them in.

Dorie presented her with the kettle. The old woman beamed. "Very good," she kept saying over and over. "Very good."

She went and called her niece to come and look at the present. The niece, Gentle Fawn, admired the kettle, holding it up and inspecting the inside. She exclaimed over how easy it was to lift. The baby on her back bounced with each jaunty movement. Then Gentle Fawn, too, pronounced the gift "very good." She smiled gratefully at Dorie, and Dorie knew she'd chosen wisely. The kettle would make the old woman's life easier.

Neighbors were called in to admire the kettle, and the old medicine woman basked in the other women's envious glances.

It was worth her best dress to see all this, thought Dorie happily.

She and Zander were about to leave when the old woman stopped them. "You eat," she said and beckoned them over to sit.

Soon a meal of fragrant stew was served, neighbors joining in with platters of roots and baskets of berries. Through the whole meal, the old medicine woman kept the copper kettle next to her side. Dorie enjoyed every bite.

"What kind of stew was that?" she asked after her second bowlful. "It tasted like deer."

"Did it?" asked Zander with a sly smile. But

when she pressed him to tell her what it was, he would only smile.

She persisted. Finally, he told her. "Bear."

Dorie swallowed and stared at her empty bowl. Next time she'd remember to ask *before* she consumed all the meat.

Dusk fell before Dorie and Zander rose to thank the old woman for the meal. She nodded, and they said their farewells. Tomorrow at dawn they would leave.

Suddenly the camp dogs began barking. "Someone is approaching," observed Zander.

Dorie stared at the figures on horseback who rode into the village. "Who is it?" she asked.

Zander shrugged. "White men. Can't tell yet if I know them."

The two travelers came closer in the gathering twilight.

"It's Burke and Campbell," said Zander.

Dorie glanced at him in dismay. "Not the two from the cabin?"

He nodded. "The same."

"Oh, no." Her heart sank. "I'm glad we're leaving tomorrow. I don't want to be around those two."

Chapter Twenty

The sun shone brilliantly on a Saturday morning. Clarence Biddle sat in a corner of the fort's trading room and hummed as he glanced over his important papers. He considered this room to be truly his; it was his sanctuary from the rest of the fort, and he was happy here. He liked the door with the little iron grill in it that kept the trappers and Indians out. *He* was the one who decided who came and went through that door.

Sometimes he would talk to a trapper or Indian through the small grilled opening; other times he'd ignore their plaintive knocks on the door and sit at his plank desk and concentrate on his precious numbers. Occasionally, he'd let a serious trapper come in, but once the trade was completed, it was a speedy "out the door with you, trapper."

On the large flat plank that served as his desk, Biddle had spread out the Hudson's Bay Company records for the fort. As factor, or chief trader of the fort, it was his responsibility to keep the records for the company and he did it very well, in his estimation. He kept track of how many carrots of tobacco were sold and how many furs were received in trade for a string of beads. He noticed that in Fort Walla Walla country, dark green was becoming the preferred color of trade beads. He wrote himself a note to order more of them.

He saw that he had axes and beaver traps, rifles and iron pots and knives in his inventory to exchange for furs. He smiled in satisfaction. The whole purpose of Fort Walla Walla, the whole purpose of the Hudson's Bay Company, was to trade cheap goods to the Indians in exchange for furs and then to sell the furs for a huge profit to England, France, and China.

He oversaw a fur inventory that included a huge quantity of beaver pelts and lesser quantities of fox, marten, lynx, and even one bear. He smiled to himself. A most profitable post, Fort Walla Walla. The company's directors should be most pleased. Biddle certainly was.

And Biddle had made his company's purpose his own. When the Hudson's Bay Company profited, Biddle profited. And since he helped make the fort, and hence the company, so profitable, why, then, it was only natural that he would want a certain share of those profits. But as he was only a chief trader in the company, his share was less than half a per cent of one share. A very meager amount, in Biddle's humble opinion. Therefore, he had been forced to find another way to ensure that he benefited from the company's huge profits.

He turned a crisp white page and ran his finger down the inked numbers until he came to his favorite account: a listing he annotated as "Extra Baggage." It was the Hudson's Bay Company's Widows' and Orphans' Fund.

Why as great a company as the Hudson's Bay Fur Company should have a fund to pay for food and clothing for useless people left over after a company employee died was something that Biddle could not understand or abide. The Company did not get any work out of the hangers-on. All the widows did was consume food that would better go to feed trappers, men who deserved it and worked hard for the company.

And the widows insisted that their children eat too. And so every dinner in the mess hall was noisy because of the constant racket of children and the constant admonishments from their mothers.

Biddle sighed. It was most distressing, which

was why he stayed away from the mess hall as much as possible. Why, he could not even bear to have his own child at his home table when he ate. Mary had been well trained to keep the child out of his sight at those times of the day.

And the widows! A sorry sight they were. They never took care of the single dress he allotted them for the year, so they were constantly looking ragged. Did not one widow know how to patch? And the mere sight of a widow at his little grilled grate was enough to ruin his day before she even opened her mouth and whined for more money.

Biddle hummed to himself as he ran his finger over the figures. If he didn't pay the widows something, he knew they'd complain and then a higher company official—someone like Chief Factor McLaren for the whole Columbia District—might hear. So Biddle saw to it that they got just enough to keep them quiet.

It was an unofficial annual event at Fort Walla Walla when, every spring, he lined up the widows—there were four of them—and handed out the annual allotment of enough bolts of calico to make one dress each. Biddle gave them all the dullest brown calico from his cheapest hoard, one he kept especially for widows and orphans. He supplied enough calico, too, for their sons to make a shirt and for the daughters to make a dress. Unfortunately, he had to give the mothers enough leather to make trousers for the sons too. Why couldn't the sons wear calico trousers too? he'd wondered time and again. But since he didn't want to rouse the suspicions of Chief Factor McLaren, he paid for the leather, though grudgingly.

At least he'd solved the shoes problem. The hangers-on went barefoot in the summer and wore old moccasins cast off by the trappers in the winter. It worked well and saved Biddle the cost of buying them all footwear.

But it was autumn now and springtime was a long way off and the Widows and Orphans Fund looked pleasantly prosperous. It should. The Hudson's Bay Company paid him ten pounds sterling per year to give to each widow. An extremely outrageous sum in Biddle's estimation, when a hard-working guide was paid twenty-seven pounds per year and the voyageurs or boatmen were paid seventeen pounds sterling annually. Fortunately, Biddle had managed to limit each widow to one pound sterling per year. That gave him a healthy profit of thirty-six pounds per year—in addition to his company wage of one hundred pounds of course.

He peered more closely at the figures. He saw that he'd been paying out to one of the widows, Mrs. McKay, the loudest complainer of all four widows, for the past ten years. He'd made a tidy little profit of ninety pounds on her account alone, not including interest. He smiled. Yes, 1826 was shaping up to be a most prosperous year indeed!

What, mused Biddle, tapping his chin, should he do with the extra money? He could save it for a trip to St. Louis. If they ever found Dorie Primfield, he could take her with him. Or perhaps he should just add it to the ever-growing pile of coins that he'd hidden in the back of his closet in his bedroom. Or perhaps he should send it to his account in England.

A knock on the door interrupted his thoughts. His head came up. He stopped humming. Since he was in an affable mood, he'd answer the knock. "Yes?" he asked in his friendliest manner.

"Mr. Biddle?"

He groaned, wishing now that he hadn't answered. "I'll be right there, Mrs. McKay." He wrote down a note to order more rope. The fort's rope supplies were almost out.

More knocking.

Grimacing, he threw down the quill pen and rose to his feet. He marched to the door and peered out the grill at the old Indian woman. He'd get rid of her as fast as he could.

"When my Charlie worked as a trapper for this company, he told me I'd be taken care of if anything should happen to him," she said.

"And you are, Mrs. McKay, you are," answered Biddle in disgust, rolling his eyes heavenward. He'd had this argument with her before, and it always started off the same way.

"My Charlie would come back and shit on you if he knew what a measly, cheap company you run!"

"I told you, Mrs. McKay. The company gives me one pound sterling a year to use for your clothes and well-being. Can I help it if that one pound is so quickly spent?" He held up his hands helplessly, as if he had no control over her free-spending habits.

He ducked when he saw her spit at him. "Mrs. McKay," he said, as slowly and carefully as he could, "I wish you wouldn't do that."

"My Charlie promised me!" she screamed.

"Sshhhhh, Mrs. McKay, let's not wake the whole fort, shall we?" he gritted. "Wait here." He went back to his plank desk and felt under it for the little leather sack where he kept pennies, pennies for buying off irritating old widows.

He made an entry in his false account book under "Bags of Flour," which was his disguised nickname for Mrs. McKay. Mrs. McFadden was "Bags of Beans," Mrs. Des Jardin was "Dried Biscuits" and Mrs. Stout was "Pounds of Lard." He picked up the pen, tallied the numbers under the Bags of Flour column, set the pen down, and walked back to the door. He opened it, placed two pennies in her palm, and quickly shut the door. "There, Mrs. McKay," he said generously. "I hope that helps meet your expenses."

She spat again and caught him off-guard. He wiped the spittle from his cheek. "Mrs. McKay," he said severely, "you won't be getting any more money for the rest of the month. You have now used up most of your account money. You have only one-quarter of your allotment remaining until spring. Mrs. McKay, do not, I repeat, *do not* come back to see me again this month!"

With that, he did something he rarely did, but he just could not have her destroying his happy mood of the day. He unhooked the solid iron-plate cover above the grill and dropped it so that he couldn't see her or hear her anymore. Conversation finished.

Humming, he returned to his plank desk, picked up his quill pen, and turned a crisp white page.

"You wanted to see me?" asked the trapper.

Biddle peered through the grate; then he opened the door. "Get in here."

The trapper scurried in and took off his dark, greasy, leather hat. He shifted from foot to foot as he waited for Biddle to speak.

"I want you to carry a certain message from

me to the factor at Fort George."

"Fort George?" breathed the trapper. "That's some long ways."

"Some long ways, it is," agreed Biddle tightly. "But the message is important. I want you to deliver this scroll to the factor at Fort George, and I want you to stop at Fort Vancouver and any missions along the Columbia River between here and the Pacific Ocean."

The man stared at him. His nervous hands twisted his greasy hat. "Fort George? The Pacific Ocean? That's a long ways away, boss."

Biddle ignored the man's hesitation. "I have an important message for you to tell the factors." He picked up an oilskin-wrapped scroll from his plank desk and thrust it into the trapper's hand. "Here is the message. Tell them that I will pay one hundred prime beaver pelts for the return of Dorie Primfield." He took a breath. "And tell them to be on the alert for one Alexander Durban. They are to notify me *immediately* if he appears at their forts." He frowned at the trapper. "Can you remember all that?"

The trapper nodded.

"You're dismissed."

The trapper turned toward the door.

"Oh, wait," said Biddle. "One more thing. Tell Clifton Ross to come to the trading room. I want to talk to him."

"All right then," said the trapper and left.

The second knock came ten minutes later. Knowing it was Ross, Biddle opened the door immediately. When Ross stepped inside, Biddle closed the door and turned to face his visitor. Biddle crossed his arms and stared at Clifton Ross for a moment. He'd known the man a long time and had sent him on many errands. Now he was about to send him on a deadly one.

"I want to hire you to kill Alexander Durban."

Clifton Ross did not even flinch. Biddle liked the way the trapper met his eye steadily.

"How much?" asked Ross.

Greed, thought Biddle. *Why the hell are so many people so damn greedy?* Then he chuckled. It was a good thing for him that they were; it made them so easy to manipulate.

"You know those forty-five beaver pelts I've been holding for you? Well, you can have them back."

"You ain't been holding them," said the stocky trapper. "You stole them."

"Ha ha, very good, Ross," laughed Biddle. Then he stopped laughing. "You cost me, Ross. If you'd brought Dorie Primfield to me in the first place, I wouldn't have to offer a damn reward of a hundred furs!"

Ross looked at him suspiciously. "I bet you're using my forty-five furs as part of those hunnerd furs for the reward, ain't you?" he snapped.

"No one said you were stupid," chuckled Biddle. "But I'll give them back to you if you kill Durban." He waited for Ross to decide.

"It's a pitiful deal," said Ross. "If I'm gonna kill Zander Durban, I want more'n the forty-five pelts that were mine in the first place!" He spat on the floor.

Biddle winced. "Keep your filthy spittle off my floor, Ross." He glared at the graying trapper. "I'll give you twenty more pelts. Prime ones."

"Ha," said Ross. "I want them hunnerd pelts you was offerin' for the reward."

"You greedy son-of-a—! I'm not giving you the hundred! How am I supposed to come up with another hundred if someone returns Dorie Primfield?"

"That's your problem."

Biddle mulled it over.

" 'Course, you can always ask someone else to kill Durban for you," suggested Ross with a sly grin. "You can ask around the fort. Lots of the fellows just sittin' around. Why, they'd be glad to do it. 'Oh, yes sir, Mr. Biddle,' " he mimicked in a high voice. " 'I'll be glad to kill Zander Durban for you. Nothin' else to do but trap and hunt and fish. Yes sir.' " He snickered.

Biddle didn't like the sound of that. "Are you threatening me, Ross?"

"Not me," said Ross, rubbing his neck. "Say, you gotta drink?"

"No." Biddle thought some more. He'd willingly pay *five* hundred pelts to avenge himself on the man who'd stolen his bride and made a fool of him!

"Listen to me, Ross," he said. "I'll give you back your forty-five pelts and I'll pay you another hundred. That's one hundred and forty-five pelts. Prime." He watched Clifton Ross's greedy eyes glitter. "One hundred and forty-five pelts to kill Durban," he repeated wearily as though Ross had dragged the very last fur from him.

At Ross's reluctant nod, he continued, "Durban was last seen at the Trapper's Rendezvous. I have reliable word that he stole Dorie Primfield." Biddle glared at Ross. "For that foul-up alone, I should charge you fifty furs."

Ross glared back but kept silent.

"They were headed for a cabin," Biddle continued. "A trapper's cabin in the mountains. Old Man Sheridan's cabin. Over by Kicking Horse Creek. You heard of it?"

Clifton Ross nodded. "I stayed there a time or two."

"They may still be there. Probably are. But just in case they're not, I've sent out a warning to all the forts to be on the lookout for them. They won't escape me!" He eyed Ross intently. "I want you to go to Kicking Horse Creek. Find Durban and kill him. Bring Dorie Primfield to

256

me and you can have one hundred and forty-five furs." Biddle grinned expansively.

"One hunnerd and forty-five?" Ross asked in dismay. "You want me to bring in Primfield too? I should get a hunnerd and forty-five for killin' Durban and a hunnerd more for bringin' in Primfield! That's the reward you posted!"

"Now, now, calm down," Biddle said, irritated. "That's what I meant. One hundred and forty-five for Durban and the hundred for Primfield. Two hundred and forty furs. That's what I meant."

"Two hunnerd and forty-*five*," Ross corrected.

Biddle gritted his teeth and nodded.

Ross watched him warily.

"It's my best offer," said Biddle firmly.

"Looks like you got yourself a deal," Ross said slowly. He walked to the door. "Better get those furs ready," he sneered. "I'm gonna be a rich man." He closed the door.

Biddle chuckled, satisfied with the deal. He put away his quill pen and put on a heavy cotton jacket. Time to go home to dinner. He closed and locked the door to the trading room. Humming, he set off at a smart pace. He'd done a good day's work.

As Biddle passed the clerk's house, he saw Prudence Pomeroy walking up the steps. "Mrs. Pomeroy!" he hailed her.

She halted. "Mr. Biddle, how are you?"

"Fine, fine," he said heartily. He peered down at her. Rather a bit too sickly and pale for his taste but big enough breasts. He licked his lips. "Mrs. Pomeroy, I have good news for you."

"What is that, Mr. Biddle?" Her hand went protectively to her bosom.

"I know where your sister is, Mrs. Pomeroy. We will have her back safely. Very soon. No need to worry anymore about your sister, Mrs. Pomeroy."

"Oh, Mr. Biddle!" she cried. "You have relieved my mind. Oh, thank you!" She clapped her hands together.

He smiled benevolently. "You're welcome, Mrs. Pomeroy. No need to worry about your sister anymore." With a friendly wave he continued on his way, humming.

Chapter Twenty-one

Dorie stood by the tepee and glanced fondly at the village around her. Though she and Zander were leaving today, she would never forget the kindness shown by the people here. Because of the old medicine woman's care, she was alive.

A movement caught her eye. "Zander?"

"Mmm?" He emerged from the tent, carrying their blankets. The packhorses stood patiently chewing on bunchgrass, waiting to be loaded.

"What are those traders doing?"

He halted and glanced to where she pointed. "What the hell?" He threw down the blankets and stalked over to where Burke and Campbell gestured at a crowd of Indians gathered around them.

"Zander?" Dorie hurried after him.

She halted behind Zander and peered over his shoulder.

Campbell held a wooden cask over a huge pot. Out of the cask poured a golden brown stream of whiskey. While Campbell set down the cask, Burke used a stick to scrape a bottle of slow, thick molasses into the pot. "Yep, this is a recipe me old Scottish granny gave me," Burke told the watching Indians as he stirred the dark brown concoction in the pot with the stick.

The sickening, pungent scent of tobacco mixed with red pepper, whiskey, and molasses emanated from the pot.

"Yer old granny never gave you this recipe," said Campbell. "We got it from them trappers on the Platte River that time we—"

"Shut yer beaver trap! These Injuns gotta think this is verrrrry good." Burke took a spoon carved from buffalo horn and dipped it in the brown water in the pot. He brought the spoon to his lips and sipped. He closed his eyes blissfully at what he'd just tasted. "Almost ready," he chortled. "Hand me them rattlesnake heads."

Campbell gave him two roasted rattlesnake heads and Burke tossed them into the pot. They bobbed in the middle, then sank.

A whiff of the concoction stirred Dorie's stomach to queasiness. She held her breath.

"Now we're ready!" crowed Burke. He held up his arms to the Indians. "Go fetch yer chief, laddies! Tell yer chief to come and talk to me. We'll drink." He laughed. "Then we'll trade!"

A man hurried off and soon returned. Behind him walked a dignified older man, his gray hair in long braids. He wore leather leggings and a leather shirt decorated with a yoke of green and black porcupine quills.

Burke grinned at him. "Och, hello there, chief. We want to offer ye a wee droppie of whiskey!"

The chief glanced from Burke to Campbell, then shook his head and said something to the Indian man who'd fetched him. "He does not want to drink," translated the man. "Says what you make smell like rotten horse meat."

Burke contrived to look insulted, but Dorie saw his lips twitch. "Why, this here is the best whiskey punch in the country! Chief should be honored I invite him to have a wee droppie with us!"

The old man with the gray braids walked away, shaking his head. A younger man joined him. Dorie recognized the young man as Gentle Fawn's husband. She was glad to see that the old medicine woman's family would have nothing to do with Burke and his whiskey.

"Well, since old chief doesna want any, all the more for us," crowed Burke. He lifted his arms and beckoned. "Gather round, Injuns, gather round. I got somethin' mighty tasty for ye right here in this pot."

A Nez Perce man walked over holding a horn cup. "I want."

"Smart man," chortled Burke, seizing the cup and scooping up a cupful of the dark liquid. He beamed at the Indian man. "Drink up hearty-like, laddie!"

The man took a drink from the cup and made a face. Before he could say anything, Burke grabbed another Indian man and pulled him over to the vat. "Ye look a likely lad," he said. He scooped up a drink with his buffalo-horn ladle. "Have a wee snort."

The Indian took a sip and Burke said, "Tastes good, eh? You like!" The Indian nodded faintly.

"Come on, lads and lassies," chortled Burke. "Come and get this good whiskey!"

Aside, he said to Campbell, "Go and get another bucket of water from the river. I'll add it to the pot after these beavershits get drunk. They willna know what they're drinkin' anyways."

Campbell hurried off.

While he was gone, Dorie noticed a tall, slender young man standing at the back of the crowd. When he saw that she was watching him, he sauntered over.

"Greetings," he addressed Zander and Dorie,

but his dark eyes were on Dorie. "You folks travelin' with these traders?"

"No," answered Dorie brightly, liking the look of the young man. His leather clothes looked clean and neat, not greasy like those of so many mountain men, and his dark brown hair was neatly groomed to his shoulders, unlike the tangled, knotted locks of so many trappers. "Are you traveling with them?"

He shook his head. "No. I know Burke and Campbell, but I am not traveling with them."

He eyed Zander for the first time. "My name's Edward Cecil," he said.

Zander introduced himself. He didn't mention Dorie's name or that she was his wife, Dorie noticed with a slight frown.

"What brings you to this village?" asked Dorie, turning her attention to the handsome young man, though she did think his nose, which appeared to have been broken once, kept him from being as handsome as Zander.

Edward Cecil shrugged casually. "Visiting relatives," he said. She saw now that while he appeared to be a white man, with light skin and brown hair, his eyes were dark and his cheek bones high. He was a mixed-blood man, she realized, but his easy air told her that he was equally at home with Indians or whites.

She glanced at Burke to see what he was up to. Several Indian men sat on the ground near the large pot, and they were drinking and talking while their women scurried to and from the tepees, staggering under heavy armloads of beaver pelts.

As Dorie watched, Burke took another scoop of whiskey punch and drank it in one long gulp. "Are you going to drink Mr. Burke's punch?" Dorie asked Edward Cecil casually.

"*Mais non!*" answered the young man. "No. I don't like to make a fool of myself." He grinned and winked at her, and privately she thought he'd never make a fool of himself. He was too confident.

Dorie liked him.

She noticed Zander glaring at Edward Cecil with hard eyes. *Why, Zander is jealous,* thought Dorie in surprise.

She averted her eyes from both men and watched Burke and Campbell cavort with the Indians. Campbell held a reluctant Indian maiden by one hand and danced awkwardly with her. Burke laughed and took another scoop of his concoction. He glanced at the Indians. "Bring on the furs," he yelled. "Bring on the dried salmon! Bring on the deerskins! Let's trade!" He clapped his hands and stomped his foot as if to an invisible fiddler while Campbell dragged his dance partner across the gravel. "I got knives to trade!" encouraged Burke. "I got traps! I got wee beads and cloth for the lassies! I got guns!"

Dorie smiled weakly at Zander. "Can we please leave?"

"Don't you want to watch the people give away their furs?" asked Zander grimly. "These dishonest traders are only doing what every other trader does—get the Indians drunk and cheat them of their furs." He narrowed his eyes at her. "Don't you want to watch?" He laughed harshly. "That's what your people do to the Indians. Or didn't you know?"

She gasped.

"No need to be hard on the lady," interjected Edward Cecil. "It is not her fault that Burke and Campbell are foolish asses."

Dorie smiled tremulously at him for coming to her defense.

Zander glared at him. "Keep out of this," gritted Zander. "This is between my woman and me."

Edward Cecil glanced at the two and grinned at Dorie. "Just wanted the beautiful woman to know that I understand," he said meaningfully, then walked away.

Zander glared at his back. "Let's go," he said, with a proprietary grip on Dorie's arm.

"I want to stay," said Dorie defiantly. She didn't and she knew she was contradicting herself, but she would not give in to Zander's rudeness. She would not! Zander glared at her, but he dropped his hand from her arm.

Dorie gave a smug little smile and focused her attention on Burke and Campbell's antics as if she was fascinated with the traders.

"Drink up, drink up!" Burke called to the Indians. Another Nez Perce man staggered up and scooped up a cupful of the wretched drink. "That's me boy," cackled Burke as the Indian drained his cup. "Have another!"

A Nez Perce woman tottered over with her cup. "More whis-key," she slurred.

Burke grinned at her as he obligingly filled her cup to overflowing. "Ye're a bonny one," he said. "Ye come and see me when we finish trading. I got a fine present for the likes o' ye." He gave her a pinch on the buttocks. The woman staggered off.

Just then Campbell, whose long legs were kicking out in his dance, accidentally slammed into Burke and the two traders fell to the ground. "What the hell you doin'?" cursed Burke, getting up.

Campbell watched his pretty dancing partner flee; he laughed and stayed sitting on the ground. "I cain't get up," he giggled. "I cain't."

"Aww, you beaverbrain, you're too damn drunk to trade," noted Burke in disgust. "Get up and start the tradin'. These Injuns is ripe to give away their furs."

Awkwardly, Campbell got to his feet. "Calico," he muttered, holding up a bolt of cloth. "Bonny calico for bonny lassies." He waved a ring at the crowd. "Rings," he slurred.

Satisfied that Campbell was doing his job, Burke turned back to the Indians. "Hey, get outta that pack," he yelled at an Indian man whose hand was stuffed into one of Burke's saddlebags. The man withdrew his hand, full of rings and beads, and ran off. "Come back here," howled Burke. "You thief, you robber!"

But the Indian disappeared behind a tepee. "Doggone it! Thievin' Injuns." Burke took a scoop of whiskey punch for consolation. He drank it down in one gulp and took another cupful. "Where's them dingdong furs you Injuns 'sposed to be bringin' me? Where the hell are they?"

As Dorie watched, a drunken man struck a woman; she screamed, and their baby, playing in the dirt, began to cry. At the next tepee, a woman lay in a drunken stupor. Two men fought with each other, cheered on by a drunken onlooker. One of the men had a knife. He struck the other, who fell to the ground, bleeding from his stomach.

He lay so still that Dorie, with a sickening dread, wondered if he was dead. Then he stirred and tried to get up.

Burke tottered past Zander and raised his tin

267

cup. "Good trading," he cried.

An Indian man brushed past him and he lost his balance, stumbling to the ground. His whiskey splashed, making a dark splotch on the front of Burke's leather jerkin. Laughing, Burke staggered to his feet.

The Indian pushed him aside and lurched over to the huge iron pot and ladled out a drink for himself.

Burke suddenly spun around. "You!" he cried. "Bring back that bolt o' cloth!"

Another Indian had picked up a bolt of the traders' red calico. Now the Indian fled, disappearing behind a tepee. Burke lurched in his direction, but stopped and turned, obviously forgetting what he had intended to do.

"You want to see any more?" asked Zander, his arms folded across his broad chest, a look of disdain on his rugged face.

"No," said Dorie meekly. "I've seen enough."

They loaded Zander's trading goods onto the mule and the packhorses, and Dorie bridled Lightning.

In the background, Dorie could hear whoops and yells as the traders and Indians kept drinking.

"I'd prefer you to ride one of the other horses," said Zander. "I don't want Lightning to throw you again. His hooves might not be completely healed."

Dorie patted the gelding's neck. "I like him. I'll ride him."

Zander lifted the saddle onto his black mare. "Dorie," he said patiently, "ride him easy then. Don't take any chances."

She smiled. He was concerned about her.

She sat on Lightning's back, waiting for Zander to finish saddling his mare. She turned Lightning's head so she could watch the Indian camp.

"Campbell and Burke are fighting," she observed. The two traders were locked in a tight grip and were pummeling each other on their backs and shoulders. They fell to the ground, Campbell on top. He punched at Burke, then got to his feet and staggered away. Burke lay on the ground, unmoving.

Zander said tersely as he tightened the cinch, "We should have left sooner."

"Well, I didn't want to," said Dorie, but secretly she wished she hadn't insisted they stay. Two Indians wrestled each other, rolling over and over on the gravel. Shouts and yells from onlookers laid wagers on who would win. Suddenly one of them pulled out a knife and stabbed the other in the heart.

"Zander!" cried Dorie in alarm.

He glanced at the Indians. "Time to go," he said with a final tug on the cinch. He mounted the horse and they headed out of camp, careful to circle the crowd of Indians, the traders, and the whiskey pot. Zander rode in the front, the packhorses followed, and Dorie brought up the rear.

Unfortunately, their trail came too close to the whiskey pot. Dorie saw that Burke was still asleep on the gravel.

She nudged Lightning to go faster. They had to get away from this camp!

They were just past the vat of whiskey when Campbell staggered up and grabbed Lightning's bridle. The horse halted and swung around skittishly. "Get off that horse," Campbell said to Dorie. "And gimme a kiss."

"Zander!" cried Dorie, but Zander's back was to her and she saw that two Indian men had just grabbed the black mare's bridle. Zander had a fight of his own.

"Get back," Dorie warned Campbell, wishing she had thought to keep her pistol with her. But it was tucked in her carpetbag, back on the mule. Lightning was pulling away from the drunken trader and Dorie was having a hard time holding the stocky horse steady. "Get back!"

But Campbell wouldn't listen. He pulled on the bridle again, then reached for her and dragged her off the horse.

Dorie struggled. "Stop it!" she cried.

Campbell put his mouth on hers, and she

gagged from the smell of whiskey and tobacco.

"Get away from me!" She pushed at him with all her strength, but she could feel his wiry muscles, stronger than hers. He threw her down on the ground and launched himself on top of her, his hands grappling with her long skirts.

Chapter Twenty-two

"No!" screamed Dorie.

Campbell's hand groped her naked thigh under her dress.

"Come on, lassie, gimme a kiss," he muttered.

She kicked and clawed at him; her nails raked his hand as she tore at his vicious grip on her limb. But she could not dislodge his hand.

Suddenly Campbell was lifted off her and thrown aside.

"Dorie!" cried Zander reaching for her.

"Oh, Zander," she sobbed, throwing herself into his arms. Then her eyes grew round. "Zander, guard your back!"

He cast her to the side and whirled, just in

time to meet Campbell, knife out, coming at him.

Campbell growled and launched himself at Zander. Zander stepped aside barely in time, but the knife grazed his bare arm, drawing blood.

Dorie crawled away, her leg throbbing from Campbell's bruising grip. "Oh, Zander," she moaned. She staggered to her feet and tottered over to the mule. "My pistol," she murmured, "oh, where is my pistol?" The mule backed away from her, jerking on the lead rein in his frantic attempts to get away from the cries and groans of the two men fighting nearby.

"Whoa," she cried, her voice shaking. The mule backed up further, sensing her fear. "Easy, boy," she said, striving to calm her voice. "Easy."

She got the mule calmed down and was rummaging through her carpetbag when she heard Campbell's coarse laugh. "There's my mark," he cried, and she turned in time to see Zander bleed from another knife cut. He was unarmed.

"Oh, Zander," she moaned, wanting to run to him. But she must stay her ground. She turned back and dug frantically through the carpetbag. She tossed dresses left and right, heedless of where they landed. When an Indian man came up and took one of her dresses and ran off, she did not bat an eye. At last she felt the hard grip of her pistol. She pulled out the pistol and glanced around. Which saddlebag was the powder in? And the bullets?

She searched frantically through one of the mule's saddlebags. Not there.

The cries of the fighting men spurred her on. "It's got to be here," she muttered. She ran around in front of the mule and searched the mule's opposite saddlebag, her fingers rummaging frantically. She found the powder and next to it, in a smaller sack, the bullets. Sweat beaded her brow, her hands shook, but she loaded the pistol.

She ran over to where the two men crouched, a mere two paces from each other. Campbell's knife weaved as he looked for an opening to stab Zander.

"Stop!" she cried, pointing the pistol at Campbell's back. But Zander was in direct line behind Campbell. If she shot and missed Campbell, she'd hit Zander. For the first time in her life, Dorie questioned her shooting skill.

Edward Cecil stood, legs apart, watching the fight, a look of amusement on his handsome face. While the two men circled each other, Campbell lunging whenever he saw an opening and Zander keeping him at a cautious distance, Edward Cecil pulled his knife out of its leather scabbard and tossed it to Zander.

"Let's make this a fair fight," said the mixed-blood man, and Dorie let out a sigh of relief. With a knife, Zander at least had a chance to survive.

She glanced down at her pistol, then at the men, her eyes narrowed to assess when she would get an opportunity for a clear, clean shot.

Now that both men were armed, it was Campbell who was leery. He lunged once, and Zander caught him by the arm and pulled. Campbell went down and Zander followed. The two men rolled over and over. Now on top, Campbell suddenly lifted his arm and brought it down. Zander parried and rolled to the side and made a quick motion.

Suddenly Campbell went still. In horror, Dorie watched him fall backward on the ground, eyes open and staring. But he didn't see her, she knew. He didn't see anyone because he was dead. Zander had killed him.

She ran up to Zander as he slowly got up. He brushed the dust off his leather pants and shook himself as though to shake off the dead man's blood.

"Oh, Zander," she moaned. "Are you hurt?"

He nodded, and put one arm around her. She could feel him rest his weight on her and she knew he was hurting. Both his arms were covered in bloody scratches from Campbell's knife. Zander tossed the knife back to Edward Cecil. "Thanks," he said.

Cecil nodded and bent down to clean the knife blade on a clump of bunchgrass.

Dorie put both arms around Zander, heedless of the blood on her brown-and-white gingham dress. "Oh, Zander, I was so frightened. . . . "

He patted her back. "It's all right, Dorie. I'll always protect you."

She lifted her teary face. "I was frightened for you," she explained, "not for me."

He grunted. "Campbell meant to rape you."

She bit her lip and hugged him tighter. "Thank you for saving me, Zander," she said. The dead man lay on the ground where he'd fallen. She buried her head in Zander's shoulder. "Let's get away from this place," she begged. Behind them, she could hear the Indians yelling and singing and arguing.

He helped her onto Lightning. The chestnut was skittish from the smell of blood. Indeed, all the animals acted nervous. As Zander mounted his black mare, Burke came staggering up. "Ye son-of-a bitch!" cried the trader. "Ye kilt my partner!"

"Your partner charged me with a knife," said Zander warily. "I killed him in self-defense."

"Ye murdered my partner!" screamed Burke. "Ye murdered him!"

Some Indian men gathered around and stared at Zander and Burke.

"Him fight with knife," said one Indian, spitting in the general direction of the dead man. "Him bad."

But Burke wasn't listening to anyone. He pointed a trembling finger at Zander. There was a wild light in his eyes. "Ye murdered William Campbell," he proclaimed, "and someday ye'll pay. Somehow, some way, ye'll pay!"

Chapter Twenty-three

Two days later

Clifton Ross sat on his horse and waited on the trail as the man on horseback came closer. The man led two mules and another horse. Draped over the second horse was a long bundle. Ross sat patiently, only a little curious, and squinted against the brightness of the afternoon sun. This man might have seen Zander Durban or Dorie Primfield. A few well-placed questions might save Ross two weeks of footwork, so he could afford to sit and wait while the sun beat down on his leather hat.

When the man was a mere ten paces away, Clifton raised his hand and hailed him.

Cautiously, the other man—he looked like a trapper—returned Ross's greeting. He was a little taller than Clifton Ross and chunky, and his wrinkled face showed he'd spent his share of years on the trapline.

Cautiously Ross got down off his horse. His loaded rifle was only a hand's reach away. "Care for a sociable chat and a plug of tobaccy?" he asked, knowing few men, trapper or Indian, could resist an offer of tobacco.

The other man nodded and dismounted. Ross reached into his saddlebag and brought out a twist of tobacco. He cut off a piece and handed it to the other.

The man eyed him carefully, then accepted the tobacco. He popped it in his mouth and chewed it.

"Where ye be headin'?" asked Ross.

The man pointed to the last packhorse. "Got a body," he said. "Takin' it to Fort Walla Walla for a decent burial."

Ross swung round in surprise and stared at the packhorse. By God, a body *could* fit into that canvas-covered bundle.

"Me partner," explained the other man. Ross watched him warily. "Kilt by a murderer."

"Too bad," grunted Ross.

The other man's jaw tightened. "He were a good man, me partner," he said. "And I aim to get the son-of-a-bitch who kilt him."

Ross nodded approvingly. He could understand such sentiments. "My name's Clifton Ross," he said, holding out his hand.

The other man took it. "Burke," he said. "Ian Burke."

"You a trapper, Mr. Burke?" asked Ross.

"Naw. A trader. Used to be a trapper, but standin' in them cold streams baitin' beaver traps got to be too much for me old bones. I do a little tradin' now." He glanced at the bundle on the packhorse. "Me and my partner did trading. Now it's just me."

Ross considered the man in front of him for a moment. Then his eyes roved over the trade goods strapped to the mules. He spotted a book and wandered over. "You trade books?" he asked incredulously. Burke did not look like the kind of man who even knew how to read.

Burke eagerly plucked the book out of the sack. "Ye wanta trade for it?" he asked. "It's a good book. Look at that fancy scrollwork. Lord Byron wrote it, ye know, the lassies' fancy poet."

Ross stared at Burke in astonishment. There were depths to this man he'd never suspected. Then Burke handed him the slim volume. Upside-down. Ross took it with a smile and corrected himself. Not so deep, after all. He opened it and read silently, "To my husband-to-be, Clarence Biddle. In happy anticipation, Adora Primfield."

Ross slammed the book shut and his jaw twitched. His heart pounded. Primfield's book! That meant Burke might have come across Primfield and Durban! Might even have traded with them! "Where did you get this book?" demanded Ross.

"Oh, it's a good book, all right," Burke assured him hastily. "Got it from the lass meself." His eyes narrowed. "Why'd ye want to know? Do ye want the book or no'?"

Ross's jaw clenched and he handed the poetry book back to Burke. So. Burke knew where Primfield was.

He turned away with a shrug. "Cain't read so good," he muttered.

Burke smiled slyly, trying to hide it as he returned the book to the sack.

Then Ross asked good-naturedly, "Bet you don't make a hell of a pile of money at tradin', do you?"

Burke glared at him. "What's it to ye, trapper?"

Ross heard the anger in the other man's voice. He held up his hands. "Just a little observation, Mr. Burke," he said. "No offense meant."

"Say what ye're gonna say, trapper."

"Well," said Ross, "what I was gonna say was this: I know a way you might make some good money. Get some prime pelts fer yerself."

"Oh?" Burke looked mildly interested. "If it's

such a good deal, why ain't ye doin' it, *Mr.* Ross?" There was a sneer in the title.

Ross restrained himself. " 'Cause I need help is why."

Burke watched him out of little blue eyes. Ross was reminded of a cat waiting to pounce.

"I'm lookin' for a man," said Ross.

"What man?"

"Name of Zander Durban. You heerd of him?"

Burke eyed him suspiciously. "Might have. Then again, might not have."

"Think about it," advised Ross. "I want to find this man and last I heard he was in the mountains, near Kicking Horse creek. Cabin up there."

Burke leaned forward. "Can I have another chaw of tobaccy whilst I think on it?"

Ross cut him another piece. Smaller this time.

Burke chewed. "Where's the furs come in?" he asked, his cheeks puffed out.

"There's a reward out for this Durban. Dead."

"How much?" asked Burke.

"Fifty furs," lied Ross.

Burke whistled. "Them's a pile of furs."

Ross smiled. "You interested?"

"Who wants to know?"

"I do." Ross smiled. " 'Course, if you ain't seen this man, then I'll just move on. No sense in wastin' your time." He made a move as if to re-mount his horse.

"Now, now," said Burke. "Just hold it a minute." He stared at Ross. "If I was to say I knowed where this man was, what would I get paid?"

"Why, Mr. Burke, you'd get half the reward. "Twenty-five furs for you, twenty-five for me."

Burke chewed, considering. "I'll tell ye somethin'," he said. "I want Zander Durban dead too. He's the murderer what kilt my partner."

Ross glanced at the body, unable to believe his good luck. He'd get Burke to tell him where Zander Durban was, then when reward time came, he'd cheat him out of his twenty-five furs. He grinned at Burke. "Well, now, why don't you just tell me where our man is?"

Burke grinned back. "Why don't ye just tell me who's payin' the reward."

The smile disappeared from Ross's face. "The factor at Fort Walla Walla. Clarence Biddle."

Burke nodded. "Done business with him a time or two. Tell you what," he said. "Why don't we partner up, ye and me, and I'll take ye to Durban?"

Ross's heartbeat quickened. This was so easy. "Let's do that," he agreed.

Burke glanced at the body. "But first I gotta take me partner and bury him at the fort. He needs a right proper Christian burial."

Ross considered. "You want to bury him at the fort?"

"Yeah. There's likely a minister of the cloth there. I want him to say the proper words. Campbell was a good man."

"I'm sure he was." Ross smiled. "You are most fortunate, Mr. Burke," he added, "because *I* am a minister of the cloth. A reverend I am, and I will be happy to bury your friend. Right here. We can bury him right here beside the trail and be on our way."

Burke looked at him uncertainly. "If ye're a minister, how come ye're huntin' a man? Maybe to kill him?"

Ross laughed. "Ministerin' don't pay much," he allowed. "And as a minister, I won't kill him. You will." He studied Burke. "That's what you want, ain't it?"

"Sure," said Burke easily. "I want him dead."

"You seen a woman with him?" asked Ross casually.

Burke peered at him suspiciously. "Yep," he answered at last. "He's got a lass with him."

"Good, good," said Ross, clapping Burke on the back. "I think we're gonna do right well together. Partner."

"I think so, too. Reverend," said Burke.

Two weeks later, Dorie crouched behind the cottonwood tree near the river and vomited until there was nothing left in her stomach. "Oh, Lordy," she muttered. "Why am I so sick?"

Aunt Hanna always said Dorie had the constitution of a horse. But Aunt Hanna would not be saying that now. Not if she'd been with Dorie for the past three days.

"Dorie?" asked Zander. He was standing over by the fire they'd cooked their—his—breakfast of fish on.

"Over here, Zander." She straightened a little, dreading another bout. But nothing happened. And her stomach felt better. Perhaps she was finished being sick. Perhaps she would be healthy now. She moved slowly over to where he was waiting, her hand on her stomach.

He eyed her. "You feeling all right?"

She met his eyes glumly. "I'm feeling better than I was earlier."

"That fall off Lightning sure did shake things up for you." Despite the light tone of his words, he looked concerned.

"I don't think Lightning had much to do with how I've been feeling," she murmured. In truth, she wondered if she might be pregnant. She wished she could talk to Prue. Prue would know. She had three children. She'd know if this sickness was related to a growing baby, as Dorie suspected.

Zander was watching her closely. She wondered if she should ask him to take her to

Fort Walla Walla. The problem was, the last time she'd asked him to take her there, he'd just laughed. But that was before—before she'd become his country wife. Dared she try again? Summoning her courage, she began, "Zander—"

"Dorie—" he said at the same time. She smiled. He continued, "Dorie, you say you want me to let you know where we're going. . . ."

She nodded, curious to know more.

"I've decided," he said firmly, "to take you to the Jesuit mission." His grin told her he expected her to be very happy about that.

"The Jesuit mission?" she repeated, dumbfounded. "Why are we going to the Jesuit mission?"

"You'll see," was all he said as he started saddling the chestnut packhorse.

"The Jesuit mission," she murmured to herself. Jesuit mission? Priests? Ministers? Weddings? Weddings!

Joy fluttered in her heart, and a tiny smile curved her lips. "Zander, do you love me?"

Chapter Twenty-four

Our Lady of Compassion
Jesuit Mission
November 1, The Feast of All Saints.

"Oh, I'm so excited," exclaimed Dorie.

"Weddings do that, don't they, dear?" Martha Whitley's blue eyes crinkled gently at the corners as she smiled indulgently at Dorie. Dorie grinned back at her. She had immediately liked the older woman. Mrs. Whitley's salt-and-pepper hair was drawn back into a tight bun, and her waist was a little wider than it might have been when she was a girl—Mrs. Whitley called herself "comfortable"—but she was a kindly woman and, truth to tell, she reminded

Dorie a bit of Aunt Hanna.

Mrs. Whitley, the wife of the factor of Fort McCraig, was visiting Our Lady of Compassion Mission for "peace and solace," as she told Dorie. But tonight Mrs. Whitley looked as excited as Dorie or any of the other young women who were to be guests at tonight's wedding. The whole mission was abuzz with excitement.

Dorie secretly wished it was her wedding. But it was not. It was a celebration of the marriage between the chief trader at Fort Scroggins and his recently imported English wife-to-be.

"Try this dress on, dear," suggested Mrs. Whitley now. Dorie took the dress she held out. It was a royal blue velveteen dress with a fitted bodice dropping into a slightly flared long skirt. "That color will look lovely on you," offered Mrs. Whitley. "I used to wear it for special dances." She sighed and smiled sadly. "But it won't fit me anymore."

Dorie ducked a flying elbow as one of the other young women—there were three others in the small room—tried to put on her own dress. Their chatter and giggles added buoyancy to the festivities.

Dorie found a quiet corner, out of the way of flying elbows, and pulled the blue dress over her head.

Once the dress was on, she looked into the large, hand-held mirror at her flushed face and neckline, and she could see that the blue dress did look particularly pretty. She smiled. "It fits," she said, "except for right here." She plucked at the stomach of her dress. "It's a little tight."

Mrs. Whitley frowned. "Why, it is," she observed, taking a pinch of fabric. Then she glanced at Dorie's flushed face. "Are you with child?" she asked quietly.

Dorie's eyes widened. "I—I don't know," she confessed. "I might be. I've been sick every morning for the past fortnight."

"Have you been tired? Lethargic?" asked Mrs. Whitley in concern.

Dorie nodded.

"When was your last flow of blood? Oh, dear," Mrs. Whitley said, "I did not mean to embarrass you. It's just that it is an important thing to know in determining . . ." Her voice trailed off in mute apology.

"I haven't had my monthly flow since"—Dorie counted back—"why, since before Zander captured—" She broke off hastily.

When she didn't volunteer anything else, Mrs. Whitley observed, "Dorie, it is very likely that you are indeed pregnant."

Her quiet words set Dorie's heart to pounding. Pregnant! With Zander's child! She clapped her hands together. "I wondered about it," she exclaimed. "I'm so happy to know!"

"It's almost time for the wedding," announced a handsome mixed-blood woman who entered the room. She, too, was visiting the Jesuit mission and had introduced herself to Dorie earlier. Her name was Maxine and she was the wife of one of the gentlemen at Fort Scroggins, the clerk, MacDonald.

"Oh, I must do my hair," exclaimed Dorie, suddenly all aflutter. Mrs. Whitley handed her a hairbrush, and Dorie brushed her thick hair back and up and twisted it. She secured it with pins, leaving wisps of hair at the sides of her face.

"How pretty," said Maxine, with a glimmer of envy in her dark eyes. "Is that a style from St. Louis, Missouri?" Earlier, Dorie had told her of her travels.

"From Rochester, Missouri," answered Dorie with a shy blush.

"Time to go, ladies," said Mrs. Whitley, and the three other women who were completing their toilette hurried out the door.

Dorie walked down the narrow hall of the mission building, letting the giggling girls go ahead. *Pregnant*, she marveled. *Oh, wait until I tell Zander!*

Perhaps, thought Dorie hopefully, as she stood in the doorway and scanned the hall for Zander, *when Zander sees the happy bride and groom, he'll want to make our marriage official, too!*

The low-ceilinged room, with long walls made of rough-cut wood, was crowded. Trappers were there, and gentlemen visiting from other forts, accompanied by their women. A few Indians hovered on the edges of the room. Monks in their black habits could be seen here and there in the press of people.

A table set to one side of the room bore a spread of food, some of which Dorie had never seen before. Plates piled high with sliced, cold venison, bear steaks, and elk meat crowded the table. Platters of root vegetables made her mouth water. There were bowls of long green pickles, a whiskey cask, and large baskets of dried fruit.

She noticed a stout man whose brown hair bunched out around his bald crown. He wore a long black robe that touched the floor. Several people listened as he spoke and his face grew redder from his exertions.

He spoke earnestly with a middle-aged man dressed in a stiff gray cloth suit. The man looked so out of place that she immediately guessed him to be the groom.

A loud gasp went up.

A woman wearing a dress the color of a robin's egg swept into the room. As she passed by, Dorie overheard two women whispering loudly.

Both women had black hair that shone in the lamplight. One wore a pale blue gown, the other a red one. Their skin was fair, their eyes dark. Mixed-blood women, Dorie realized.

"The bride looks lovely, don't you think?" said Blue Dress.

"She should. He paid enough for that dress! It's from St. Louis, you know," answered Red Dress.

"St. Louis! My goodness!" Blue Dress looked properly impressed.

Dorie stared at the bride. She wore a thick white ribbon at the snug waist of her wedding dress. Her blond hair curled in ringlets at the side of her face, and a little white hat perched on her head. She wore a happy smile on her pale, pretty face. Her husband-to-be eagerly reached out his hand to greet her.

"I bet Abby would like to claw the bride's hair off," giggled the woman in the red dress standing next to Dorie.

"She should! I would if I were her." Blue Dress looked most affronted and crossed her arms. "Just look at him. I think Abby should shake *him* bald, too!"

Puzzled, Dorie stared at the bridal couple. Who was Abby? And what had they done to offend her?

The priest held up both hands to get the attention of the gathered people.

"Ladies, gentlemen," he began. "Tonight we celebrate the nuptials of the lovely Miss Gwyneth McFee and Mr. Hedley Darlington, assistant factor and clerk at Fort Scroggins!"

There was a loud clapping of hands and stomping of booted feet.

"Gather closer," continued the priest, "and we will witness the uniting in marriage of this blissfully happy couple."

The ceremony was over in mere minutes. The groom flushed as red as a berry and his voice cracked once; the bride looked pale and her voice was a choked whisper. Amused, Dorie decided she would be sure to raise her voice when *she* pronounced *her* vows.

She wandered through the room. When she spotted Zander, she lifted the front of her skirts and made her way over to where he stood. "Hello, Zander," she said, conscious of the new life she carried—new life that *they* had made.

His eyes fixed on her face, but he did not speak. Now she forgot everything but him. In the light of the lamps, his black hair shone as lustrously as a raven's wing. His eyes were dark, burning, drawing her closer.

"Zander?"

"Dorie," he breathed. "You look lovely."

She smiled. She felt lovely too. He took her hand and drew her to his side, his eyes holding hers captive.

Her heart pounded. The evening passed in a blur for Dorie. She did not even hear the people talking around her. All she heard was Zander's even breath. All she felt was Zander's warm hand, holding hers secure, and Zander at her side as she floated in a happy haze.

"Shall we dance?" His words drew her out of her haze.

"Oh yes," she whispered.

The musicians, two fiddlers and a flutist, played a waltz. Zander took her in his arms, and she stared up at him; her breath caught at the look of promise in his eyes. *A promise to love me? A promise to marry me? Oh, Zander, what is your promise?*

He moved with her easily, his steps slow and sure. She followed and they glided gracefully around the room. Two couples moved aside and watched, but though Dorie felt the admiring eyes, for her the only person in the room was Zander. Always Zander. *Oh, Lord, how I love him,* she thought.

They waltzed as one being; her blood pounded in time to the music. Too soon the waltz finished, and the fiddlers played a faster tune.

"Let us walk outside," he suggested.

Wordlessly, her hand in his, she followed him through the packed crowd and through the door out into the evening air. Silver stars

296

pierced the night sky above them.

She took a breath and held it, wanting to stand here with Zander under this beautiful sky, wanting this evening to last forever.

"Dorie, I want to tell you—" he began.

A sobbing cry caught her attention. Near the garden sat a woman with a baby on her lap. The woman's head drooped, and her slumped shoulders shook with each sob. She cried as though her heart were breaking.

"Zander?" murmured Dorie. "That woman. She's crying." Dorie felt a rush of sadness that such a beautiful night for her should be such a sorrowful night for another. "Let us help her."

"Dorie," he said, taking her arm. "Leave her be. Leave her be in her grief."

"I can't," she said, pulling away.

He followed. "Dorie, don't!"

"Zander, she's crying!" exclaimed Dorie over her shoulder, hurrying over to the woman. "Perhaps she needs my help."

"Dorie," he tried again. "Get one of the other women to help her." There was an urgency in his voice that she did not understand.

"She needs someone to help her, Zander," Dorie said crisply, "and we are the ones available."

Resigned, he followed her.

As Dorie approached the woman, she saw the short, thick black hair and high cheekbones. The woman was Indian. The child in her arms slept, which was probably a mercy, thought Dorie. At least the poor woman did not have to contend with a crying child as well as her own sorrow.

"What's the matter?" asked Dorie kindly. "Why are you crying?"

The woman glanced up and wiped at the tears on her face. Her face took on a stoic look, and Dorie thought the woman had assumed she was alone.

Dorie sat down beside her, heedless of wrinkling her blue dress, and said gently, "Please. I want to help. Can you tell me why you're crying? Are you hurt?" She glanced at the woman's hands and arms. Nothing looked cut or broken.

The woman met her eyes. What she read in Dorie's must have decided her, for she said in slow English, "I cry because that is my husband getting married."

Dorie stared at her in astonishment. She must have misunderstood the woman.

"Your—your husband?"

The woman nodded. "Yes."

"But—but how can that be? How can he marry someone else if he's married to you?" Her eyes jerked from the woman to the sleeping baby. "And you have a child. How can—?"

The woman's face closed. "He will never marry me! I am only his country wife!"

Chapter Twenty-five

Dorie sat on a wooden bench in a small room in the mission, enfolded in Mrs. Whitley's motherly arms. The furnishings were simple—two beds built into the wall, a table, and two chairs.

"How could he?" sobbed Dorie. "How could he do this to me?"

"There, there, child," soothed Mrs. Whitley, patting Dorie's shoulders.

"How could he?" demanded Dorie, straightening. She sought Mrs. Whitley's grim blue eyes for an explanation.

"I've seen this happen before," confirmed the older woman. "I've seen men do this to women."

"But," sobbed Dorie, "this is *me*! This is *me*

who is hurting! Don't you understand?"

"Alas, child, I do," said Mrs. Whitley gently.

Dorie burst into fresh sobs. "I loved him," she said, her voice rising. "I *loved* him!"

Mrs. Whitley continued to pat Dorie's shoulder patiently.

"I thought he loved me, but I—I was just his country wife." Dorie wiped at her eyes with a lace handkerchief that Mrs. Whitley had given her. "I told myself he loved me. I believed he loved me!" she wailed. "I thought we were going to be married. That we were as good as married. I thought we were just waiting until we found the nearest minister to marry us. I thought—"

"There, there, child," soothed Mrs. Whitley. "Don't keep blaming yourself. He had a part in this too." There was a hardness in her voice, out of keeping with the gentle lines of her face.

"He lied to me!" cried Dorie, her face in her hands. "He lied to me, over and over. I meant nothing to him. Nothing!"

She withdrew from Mrs. Whitley's comforting embrace and huddled, knees up, in a tight lump on the bench. "He lied to me, Mrs. Whitley!"

"Call me Martha," she said, patting Dorie's shoulder. "And yes, he did lie to you. Perhaps not with words," she explained, "but his actions were certainly deceitful."

"They were! Oh, yes, they were," nodded Dorie. "He was so kind to me. Staying with me after I fell off the horse . . . saying kind things . . . 'Oh Dorie, you look lovely'," she mimicked bitterly. "And all the time he knew! He *knew* we weren't married. He knew!" Fresh sobs shook her body. She tightened her fist. "He never *intended* to marry me! Oh, I am such a fool!" she cried. "Such a fool!" She pounded her fists on the bench beside her.

"Hush," scolded Martha gently. "Do not berate yourself, child. You're not the first woman deceived by a handsome face. You won't be the last. Unfortunately," she added regretfully.

"He brought me to this place to flaunt his lies," cried Dorie. "He brought me here to say 'This is what you'll never have, Dorie Primfield. You'll never be married'! I know he did!"

Aghast, Martha looked at her. "Is he that cruel?" she marveled.

"Yes," answered Dorie, stoutly. "He is."

"Men!" sneered Martha, the curl of her lip out of place on her kind face. "He doesn't deserve you. You are a fine person, Dorie Primfield. You deserve kindness and fairness—and a man who loves you and treats you with respect." Martha twisted her hands together. She looked overwrought. "And you deserve marriage," she added.

"Well, I don't have it!" howled Dorie at the low wooden ceiling. "And I'm pregnant!"

"There, there," soothed Martha again, patting her.

Dorie took her hand. "Oh, Martha, what would I do without you?" she asked. "Here I am, far away from home, from my family, from my sister, Prue—" Tears welled again and she broke down and cried. After a time, she gulped, "You're being so kind. . . . "

"There, there," said Martha. "We women must stick together."

"Yes," said Dorie, thrusting her chin out. "We must."

She glanced across the room at her carpetbag. Slowly she unfolded her limbs from their cramped position. She got off the bench and shuffled over to her bag. Opening it, she sorted through her possessions, at last drawing out a dress.

"This," she announced to Martha as she held up a yellow-and-white gingham dress, "is my best dress. I am going to give it to that woman with the baby. The country wife. I believe her name is Abby." Dorie tottered over to the bench and collapsed on its hard frame, clutching the dress.

"That is a kind thing to do," said Martha. "I'll give it to her, if you like."

Dorie nodded and handed her the dress. Martha took it and started to rise, then sat back down. "What are *you* going to do, dear?"

Dorie glanced at her, uncomprehending.

"You have to make a plan," prodded Martha gently. "If you make a plan to help yourself, you'll do better. You won't be at loose ends or," she added firmly, "at the whim of a man."

Dorie stared at the wooden floor and forced herself to think of her choices. "I want to go to Fort Walla Walla," she surprised herself by saying. "I want to go and find Prue. She'll help me."

"Your sister? Yes, I'm sure she would," agreed Martha, nodding her head vigorously. "That's a good plan."

"I'll wait until Zander leaves the mission," continued Dorie.

"Why not go now?"

"I don't want to see him—ever again!" said Dorie vehemently. "I don't want to have even the *chance* of accidentally seeing him again. No, I will stay here until he's gone, then I'll go ahead to Fort Walla Walla."

"I'm sure one of the good fathers at the mission here will escort you or—" Martha put her finger on her chin and tapped it consideringly. "I know some trappers from my husband's fort. They're here. We can ask them to accompany you—"

Dorie nodded. "That sounds fine, Martha." She smiled at her friend apologetically. "I just want to lie down. I am so tired. . . . "

"Of course, dear," agreed Martha, standing

up hastily. "You must get your rest. You've got yourself and the baby to think of. Rest is very important."

Dorie smiled wanly. "And if you see Zander anywhere around the Mission, shoot him for me, would you?"

The older woman's jaw went slack for a moment. Then she snapped it shut. "Oh. A joke."

"A poor one," admitted Dorie, eyes brimming.

Martha patted her hand. "Go and lie down and get some rest," she said kindly. "I'll take this dress to Abby and I'll see if I can find those trappers I know." She smiled, and her eyes crinkled at the corners. "Don't worry. Things will look better for you after you've rested."

Dorie felt a surge of gratitude for the older woman's concern. "Thank you for all you've done," she murmured.

Martha smiled back. "We women have to stick together," she answered.

Zander leaned one shoulder against the rough wooden wall of the men's quarters and stared moodily across the mission grounds at the log walls of the women's accommodations. Dorie was in there. She had to be.

At the end of the grounds, against the far walls, was a long, low building. The monks' quarters.

Next door to that was the chapel. He could

hear several people inside, singing, at mass. He wondered idly if Dorie was among them.

No, he thought. He hadn't seen her go in. And he'd been waiting outside the women's quarters for most of the day. At this mission, the men were housed in separate quarters, across from the women. So he'd spent most of the day leaning against the men's quarters and glaring at the door of the women's quarters. What was taking her so long? She had to come out. She had to.

And when she did, he would convince her that all along he'd intended to marry her.

He squirmed a little inside, wondering how she was feeling. It was damned unfortunate that she'd learned the meaning of "country wife" the way she had. But it wasn't like that between them. No. Not like it had been between his father and mother. No. Not like that at all.

He clenched his fist for the fiftieth time that day. If only she hadn't found out what a country wife was! If only he'd gotten her to the priest before she discovered the meaning of the words. He'd been so close, so close to getting her to the altar!

Last night, at the wedding, when he'd seen her floating toward him in that dress, he'd realized how much he wanted her.

He'd meant to talk to the priest so that today would have been *their* wedding day. If only Dorie hadn't talked to the country wife, the poor

305

woman with the baby. He'd tried to stop her, tried to get her away. He'd taken one look at the woman and the baby, and he'd known what she was crying about. Exactly what had happened to his own mother. Exactly what he'd prevented happening to Mary.

His lips tightened. Yeah. He knew.

And as for Dorie Primfield . . . Dorie was a headstrong woman who would do things her own way. He'd learned that.

Earlier he'd gone to the women's quarters to talk to her, and a gray-haired woman had refused to let him in, chasing him away with a broom, much to the amusement of some visiting trappers.

He idly watched a monk lead a bay horse along the little path that went down the center of the mission grounds. Eight-foot walls surrounded the mission, and the gates closed at dusk. There was a blacksmith shop, a poultry building, a large garden, and a winery at Our Lady of Compassion Mission.

Zander sighed. He wished *his* lady would have compassion for him.

Impatiently, he shoved himself away from the wall. Damn, where was she? She couldn't have left the mission without his seeing her. He fidgeted with his possibles bag. No tobacco in it. Tired of his long vigil and wanting a short respite—he'd been waiting since early morning—

he ducked into the men's quarters and found his saddlebags. He'd just cut himself off a piece of tobacco when he glanced out the open door. Dorie!

He dropped the tobacco and ran after the bonneted woman. "Dorie! Dorie, wait!"

He raced after her as though wolves chewed at his heels. "Dorie!"

He skidded to a halt when he caught up to her and stared in astonishment at the woman. The woman was wearing Dorie's yellow-and-white gingham dress, all right, but it wasn't Dorie. It was the Indian woman, the country wife. "You!" he cried.

She glared at him disdainfully. It was obvious that she, too, recognized him. She said nothing.

"Beggin' your pardon, ma'am," he stammered. "I—I thought you were someone else. Someone I know."

The Indian woman stared at him in mute reproach.

"You're wearing Dorie's dress," he said. "Do you think she'd talk to me? Could you tell her I've got to talk with her? Please?" God, he felt like a fool begging this woman, but he had to talk to Dorie. He had to!

The woman sniffed and took a step toward the women's quarters. She increased her pace and he hurried after her. "Please?" he called.

"Ma'am? Please, won't you at least talk to her for me?"

She whirled and faced him, her black eyes spitting fury. "Why should I help you? You'll set her and your child aside when it's convenient for you, just like all the rest!"

Chapter Twenty-six

Evening descended on Our Lady of Compassion Mission. Two bedraggled-looking trappers strolled through the mission gates just as one of the monks was starting to close them for the night.

"Ye sure we can sleep here tonight?" Burke asked Clifton Ross.

"I done it afore," answered Clifton Ross. He pointed at the men's quarters. "Over there. Them's the men's quarters. We'll get a bed there and a meal in the dining hall."

Burke grinned. "Ye think these Jesuits will feed ye?"

Ross looked at him blankly.

"Ye bein' a reverend and all. Ye're no' a papist."

"I've stayed here afore," said Ross stubbornly.

"Ye mean these Jesuits will feed just anybody?" asked Burke in astonishment.

Ross grimaced but said nothing.

They unloaded their horses and pack animals and left them at the corral, then headed for the men's quarters. Suddenly Burke halted in midstep. Ross bumped into him from behind. "Damnation! Cain't you get out of a man's way?"

"Shut yer beavertrap," said Burke tensely. "Take a wee look over there." He pointed surreptitiously. "Who do ye think that is?"

"Who?" demanded Ross irritably. He peered into the gathering gloom. "Some monk, I suppose."

"Look again," said Burke with a satisfied smirk. "That is our quarry, Reverend."

"Our what?" Ross blinked. "Who?" He grabbed Burke's arm. "It's Durban!"

"Right ye are." Burke gave a happy little hoot.

Clifton Ross stared at the tall man lounging against the men's quarters. "Well, I'll be! This makes our job a mite easier," he breathed.

"I can feel those furs already. Can't ye?" asked Burke.

"Huh?"

"The reward. Remember? Och"—Burke

squinted at Ross—"are ye still gonna let me kill him?"

"Yep. That's the deal."

"Good!" Burke spat out some chewing tobacco. "Wouldn't want ye to deprive me of my revenge. Don't want ye drinkin' o' the milk o' human kindness while we're here."

"What are you talking about?"

"Why, this is a mission, Reverend. A religious community. I dinna want ye goin' and gettin' all holy on me and forgivin' that son-of-a bitch or somethin'." Burke sounded genuinely concerned.

Ross laughed. "No chance of that, partner. We found him. Now he's all yourn."

There was a knock on the door of Dorie's small room. She got off the bed and answered it. A frail monk in a long black robe said, "There is a gentleman caller for you."

"I don't want to speak to him," said Dorie as calmly as she could. If Zander thought he could talk his way back into her life, he could think again! Aunt Hanna always said "Once a snake, always a snake."

The monk looked at her calmly. "I will tell him to go away." He left.

Dorie smiled grimly at Martha. "I don't want to see him, Martha. Ever again."

Martha, sitting on the bed reading her Bible,

nodded her head vigorously. "I think that is wise, dear."

A knock came on the door again. Dorie jumped.

"I'll get it," said Martha, rising imperiously. Her face settled in grim lines as she sailed toward the door, prepared to do battle. Dorie smiled secretly to herself. She was so glad she had Martha Whitley for an ally.

"She is not to be disturbed," said Martha, swinging open the door.

The same monk stood there. "He said to tell you his name is Edward Cecil," said the monk mildly.

Martha glanced at Dorie. "Do you know an Edward Cecil, dear?"

"Edward Cecil," Dorie mused. "Hmmmm. Edward Cecil." Then, "Oh, yes, I know him. I met him at the Indian village." She made a decision. "Tell him I will meet with him," she said to the monk.

He glided away.

Dorie smiled at Martha. "I met Mr. Cecil once before. He is a decent man."

"I hope so," murmured Martha. She sat down on the bed and picked up her Bible. "Did you want me to accompany you?"

"In case Zander is lurking around?" asked Dorie. "No. I believe this is not a trick. I will speak with Mr. Cecil a short while, then I'll return."

She gave a shudder. "I do not intend to bump into Zander Durban, and I will not give him any excuse to talk to me. Whatsoever."

Martha stared at her curiously. "As you say," she offered at last, then resumed her reading.

Dorie hurried out the door. She gasped when she caught sight of a tall form lounging against the building opposite. "Zander!" she murmured. It was a trick, after all! She whirled to run back to her room when a deep voice said, "Dorie? Don't go. It's me, Edward Cecil."

She halted; he'd been waiting just outside the door. He bowed and her heart stopped its frantic racing. "Mr. Cecil," she acknowledged. "I hope you will be quick about what you have to say." She glanced across the yard at the lounging man. "I do not wish to visit long."

He too glanced at Zander. "I understand," he said softly. "I stopped by to give you my deepest regards. I heard you were here and I remembered how delightful—"

"Mr. Cecil," said Dorie. She could feel her cheeks flush. "It is not necessary to resort to flattery."

"Of course not," he said hastily. "I but wished to let you know that I am at your disposal." He took her hand and bowed over it.

"Wherever did you learn such courtly manners, Mr. Cecil?" she inquired curiously.

"My father was a French gentleman in the

North West Fur Company. He taught me to always honor a beautiful woman."

She eyed him in amusement. "My, how those smooth words roll off your tongue, Mr. Cecil."

"True words, Dorie," he corrected earnestly. He touched his lips to the back of her hand. "Please. If you need anything, anything at all, please call upon me. I am at your command." He straightened and regarded her out of sparkling black eyes. "I have learned a little of your predicament—"

Her eyes widened at his presumption.

"Ah, only a little," he cautioned her. "Enough to offer my services should you need an escort away from this mission or anywhere else."

She regarded him thoughtfully. "It is true that I seek an escort to Fort Walla Walla," she allowed.

"Let me help you," he urged. "I know the way, and I will hire good men to go with us."

She glanced across the yard. He was still there, the snake.

Tears stung her eyelids. She blinked them away and turned back to Edward Cecil. "My—my sister is at Fort Walla Walla. I would dearly love to see her."

"And you shall, *ma chère*. I will be happy to escort you."

Dorie thought about it. She knew Edward Cecil and was impressed with his manners and his thoughtfulness. Yes, she could trust him. Unlike the *rat* across the yard!

"Thank you," she said, "I will accept your kind offer."

He kissed her hand again and released it reluctantly when she gave a little tug. "When did you wish to leave?"

Her glance slid to the wall opposite, then back to Edward Cecil. "I—uh, wanted to wait for a day or two," she said awkwardly.

"Bien," he answered. "That will allow me time to find the men we need. I like to have trustworthy men at my back when I travel." He grinned.

"Very well. Thank you, Mr. Cecil," said Dorie with as much dignity as she could muster. She took a step into the women's quarters.

"Dorie," he said, and she halted at the urgency she heard in his voice. "I would never leave you to face anything alone. I would always be at your side, if you were *my* wife."

Her eyes widened. "Mr. Cecil! You forget yourself!"

"I'm afraid I do," he said sadly. He touched his heart. "Your beauty causes me to lose control of my thoughts and my tongue." He grinned. "But it troubles me very much, *ma chère*, to even think that you have been poorly treated."

Just how much did he know about her circumstances? she wondered.

Emboldened by her silence, he continued, "Let me but say this, *ma chère*, and then no more words will fall from my lips—if you were to look for another husband, you would not have far to look."

He means himself, she thought. "Thank you, Mr. Cecil," she said as primly as she could. At least he did not know she was not married to Zander, she thought in relief. Then she scolded herself. It didn't matter what he thought. She had no intention of marrying him!

She stepped inside the doorway of the wooden building. "I bid you good-bye for now, Mr. Cecil," she said firmly, then closed the door.

Zander clenched his fists as he watched Edward Cecil saunter away from the women's quarters. He recognized the man from the Indian village. What had he told Dorie? What had she told him? The questions burned into his mind as he glared at the retreating back of the tall man. Finally, he strode after him.

"Cecil!" he called.

Edward Cecil swung around. "You called me, *ami*?" he asked pleasantly.

Friend? What game is this he plays? wondered Zander.

"What were you talking to my wife about?" demanded Zander.

"Your wife?" asked Cecil thoughtfully. "Strange. She did not tell me she was your wife."

"You know she's my wife!" thundered Zander.

"Then why is she asking *me* to take her to Fort Walla Walla, eh?" inquired the mixed-blood with a smile.

"Fort Walla Walla!" Zander repeated angrily. "You stay away from her, Cecil. She is *my* wife!"

"Not any longer," he answered with an impudent grin.

Zander glared at his rival and tried another tack. "It will not do you any good to take her there. Biddle won't want her now that she's been mine."

"She is not going to see Biddle. She wishes to see her sister."

Zander ground his teeth.

"It would seem, *mon ami*, that you have not treated the lady very well, eh? And now you have lost her."

Zander clenched his jaw. "That is none of your goddamn concern!"

"Oh, but I think that it is," sneered Cecil. "She tells me she does not want you." He jerked a thumb at his chest. "It is *me* she wishes to marry!"

Chapter Twenty-seven

Zander rode Shadow away from the Mission of Our Lady of Compassion. His packhorses followed behind him in single file, with all his trade goods piled upon their backs.

He was going to have to kidnap Dorie Primfield *again*. He clenched his teeth as he thought about it. She was carrying his child, and by God, she was his wife and he wanted her with him!

He glanced back at the mission gates. It was late morning and everyone at the mission could have seen him ride away. Which was what he'd planned. Then word would get back to Dorie that he'd left. He wanted her to think he had given up all hope of talking to her and had quit the mission.

"She's pregnant. She won't talk to me. What is a man to do? There is no reasoning with her!" he told the black mare as he rode in the direction of Fort Walla Walla. The horse plodded steadily onward. "I have no choice but to kidnap her, Shadow. I have to make her listen to me!"

The sun was low in the western sky behind him when he reached a heavily bouldered area not far from the river trail he'd been following. He spotted a group of large rocks and headed for them. That would be a good place to make camp, he thought.

He dismounted from the mare and took off her saddle and unloaded the packhorses. He tied the mare, mule, and other horses to a scrawny greasewood tree out of sight of the trail. Then he gathered driftwood along the river, enough to make a fire, and muttered to himself all the while.

The wood gathered, he made a small fire and smiled grimly. He would be ready when Dorie and that fool, Cecil, came by.

"Zander Durban has left the mission," Edward Cecil announced importantly.

Dorie regarded him hopefully. "Are you certain?"

"*Oui*! He's left the mission and he will not be returning."

"Oh? How do you know that, Mr. Cecil?"

"Because *I* chased him away. You should have seen how afraid he looked once I told him to get out." Edward grinned. His chest actually puffed out.

Dorie frowned and shook her head. She wondered if she had made a mistake in accepting Edward Cecil's offer of escort to Fort Walla Walla. The man was turning out to be a braggart. Also, it surprised her to learn that Zander was afraid of Edward Cecil.

"I've hired the men to accompany us to the fort," continued Edward Cecil. "Good, reliable men. They'll help protect you." He smiled confidently. "We can leave tomorrow, if you desire."

Did he know she'd been waiting for Zander to leave? wondered Dorie. She was a bit ashamed of hiding in the women's quarters the whole time. It wasn't like her. "The soonest faced, the soonest finished," Aunt Hanna always used to say. But Dorie had her growing baby to think of. And she did not want to see Zander Durban ever again. The skunk! Just thinking of that man set her teeth on edge.

"I have sent some scouts ahead to pick the best trail," continued Edward Cecil.

She glanced at him. Obviously he expected her to be interested in their traveling plans.

Very well. "Who?" she asked.

"They are two very respected men in this territory," he answered with a knowing smile. "Ian Burke and Clifton Ross."

Dorie stared at him. Not the Burke she'd already met at the cabin? And Clifton Ross? She knew him and did not consider him very respected in the least! The thought niggled at her that perhaps she had made a *big* mistake by agreeing to go with Mr. Cecil. Perhaps she should ask Martha to arrange an escort with the men she knew.

"Dorie?" Edward Cecil must have asked her something because he had an expectant look on his handsome face.

"I—I beg your pardon, Mr. Cecil. What was it you said?"

"I said I have the horses ready and the men. I'd like to leave at dawn tomorrow." He smiled pleasantly.

"Very well, Mr. Cecil. I'll be ready at that time." She backed into the women's quarters, anxious to get away from him. She needed time to think, time to plan. But he was giving her very little time. Perhaps she should just go along with what he'd planned. She was reluctant to bother Martha with her problems. After all, she'd already relied on that good woman so much. . . .

He gave her a courtly little bow. "I will see

you at dawn," he said and strode away.

She watched him go. She supposed she should be grateful that he was helping her. Grateful for his interest in her welfare. But instead, she was becoming suspicious. Oh, dear. What was happening to her? All she wanted to do was get to Fort Walla Walla and see her sister. Why should that be so difficult?

"There he is," whispered Burke eagerly. He and Clifton Ross halted their horses. They dismounted so they could walk quietly on foot. That way their quarry wouldn't hear or see them.

"I wondered how long it would take us to find him," murmured Clifton Ross.

"That was a good idea you had, partnerin' up with Edward Cecil," commented Burke. "He gets the Primfield lass, and we get Durban. And the furs, o' course."

"Of course," answered Ross shortly. Burke harped constantly about the furs—at least ten times a day. By God, Ross would be glad to be rid of this "partner," but he needed Burke for just a little longer. Ross fought to rein in his impatience. "I'll hold the horses while you sneak closer," he offered at last.

Burke snorted. "Ye ain't a coward, is ye, Reverend?"

"Stop calling me that," snarled Ross.

"Coward?" drawled Burke irritatingly.

"No, the other."

"Reverend?" asked Burke in surprise. "That's what ye are, ain't ye?" He watched Ross out of beady little eyes.

Ross gritted his teeth. "Yeah."

"Well, then, get used to it," advised Burke. "How long you been a reverend anyway?"

"Not long," gritted Ross. "Can we get closer to Durban? I want him killed and done with."

"Anxious for them furs, are ye?" chuckled Burke.

They hobbled their horses behind a large boulder, at some distance from Zander Durban. He was setting up camp near some pine trees and boulders. "Lucky we saw him ride in there," observed Burke at Ross's elbow. "Else we coulda ridden right by and missed him."

Ross snorted, trying this time to rein in his irritation with his talkative partner.

They waited for a while. "We wait much longer and it's gonna be dark," warned Burke.

"What do you suggest?" bit out Clifton Ross. "God, I could use a drink."

"Me, too," answered Burke. "But I left me whiskey flask on me horse. Why don't we creep closer to Durban and then I'll plug 'im." Burke was loading his flintlock.

"You gonna use that thing?" demanded Ross.

"I am," assured Burke. "What's wrong with it?"

"Too loud, ain't it? A knife's quieter."

Burke paused as he considered. "Yeah," he agreed at last. "But you have to get very close to use a knife. I thought we might kill him from a distance. Less blood."

"Less danger, you mean," taunted Ross.

Burke halted in the act of ramming the bullet down the long barrel. "What do ye mean?" he asked ominously.

"Nothin'," Ross answered hastily. He glanced around nervously. "This is a well-used trail. Anyone might come by at any time. If we use the flintlock, the noise of the shot will draw anyone in the area."

"Good thinkin', Rev. The knife it is." Burke withdrew the ramrod after only two thrusts, not enough to lodge the bullet. He set the rifle aside.

"What the hell? Finish loading it," Clifton ordered irritably. "I'll use the rifle on Durban if you get into any trouble."

"Watch yer language, Rev."

"We're planning to kill a man, and you're telling me to watch my language?" Clifton Ross shook his head in disbelief. He was sick unto death of the whole "reverend" pretense. How could Burke be so stupid as not to guess the truth?

Burke picked up the ramrod and rag and finished tamping the bullet in place. He was in no hurry, Ross noticed in irritation. "Work a little faster," he urged.

"Ye just hold the horses, Rev, and leave the real work to me." Burke eyed him coolly.

Ross subsided and had to content himself with cracking his knuckles and fingers in irritation.

At last the rifle was loaded and Ross reached for the weapon. Burke jerked it out of his reach. "I'll just keep it," he said cautiously, "til we get a wee bit closer."

They sneaked past boulders and drew closer and closer to where Durban was sitting at his campfire, drinking from his tin cup. The smell of coffee hovered in the air.

"Wish I had a wee droppie," whispered Burke.

"Just kill Durban," said Ross in a low voice. "Then we'll drink."

"Yeah."

That was one thing he liked about Burke, Ross admitted. The grizzled man was a good drinking companion.

They waited until they saw Durban get up to check his livestock. While Durban was talking to a big black mare, Ross hit him on the head with the stock of the rifle and Burke plunged the knife into Durban's back. He dropped like a hamstrung horse.

Ross stared at the man lying on the ground. "He dead?"

"Don't know," Burke answered. "Let's make sure." He kicked at Durban, finally rolling him over onto his back.

"Looks like he's still breathin'," noted Ross angrily. "Hell of a sloppy job you did! Hurry it up!"

Burke raised the knife to stab Durban right in the heart.

"Hey!" cried a deep voice behind them. "What are you doing?"

"We been found out!" cried Ross. He dropped the rifle and started to run. Behind him he could hear groans and grunts as Burke fought with whoever had attacked him. Suddenly Ross was grabbed by the waist and swung around. His head crashed against Burke's and he knew nothing more.

Chapter Twenty-eight

Zander awoke to a humming sound and thought it was his head at first. But it wasn't. It was a trapper beside the fire. The man hummed as he stirred something steaming in the pot on the fire.

Zander fell asleep once more.

When he awoke again, he realized that it had not been a dream. There really was a trapper and a fire. Only this time the trapper squatted beside him.

"You waking up?" asked the trapper in surprise. Tight black curls peeked out from under his battered leather hat. He was a large man; his skin a deep brown that almost matched his robe. Why was a trapper wearing a black robe?

puzzled Zander groggily.

"Who the hell are you?" Zander blinked and stared up into a large black face.

A grin split the man's face. "You're alive!" He bent over Zander and peered into his eyes closely, peeling back the lids. Though his shoulders were huge and his arms powerfully built, his touch was gentle. "Ah'm Father Bartholomew," he added in a soft drawl. "Ah live at the mission but was at a nearby Indian village to heal the sick. Ah was on my way back to the mission when Ah saw those robbers attack you."

"Heal the sick?" repeated Zander in bewilderment. "What robbers?"

The Jesuit said, "Bad men, those two." He jerked his chin in the direction of two slumbering bodies, sprawled on the ground.

Zander slanted a glance at them. Burke and Clifton Ross. He tried to rise. "I've got to get up, got to find Dorie—" Dizziness swept over him. "Ohhhhhh," he groaned.

"Let's take off your coat," said Father Bartholomew. Carefully, he pulled the thick leather garment off Zander. "Lucky you were wearing the coat and shirt when that coward stabbed you," he observed. "The knife didn't go so deep."

"It feels like it went plenty deep," observed Zander dryly.

"It is bleeding a mite," admitted the Jesuit,

and Zander could hear the concern in his voice. "Wait here." He disappeared from Zander's vision.

When Zander awoke again, he was lying on his stomach and Father Bartholomew was pouring molten liquid on his back. Zander cried out at the burning pain. Then he felt the skin being pricked. *He's sewing me up*, thought Zander dully. He could see a long white cotton thread in the Jesuit's hands. And God, how his back hurt!

"Drink this," said Father Bartholomew. He held a cup of steaming liquid up to Zander's lips. Zander took a sip and spewed it out. "Arrgh, that tastes like—"

"That is good tea, Ah'll have you know," said the Jesuit mildly. He chuckled. "It's got healing properties."

Zander shook his head. "I'll heal without it, thanks."

Father Bartholomew looked serious suddenly. "Ah've got to get you back to the mission before those two wake up." Zander felt himself being lifted and carried as though he was but a child.

"Who are you?" Zander asked, bewildered. "Where are you from? I can't be dead. I hurt too much."

Father Bartholomew chuckled. "Ah ran away from a plantation down south. Ran off into the woods one day and became a free man. Then Ah came north and met the Jesuits. Liked them, and now Ah'm one. It's a good life."

Zander shifted a little. He had never liked slavery. He remembered a talk he'd had with old Father Ambroise about whether it was right to keep men and women as slaves. The good father said that the Bible told slaves to honor their masters. Zander had answered that it was not right for people to own one another. Father Ambroise's eyes had twinkled as he replied, "I agree with you, son. A loving and compassionate God would not ask his children to live a painful, degrading existence. He would want them to be happy and free."

"Yet slaveowners quote the Bible to justify slavery," Zander had answered.

"Yes, they do. And the problem," retorted Father Ambroise, "is that God speaks symbolically. That's where many people make their mistake—when they take the Bible so literally."

"How do you know if an action is of God?" Zander had wondered aloud.

"That's easy," Father Ambroise had laughed. "If it is compassionate and loving and just and true, then it is of God. If it hurts people and is cruel or lying or condemning or shaming or life-destroying, it is not of God."

Zander frowned. "That is not easy at all, Father Ambroise."

Father Ambroise chuckled, then sobered and replied sadly, "No, it is not, my son."

Zander's reverie was interrupted when he was jostled and draped over a mule. The mule, too, was huge. Zander groaned.

"Ah know it hurts," said Father Bartholomew, throwing a blanket over him, "but Ah think the mission is the safest place for you."

Zander felt his body jerk with every step the mule took. He blinked as darkness first surrounded him, then swallowed him up.

It seemed they rode for a long time. "We're near the mission," he heard Father Bartholomew say. Then he surrendered to the darkness once again.

He woke again. It was light, probably early morning. He heard voices. They spoke as he bumped along.

"Mr. Cecil, when can we expect to get to Fort Walla Walla?" Dorie's voice. Zander fought against the overwhelming darkness. Dorie! He had to find her. . . .

"Takes about two days, Miss Primfield." Edward Cecil's voice. Zander struggled to wake up, tried desperately to lift himself off the mule's back. But it was hopeless; his muscles refused to move.

"Oh, look at that poor man over there, across the back of that mule. I wonder what happened to him?" Dorie sounded genuinely concerned.

"There now, miss. Father Bartholomew will help him. Probably just some poor trapper. Probably dead, too. Wouldn't worry about it." Cecil again.

Then Zander lapsed into unconsciousness.

Two mornings later, he was feeling better. A knock came at the door of his tiny cell at the Jesuit mission.

He got out of bed and reached for his leather trousers and red shirt.

"Time for your morning tea," said a deep voice on the other side of the door.

Zander hastily finished buttoning his shirt and swung the door open. "Not your tea!" he exclaimed halfheartedly, knowing there would be no reprieve.

"Drink it," Father Bartholomew ordered sternly, holding out a tin cup. "This tea has saved many a man."

Bravely Zander raised the cup to his lips and drank. The bitter brew scalded his tastebuds. "Whew! That tea tastes like beaver piss!"

"There is nothing wrong with beaver piss," said Father Bartholomew solemnly.

Stiffly, his back still sore, Zander slowly followed the huge Jesuit to the small eating room where the priests gathered for their morning meal. He sniffed the air. Cornbread.

They were just finishing the meal when a loud

disturbance at the front door of the priests' quarters caught Zander's attention.

Several trappers entered and sat down at the benches alongside the table. They started helping themselves to the cornbread and coffee. One of the men dressed in a trapper's leathers looked distinctly Chinese.

Father Bartholomew greeted one of the newcomers, a tall, husky man whose black hair and brown eyes made him look almost Indian. Almost.

"Meet my old friend Sam," said Father Bartholomew as he introduced Zander to the man. "Sam and his brother Charlie are visiting from the Sandwich Islands. They ship over on the trading ships, running silks from the Orient to Fort George. Now and then they pick up furs for their ventures back."

He slapped the big man heartily on the back. Zander was surprised that the big Islander didn't keel over from the force of the good father's greeting.

Sam sat down next to Father Bartholomew, and Zander asked, "I don't suppose he saved your life, too?"

Sam laughed. "Yeah, as a matter of fact, he did. I was dyin' of the fever."

Father Bartholomew stared modestly at his tin cup of coffee.

Sam eyed Zander's cup. "Say, does he make

you drink that godawful tea? Tastes like beaver—"

"Mr. Durban likes my tea," interrupted Father Bartholomew. "It happens to be a fine tonic, and Ah strongly recommend *you* drink some."

Sam held up his hands to ward off the priest. "Naw, Father, there ain't nothin' can make me drink that tea. 'Cept facin' certain death, of course."

Father Bartholomew smiled. "Of course."

Zander took a sip of coffee. "How long since you been to Fort George?"

"Just came from there, five days ago," came the answer. "Me and my brother and the others stopped two nights at Fort Vancouver. Rest of the time, we just paddled the old Columbia." Sam waved to another priest across the room. There was loud jocular talking in the small room.

"I don't suppose," said Zander casually, though his heart was pounding, "that you knew an Indian there, a Willie Durban?" It had been three years since he'd seen his brother.

"Willie? Willie Durban? Yeah, I know him. He's the one that's got that farm, right? He got a wife and little kid?" Sam frowned pensively. "He's got a sister livin' with them, too, I think."

Zander nodded. "Lena. You say he has a wife and child? Willie?"

"If it's the same man I'm thinking of, he sure does. She keeps him on a tight trapline, too.

336

Don't let him out to party and gamble. 'Course, once in awhile he escapes to the fort and we have a card game and a drink or two. That's where I met him."

"Sounds like Willie," said Zander quietly. "He's my brother."

"He's doin' fine from what I can tell," answered Sam.

Zander took another sip of coffee. "What's his wife's name?"

Sam shook his head. "Don't remember."

Zander nodded. So Willie was taking care of Lena and had married and was the father of a child. Suddenly Zander felt very, very old.

He rose from the wooden bench and stretched carefully. If he moved too fast, his ribs still hurt. His back too. "I've got to get going," he said to Sam. "Obliged for the information."

Sam nodded. "You heading out to Fort George? You're welcome to travel with us. We're just gettin' us some good pelts, then headin' back."

Zander shook his head. "No thanks. I'm heading the other way. Fort Walla Walla."

Sam nodded. "I hear there's some fine pelts there."

"There are, but it's not the pelts I'm after," said Zander grimly.

Sam gave a roar of laughter. "Must be a woman, then!"

Zander stalked from the room.

337

Chapter Twenty-nine

Dorie peered out over the land. From where she sat, on her horse on the crest of a hill, she had an excellent view of the Columbia River, the brown hills in the distance, and the surrounding territory. Beside her, mounted on his horse, sat Edward Cecil. Two other men, who rode with them as protection, straggled up the hillside. To her relief, Edward Cecil had hired them as last-minute replacements when Burke and Ross could not be found.

Edward Cecil raised a hand and pointed out the high log palisade around a fort. "There it is."

"At last," she breathed. "Fort Walla Walla!" And Prue!

Excitedly, Dorie kicked the sides of her

mount and the horse trotted forward. They slid and galloped down the gravelly hill to the shore of the Columbia River, which was as calm as a lake where it fronted the fort. As they passed through a copse of yellow cottonwoods, a deer bounded out. Edward Cecil, who always kept his flintlock loaded, took aim and fired.

There was a bright flash and nothing happened. The gun refused to fire.

"Flash in the pan!" he exclaimed. "The flint must be wet." He shrugged and gave Dorie a boyish grin.

He was charming, there was no doubt about that, and sometimes flintlock guns *did* misfire. But she'd noticed he'd missed his target four other times on their two days of travel from the mission. Edward Cecil, she decided, was *not* a good shot.

They galloped up to the fort and slowed the horses to a walk as they entered the open gates. Dorie glanced around. The fort was large, with buildings on the east and west sides and at the back. She admired the four large towers at each corner. So this was where her sister lived! Fort Walla Walla. At last!

There were only two buildings that looked like houses in the whole fort. Edward Cecil stopped in front of the smaller one. "This is the Pomeroy residence," he said.

Dorie dismounted and her legs shook—from

the riding ar d from the anticipation of seeing her sister.

"Prue!" she called, unable to wait. She tottered up the steps. Edward Cecil bounded right behind her. A fat, frisky, brown-and-white puppy lolled on the steps, and Edward almost stumbled over it. He swore and kicked the dog aside.

Dorie stared at her escort in shocked surprise.

Then her attention was caught by the door opening. A woman's head poked out. "Prue!" cried Dorie.

"Adora?" Prue stepped onto the porch, her arms wide open. "It *is* you!"

Dorie laughed and threw herself into her sister's arms. "Oh, Prue! I've missed you!" cried Dorie, her arms flying around her sister.

"I've missed you too!" Prue was laughing and crying, hugging Dorie and doing a little dance, then hugging her again. "Oh, Dorie!"

The sisters clutched each other as though they would never let go. At last, reluctantly, Prue released Dorie. "Let me see you," she said, taking a step back and eyeing Dorie from head to toe. "You've grown! You're a woman!"

Dorie laughed. "Of course." Then she remembered she hadn't seen her older sister since she was but thirteen. And she was twenty now. That made Prue twenty-seven. "Oh, Prue," she hugged her again. "I've missed you so!"

"Come in, come in," urged Prue.

Dorie suddenly remembered that Edward Cecil was still standing there, and she introduced him. Prue politely invited him to join them.

"Thank you, no, ladies," he answered. "I will take care of the horses. But I would like to call upon you later this evening, Miss Primfield, if I may."

Reluctantly Dorie gave her consent. Then Prue ushered her into the house in a swirl of hugs.

Inside, it was clear that Prue had made the log dwelling into a home. It was one large room and there were blue-and-yellow quilts on the corner beds. White lace curtains hung at the two windows. A clay vase with a bouquet of dried sage graced the plank table, and a blue-and-yellow hand-braided rug lay on the floor.

A young Indian woman placed several pieces of chopped wood beside the fireplace. "That will do, Madeline," said Prue. "You may make us some tea." Madeline glided silently over to do as her mistress requested.

In the middle of the blue-and-yellow rug sat a plump baby about nine months old. He sucked on a biscuit.

"Oh, he's beautiful," cried Dorie, running over to pick up the baby.

Prue laughed. "He is," she agreed happily. "My two older ones, Susan and Peggy, are out digging turnips from the garden. They'll be back soon."

Dorie smiled and kissed the baby on his fat little cheek. He drooled some biscuit on the front of her dress.

Prue laughed and plucked him out of her sister's arms.

"I had better get used to drooling babies," observed Dorie quietly.

Her sudden seriousness caused Prue to turn her head in alarm. "What do you mean?"

"I mean," said Dorie steadily, "that I will soon be having my own."

"Of course you will," said Prue. She gave a light trill of laughter. "Once you're married to Mr. Biddle."

Dorie shook her head. "No, Prue. I have no plans to marry Mr. Biddle. And I am pregnant."

Silence. Prue put down the baby. "Adora?"

"It's true, Prue. I am expecting a child."

"Oh, Lord," groaned Prue. She touched Dorie's cheek gently and Dorie started to cry. All of a sudden, it was too much—the baby, the trip from the mission, Zander's betrayal. She leaned into Prue and felt her sister's arms creep around her, not in joy now, but in comfort and perhaps even in pity. And Dorie cried.

* * *

Dorie and Prue sat at the table drinking black tea. Prue nursed her baby, Peter, while Dorie told her sister of all that had happened. She even told her, briefly, about Zander.

"Please go and fetch Susan and Peggy from the garden so that they can meet their aunt," Prue directed Madeline. The young Indian woman nodded and slipped quietly out the front door.

Prue reached over and took Dorie's hand. "I know this must be a difficult time for you," she said, "but I want you to know that Leland and I will do everything we can to help you."

Dorie smiled gratefully and patted her sister's hand. "I know you will," she said. She sighed. "I am so fortunate to have you to help me. And I met another kind woman, a Mrs. Martha Whitley, at the Jesuit mission. Do you know her?"

"Mrs. Martha Whitley," Prue mused. "Yes, I believe I met her once or twice. Her husband is a chief trader, if I am not mistaken."

Dorie nodded. "I feel so fortunate that there are such caring people here." She smiled at Prue and Prue smiled tremulously back and dabbed at her teary eyes with the new handkerchief Dorie had given her.

There was a knock at the door.

Dorie glanced up as two men entered. One was tall with blond hair. He had kind blue eyes and looked to be about Prue's age. He would be

Leland Pomeroy, she guessed. The other man was shorter and rounder and wore glasses. He frowned fiercely at the two women.

"Why, Leland," said Prue in surprise, hastily tucking her breast into her dress. Fortunately, little Peter had fallen asleep. "And Mr. Biddle, too."

The taller man nodded. " 'Lo, Prue. I brought Mr. Biddle over. He wants to have a word with your sister."

"Oh! Yes, of course," said Prue, glancing at Dorie. Her glance sent a plea: *Please speak with him*.

"I will talk with him," answered Dorie slowly. Inwardly she dragged herself into some semblance of order. She had completely fallen apart and cried and cried while Prue had consoled her. Now she felt drained of all emotion. Her eyes must be red and swollen from the tears.

Clarence Biddle's eyes, however, were angry behind the round glasses. *Why is he so angry?* Dorie wondered. *He wasn't the one who was kidnapped!*

Slowly she rose to her feet. She was taller than he by four inches. She grimaced, glad now that she would not be marrying him. The difference in their heights she could have borne; the constant angry look on his face she could not.

"What do you mean by coming to the fort?"

demanded Clarence Biddle.

"I came to see my sister," answered Dorie coolly. Prue watched them with wide, worried eyes.

"You have no business coming here!"

Dorie frowned. "This was my destination in the first place."

"Yes, before you were kidnapped! But now that your reputation is sullied, I don't want you!"

Dorie glared at him. "That suits me well. I have no intention of marrying you, either." She slid a glance at Prue. How could her sister have thought she would ever be happy married to this pompous—

"I understand you are pregnant," continued Biddle.

Both Dorie and Prue gasped.

"Madeline," whispered Prue, her stricken eyes meeting Dorie's. "She must have gossiped. Oh! I will dismiss her immediately. A pity, she is so good with the children. . . ."

Too late now, thought Dorie, wishing she had not confided in her sister while others were around. In truth, she had not even noticed Madeline.

"Whether I am pregnant or not, sir, is none of your concern," ground out Dorie.

"It is," cried Biddle in a shrill voice. "You have damaged my reputation with your carelessness!

Made me a laughing stock of the fort! Did you know I promised one hundred furs for your safe return? One hundred furs!"

Dorie shrugged.

"And now I have to pay it! To Edward Cecil." Biddle's huge eyes glared from behind his shiny glasses. He looked even angrier than before.

"It is wise to pay your debts," advised Dorie. Aunt Hanna would have said something like that at a time like this.

"And I still don't know where Zander Durban is!" Biddle complained.

Dorie narrowed her eyes. Biddle certainly seemed to know enough. She put her nose in the air. "I have not the least interest in Mr. Durban's whereabouts." She decided to refrain from mentioning that she'd last seen Zander at the Jesuit mission.

Biddle grabbed her arm. His voice and face turned ugly. "I won't have you making a fool of me!" he announced, his voice scathing. His grip tightened. "Pretty though you may be, don't expect me to marry you!" He flung her arm away from him. "And keep out of my sight!"

Then he turned on his heel and waddled out the door, slamming it behind him.

"Oh dear," said Prue.

"Dorie? There's someone here to see you," said Prue later in the evening.

Dorie's heart beat fast. Zander? *No*, she scolded herself. *He doesn't love me, doesn't care. He is out of my life!*

Composing herself, Dorie rose from where she was playing cat's cradle with her nieces on the floor. Susan and Peggy gave little cries of disappointment that now they'd have to go to bed. "I'll be back soon," she promised them over her shoulder. They were such sweet little girls. So playful, too.

"*Bonjour*, Dorie."

"Oh. Mr. Cecil." Her mouth turned down. How could she have forgotten that he had said he was going to visit her this evening? She sighed. There was too much on her mind. She was getting forgetful.

"Come in," she said helplessly, holding the door open.

"Why do you not get your cloak?" he asked. "We will go for a walk. It is very fine this evening."

Reluctantly, she got her cloak and kissed her nieces good night, closing the door behind her. She didn't know if she should be alone with Mr. Cecil, but since her reputation was now in tatters—according to Clarence Biddle—she supposed a walk in the evening air could not plunge her name any further into disgrace.

They walked for some time around the inside perimeter of the fort. The fort was quiet everywhere except the men's quarters, from which raucous laughter issued forth.

"The men, they are happy tonight," Edward observed.

She nodded. It had been a mistake to come out. She had nothing to discuss with this man. "I want to return to my sister's residence," she told him finally.

"Wait." He placed a restraining hand on hers. "Do not go, not yet. I must tell you something."

She glanced around, a wave of discomfort rushing over her. There was no one else about, just the two of them.

"I must tell you this: I want to marry you." He kept her hand in his and looked into her eyes pleadingly. "You are very beautiful. I find I want you for my wife."

He was making her an honorable offer, she realized. Unlike Zander. But when she met Edward Cecil's black eyes, there was no surge of excitement inside her, no surge of love, nothing like what she'd felt when she'd looked at Zander. She raised her other hand and touched his cheek.

"Thank you," she whispered. "Thank you for asking me."

"You will marry me then?" She heard the hope in his voice.

She shook her head. "I find I cannot," she answered truthfully.

"Dorie," he said softly. He leaned over and kissed her. Though his lips moved across hers, nothing happened inside Dorie. Nothing at all. It was as though she had kissed an acquaintance, not a lover.

After a moment, Edward Cecil broke the kiss and sighed. His disappointment lay heavy between them. At last he said, "Come. I will take you back to your sister's."

She was grateful that he had accepted her answer. Another angry male would have been more than she could tolerate in one night.

They walked in silence back to the Pomeroy house. When they reached the front steps, he bowed stiffly. "I wish you well, Dorie Primfield." She heard the regret in his voice and closed her eyes. She too had regret—that she could not accept an honest, honorable offer, that she did not love him.

She went up the steps. "Good night, Mr. Cecil," she said into the cool evening air. He stood watching her, as if waiting for her to reconsider. But he said nothing, and so she said nothing. She opened the door.

"Farewell, Dorie."

"Farewell, Mr. Cecil." Once inside, she closed the door behind her and leaned against it, eyes squeezed tight, a sadness enveloping her. Edward Cecil was not strong enough for her. At some deep level, she sensed it. And besides, she was a better shot than he was.

Dorie had been at Fort Walla Walla for a fortnight now. She decided to go for a walk around the fort's large yard. Heartily in need of amusement and distraction, she had already stretched the fort's meager sources of entertainment. To fill the long day, she had even promised to take her nieces, Susan and Peggy, for a walk later.

As she was sauntering in the direction of the trading room, she heard a terrible caterwauling. She almost ran back to the Pomeroy residence, but something stayed her. The caterwauling rose and fell in a faintly musical way. She searched the grounds for the source of the noise, then realized it was coming from outside the palisade walls. Curious, she ran to the ladder that led to the second story walkway around the fort. She climbed the ladder and peered over the pointed logs.

To her astonishment, she saw a strange parade making its way around the walls of the fort. And the source of the wild noise was a man who puffed his cheeks mightily in and out as he played a musical instrument. "Why, it's the bagpipes," she breathed. A sharp, clear trumpeting drifted across to her.

Leading the procession marched a tall trapper, his back laden with the furry goods of his trade. He marched most solemnly and carried a pole with a red square of cloth fluttering from the top.

Another trapper with long white hair and a full white beard raised a brass horn to his lips and blew a blast. She closed her eyes and covered her ears at the squawking sound.

Beside him marched a very skinny trapper beating a stick upon a short log he held in one hand. His leather clothes sported red and blue ribbons tied to the leather fringe, and his dark hair was tied to one side with a thick green bow. With each puff of wind, the ribbons fluttered.

Open-mouthed, she watched the parade. With each puff of the bagpiper's cheeks, the screeching sound rose and fell. Then several men striding behind him raised their voices and sang along with the noise. As Dorie listened, she was able to detect a repeated sound and realized it was music, of a primitive sort. An inexplicable thrill ran through her at the wail.

The jostling parade marched twice around the fort's walls. Six trappers standing on the palisade walkway loaded their flintlocks and, at a command from Clarence Biddle, fired off a small welcoming cannonade. Then the parade marched through the gates and up to the trading room.

While she had no wish to meet Clarence Biddle, curiosity compelled Dorie to scramble down the ladder and run over to the trading room.

The room was crowded, and Biddle busied himself shouting orders to the newcomers to line up. She wandered through the room and nodded pleasantly at Leland, her brother-in-law, as he tried vainly to discourage a huge, ham-fisted trapper from picking up every single carrot coil of tobacco and sniffing it.

There was a marvelous array of items. There were blue and pink and red glass bead neck-laces. There were antler handles for knives. Several bolts of blue, black, and red calico were neatly laid on rough plank shelves. Shiny kettles sat on the floor, next to a large iron pot filled with brass bracelets. Another large iron pot held an assortment of red and black and green and brown buttons of all sizes. Pretty green and blue bottles sat at the back of a shelf. Five hoes were lined up neatly against the shelf next to five iron axes. Dorie almost tripped over a plow as she wandered past all the items.

As the room grew quieter, she glanced around. Seeing the newcomers' eyes upon her, Dorie edged toward the door.

"Where you going, pretty lady?" cried a trapper.

"Come on back. I'll buy you some beads," joked another.

"I ain't seen someone like you since I left St.

Louis," yelled a third. Another trapper reached out to pat her arm as she hurried past him.

Her cheeks red, Dorie fled the trading room. Obviously, a white woman was a rarity in this frontier land.

She hurried back to Prue's house and collected Susan and Peggy. "It's time for our walk," she said with forced gaiety. Her visit to the trading room had unnerved her, but being with the two little girls would restore her spirits.

They decided they wanted to pick wildflowers and they also wanted to take their puppy for a walk, so Dorie tied a rope around the fat little animal's neck. They said farewell to Prue and strolled towards the fort's gates. As they were passing the gates, a trapper, who appeared to be on sentry duty, called down to them. "Don't be gone long, ma'am, and don't go too far," he ordered briskly. "Two horses were stolen last night. Injuns done it."

Susan and Peggy looked a little pale at the news, but Dorie said, "We will return presently."

He nodded and gave them a wave.

Dorie said to the girls, "We'll just pick some flowers along the river. We won't go too far."

"I can run fast," Peggy, who was five and had brown hair and freckles, assured her. "I can run faster than Indians."

"*I* can run faster," protested Susan, who was

two years older and had blond hair and green eyes.

Dorie chuckled. "Let's hope none of us has to run from the Indians today!"

Susan tugged on the puppy's makeshift leash. "I'll carry our puppy if the Indians come for us. They can't steal him!"

Peggy nodded solemn agreement, and Dorie had to hide a smile.

They reached a copse of cottonwoods and the girls happily picked two huge bouquets of yellow and white flowers. "Mama will like these," said Susan, burying her nose in the handful of fragrant yellow.

"I'm going to give all my flowers to Mama," said Peggy.

"No, you can't. I'm going to," pouted Susan.

"Girls, girls," said Dorie, "your Mama will be happy to receive bouquets from *both* of you."

They looked at her doubtfully, but at least they stopped arguing.

They wandered alongside the river, which was as placid as a lake. Suddenly the puppy began to bark, and Dorie spotted a man walking toward them. As he drew nearer, she recognized Edward Cecil.

He approached them, a smile on his handsome face. "Good day, Miss Primfield," he said genially. "I see you ladies are enjoying the day."

"We're picking flowers," said Susan.

The puppy lunged for Edward Cecil's feet and Peggy, who was holding the leash, was dragged along. Edward Cecil glanced distastefully at the fat brown-and-white dog and moved away. Dorie quickly took the leash from the little girl. "It's time to return to the fort," she announced.

"Very good," approved Edward Cecil. "There have been reports of marauding Indians in the area. And two horses were stolen last night."

Dorie felt grateful for his protection as they walked back to the fort.

"Have you thought any more of my marriage proposal?" asked Edward Cecil wistfully.

Dorie stared at him in surprise. She was certain she'd already turned him down. Before she could say anything, he urged, "Come for a canoe ride with me."

She glanced at the girls. Well, why not? Perhaps she needed to be clearer with him, set things straight. There was nothing between them—nor could there ever be. She must tell him.

"After you return them to their mother, of course," he amended.

She delivered the girls and puppy to Prue, then she took up her cloak. "Mr. Cecil has invited me for a canoe ride with him," she told Prue.

Prue, who was changing the baby, nodded absently. Dorie left the house with the vague feeling that Prue had not really heard her. Truth to tell, she'd settled into a quiet life at the fort, but she felt like an appendage of Prue's family, someone who was there, and tolerated, but that was all. Sometimes, since she'd been at Fort Walla Walla, she found herself longing for Zander and a life of their own. When that happened, she had to remind herself severely of his betrayal. He'd used her and deceived her! She would not share her life with such a man! She deserved better.

And most times she could make herself believe it.

Dragging her thoughts away from Zander and his cruel betrayal, she summoned a smile for Edward Cecil.

At his behest, two trappers carried a canoe down to the water. Edward Cecil dismissed them and then Dorie got into the front of the craft. He handed her a paddle and then pushed them off.

They glided along the water and Dorie smiled to herself. "Everything is so peaceful when one is on the water," she remarked, beginning to relax.

Edward Cecil nodded. His strong thrusts of the paddle sent them skimming across the river's surface.

They talked occasionally, and Dorie felt herself relax more. If only her time with Zander was this easy, she thought. But it wasn't. He had deceived her and betrayed her and she must push him from her thoughts forever.

All too soon the canoe ride was over, and they were paddling up to the gravelly shore in front of the fort.

"Thank you," said Dorie.

Edward Cecil looked at her sadly out of brown eyes and for a moment, absurdly, she was reminded of the lolling puppy. Edward Cecil still wanted her to marry him, she realized, meeting the mute reproach in his eyes.

She sighed. She liked him and was grateful to him, but she didn't love him. Not like Zan—Stop it! she warned herself. Zander was gone from her life. It was best that way.

"Mr. Cecil," she said firmly. "I am honored by your request of marriage. But I simply cannot marry you." She held his gaze, her jaw clenched.

"Very well," he answered softly.

"Thank you," she said. He regarded her sadly. She would not feel sorry for Edward Cecil and his hopeless marriage suit. She would not! Someday he would find a fine young woman to marry. But it would not be Dorie Primfield!

When she arrived back at Prue's, she discovered that one of the trappers in the parade had delivered a letter to Prue. It was from Aunt Hanna and Uncle Albert.

" 'Give our love to the children,' " read Prue. " 'The girls must be quite grown by now. How we would love to see them! And tell your sister, Adora, that we love her'," continued Prue. " 'I know she will have reached your fort by now. Tell her to write. Your uncle and I spend very quiet days now. We are very happy at our farm. We sit on the porch at sunset and hold hands like we used to do in our courting days.' " Prue giggled. "It's hard to imagine Aunt Hanna and Uncle Albert courting, isn't it?"

Dorie said nothing as Prue read on, but she remembered her own happy days with her aunt and uncle. Suddenly she missed them deeply. She wondered sadly what Aunt Hanna would say if she knew Dorie was pregnant. And unmarried.

Later that night, Dorie and Prue were washing up the dishes from the evening meal. "Prue," said Dorie, "I want to go back home to Rochester."

"Rochester?" Prue looked startled. "Why, I thought everything was fine, that you liked it here with us."

"I do," said Dorie, "but I want to go back. I— I want to see Aunt Hanna and Uncle Albert."

Prue eyed Dorie's stomach. "Won't be easy traveling," she said at last.

Dorie flushed. "I'm returning in disgrace, you mean. Well, you're right. I am going back to them with a baby. But there's nothing for me out here. And the baby's due next spring. I still have time to get to Missouri."

"Winter's coming. It's going to snow. There will be blizzards. You don't want to be traveling in the snow."

"No, I don't," answered Dorie honestly. "I want to leave soon."

"When?"

"Very soon. Within a fortnight."

"Two weeks?" Prue thought about it. "I suppose Aunt Hanna and Uncle Albert will help you once you get there," she admitted grudgingly.

"That's what I think, too," said Dorie quietly, sensing her sister's capitulation. "I've tried it here, Prue. I tried to live at the fort. I tried to live in the Western territories." She shook her head sorrowfully. "But I just can't do it. If I was alone, perhaps I'd do better, but I have a baby to think of now. A baby with no father to help me raise him."

"You could marry someone else."

"Edward Cecil you mean?"

Prue wouldn't meet her eyes, and Dorie guessed that somehow Prue had learned of his proposal. Were there *any* secrets in this fort? "No," Dorie said firmly, "he is not the man for me."

"Who is?" demanded Prue.

Zander is, Dorie wanted to cry. She'd had time

360

to think about him, to remember him, and it was the caring moments she remembered. The time at the cabin, the time he'd saved her life, the time at the Indian village . . . But aloud she said, "No one."

Prue attacked the dish she was washing as if she would scrub the very design off the plate. "Very well," she said at last. "You are an adult now. You have to make your own decisions." She sighed. "But I wish you would stay. I—I worry about you."

Dorie hugged her. "I know you do. But you are right. It *is* my life and I have to make the best decisions I can." *But I haven't been making very good decisions when it comes to men,* she thought. *Not at all. My judgment of their character is very wrong. First Zander, then Edward Cecil. Even Biddle.*

Clarence Biddle was actually one of the reasons she was anxious to leave the fort. Every time she saw him, he watched her out of contemptuous eyes, and she knew he despised her.

Glumly, Dorie picked up a dish and dried it. "It will be good to see Aunt Hanna," she said dully.

"Yes," agreed Prue, just as dully.

They worked in silence. Dorie felt humbled and defeated. She'd come out West to make a new life and now she was going to return to Rochester, Missouri, in disgrace. Old Aunt

Hanna and frail Uncle Albert would have to
work harder than ever on the farm to help her
support the baby.

"I guess Leland had better tell Mr. Biddle that
you're leaving the fort," said Prue at last. "He'll
want to know." She sounded deflated.

So Prue had still harbored hopes that she
would marry Clarence Biddle, marveled Dorie.
She shook her head in amazement before she
replied, "That would be for the best."

The baby started to cry, and Prue hastily
dried her hands and ran over to him.

Dorie washed another dish. As she was lifting
it onto the counter, it slipped from her wet
hands and shattered on the floor. She stared,
tears blurring, at the broken shards. Where, oh
where, had her life gone so wrong?

Chapter Thirty

Biddle pounced on Clifton Ross and Ian Burke the minute they walked through the gates of Fort Walla Walla, their weary horses in tow.

"Where's Durban?" demanded Clarence Biddle.

Ross shrugged. "Not here."

"I know he's not here, you fool! Where is he?"

"Probably at the Jesuit mission," said Burke.

Biddle glared at Burke. "Who the beaver dung are you?"

"He's my—er, partner." Ross shifted from foot to foot. "When Billy Bow headed back to St. Louis to visit his sick mother"—Ross spat to indicate his contempt for any partner who would do such a thing—"I needed a new partner. Burke here was gonna help me kill Durban."

Biddle eyed the gray-haired trapper from floppy leather hat to thick boots. "Does he know what the hell he's doing?"

Ross shrugged. "Sometimes."

Biddle rolled his eyes. "What's this about Durban being left at the Jesuit mission?" Biddle was so angry, Ross could see the cords stand out on his neck.

"Can I unsaddle the horses?" asked Burke. "They're a wee bit skittish." It was unlike Burke to think of the animals, thought Ross snidely. He was probably just trying to get away from Biddle and his wrath.

"No, you cannot unsaddle the horses," snarled Biddle. "Not until I know where the hell Durban is!"

"He might be daid," ventured Burke.

"Might be? Might be? What do you mean, he might be?"

"Well, last we saw of him, he looked pretty daid." Burke wouldn't meet Biddle's angry eyes.

Biddle started to calm down. "Dead? Are you sure he's dead?" he asked eagerly.

Ross glanced at Burke. He knew the Scots trapper wanted to say yes. But if they told Biddle that Durban was dead and it turned out Durban wasn't, there'd be hell to pay. On the other hand, they might get the furs and get away in time . . .

"He's daid," said Ross confidently.

"He isna daid," said Burke at the same time.

"Which is it?" Biddle's head swiveled back and forth between the two. His glasses caught the late afternoon sun; his lips pursed tightly.

Ross grimaced. He could have had those furs and been gone from the fort within the hour.

"We jumped him," said Burke. "I stabbed him. He looked daid."

Biddle glared at Ross. "Well?"

Ross cracked his knuckles as he thought up a suitable reply. Damn Burke for telling the truth.

"Ross. You tell me what happened," ordered Biddle. "And none of your lies. Remember, I'm holding your furs."

Ross sighed. "Two days ago, we jumped him. Then our heads were bashed together. When I woke up, Durban was gone."

"So he's not dead."

"No. Probably not. Unless someone dragged away his body," Ross added.

"Why would anyone drag away his body?"

"For the reward?" suggested Ross.

Biddle considered this. "You're the only one who knew I wanted him dead. Everyone else thought the reward was for Adora Primfield's return." He glared at the two trappers. "Which I now have to pay to some Injun named Cecil

because you screwed up! You didn't find Primfield, and now you've loused up killing Durban!
What the hell am I paying you for?"

"Don't know," said Burke, shaking his head.

Ross wanted to shut him up. But he had no
chance. They had to stand there while Biddle
ranted and raved at them. Finally he was done.

"Er, can we go now?" asked Burke. "The
horses . . ."

"Take your damn horses and get the hell out.
I don't want to see you two asses in this fort."

"But my furs . . . You cain't just keep my
furs," pleaded Ross. Would he ever get his furs
back?

"I *can* keep them and I will!" Biddle stomped
off.

Ross and Burke watched him leave. "Whoee,"
said Burke. "That man is like an angry bear that
just had his food snatched away. He always like
that?"

Ross shrugged in frustration. "Sometimes
he's worse."

"Ye gonna get your furs back?" Burke asked.

"Yeah. I am." Ross gritted his jaw. He'd get
his furs back if it was the last thing he did!

"How?"

"Don't know yet. Somehow."

Burke guffawed in contempt. "Och, ye son-of-
a-beaver! Ye ain't no reverend! Ye're some
kinda trapper, same as me. And those words

366

you said over poor, daid Campbell dinna count for beaver shit! I coulda done as well!" He stomped off angrily, leading his horse to the corral.

Ross watched absently as his "partner" led the horse away. Burke's anger meant nothing. It was Biddle he had to talk to. One more time.

"Dorie," said Prue, handing her a tin pot. "Would you go and get some chicken feed for my hens? Now that I've dismissed Madeline, there is more work for me to do," she added apologetically.

"I'll be glad to help," said Dorie, embarrassed at the reminder of just how Madeline had lost her position in the household.

Dorie took the pot and headed toward the small building next to the trading post where some of the fort's supplies were kept.

As she walked across the yard, she spotted Mary walking with one of her children. Prue had pointed Mary out to Dorie on the second day she was at the fort. Dorie had not known that Biddle had a country wife until that time. When Prue admitted as much, Dorie had been curious to meet the woman she was intended to replace. Prue had reluctantly introduced her.

Dorie had been surprised at how young Mary appeared. Only a girl, really. And she had liked Mary. The dark-haired young woman was quiet and very caring of her little daughter. Later, Dorie had had strict words with Prue about what it was like to be a country wife. Prue had shrunk a little into herself after that, but Dorie did not spare her. It was one of the few disagreements she and Prue had. Prue had claimed not to see any problem. But Dorie had assured her that never, ever, would Dorie Primfield be party to replacing a country wife!

Dorie thought about speaking with Mary now, but the Indian woman seemed to be in a hurry and she walked with that strange duck walk that women have when they are pregnant.

Mary had all of Dorie's sympathy. From what she'd gleaned from Prue, Biddle treated her carelessly.

Dorie was musing on the amazing abilities of men and women to hurt each other when she entered into the dark little shed that was the supplies room. She felt along the wall for the corn barrel. She took a step and stumbled. A rake handle came up and hit her in the forehead.

"Ouch." Someone had neglected to put it away carefully. She fumbled in the dark, trying to lean the rake against the wall and keep the sharp tines out of the way of her feet. Once the rake was placed against the wall, she continued to feel her way along, touching the contents of each barrel until she found the one with the parched corn. She scooped up a potful and was just about to leave when she heard deep voices talking just outside the open window. The window had no covering of any kind.

"I tell you, I want my furs."

Dorie froze. She recognized that demanding voice. It was Clifton Ross.

"You aren't getting anything—no furs, no money, nothing, until you bring me Zander Durban's body. Dead!"

That voice belonged to Clarence Biddle! And they were arguing about Zander. Biddle wanted him dead!

Dorie's pulse pounded in her throat; what should she do? If she ran out of the shed, she risked their seeing her. And if she stayed where she was, they might see her. . . . But then again, they might not! Convinced that Zander was in grave trouble, she sank down beside one of the barrels, just under the window; that way she could listen better and find out their plan!

"I know you're up to somethin'. You got that crafty little smile on your face," Ross said insinuatingly.

"You saw me working on the company's accounts. That's all. Part of my job," protested Biddle.

Just then, a cat wandered into the shed. Spotting Dorie, it hurried over and began meowing loudly.

"What's that?"

Silence.

"Just a cat," said Biddle irritably.

"Shhh, kitty," mouthed Dorie urgently, stroking the animal to quiet it.

"I knows what yer big secret is." Clifton Ross's voice sounded sly. "I can read, you know."

Biddle cleared his throat. "That's unusual in a man of your—er, trade."

"Ain't it, though?" Ross seemed to be enjoying himself, Dorie thought.

"Look, Mr. Biddle," said Ross, getting serious. "I want my furs. You gotta give them to me."

"You loused up the Durban murder. I don't have to give you anything!"

Dorie put her fist over her mouth to stifle her gasp. Durban murder? Was Zander dead? Oh, Lordy. But wait! Biddle had said Ross had "loused up" the murder. Did that mean Zander was still alive? Hope sprang into her heart.

"I want them furs!" Ross sounded desperate.

"I'm not giving them back. Not until I decide what to do."

"What's that mean?" Ross sounded a little less desperate.

"It means I have to think if I can use you. If I can get my money's worth out of you."

There was a silence.

"You ain't plannin' on givin' me my furs, are you?" Ross's voice was cold.

Biddle remained silent.

"I knows somethin' about you," said Ross slowly. "You're stealin' somehow from the widders and orphans."

"You know nothing!" said Biddle savagely.

"Oh, yes I do," returned Ross. "I had a friendly chat with the chief trader at Fort McCraig."

"No chief trader's going to talk to *you*," scoffed Biddle.

"He is when he wants me to do a little job for him."

Biddle did not reply to that.

"We was havin' a drink and a chat," continued Ross, " 'bout them poor widders at Fort Mc-Craig and about how the company pays ten pounds sterling every year for their pension."

Biddle remained silent.

"I said, 'Are you sure it's the Hudson's Bay Company payin' so generously for them widders and orphans?', and he says 'Yeah. Company policy. They pay that at all the forts,' he says."

There was another silence.

The cat rubbed against Dorie's hand, and she was forced to pet it for fear it would meow again.

"So I thinks to meself, 'Clifton, there ain't no ten pounds a year goin' to them widders at Fort Walla Walla, no sir.' " He cackled. " 'Bet it's all goin' into Clarence Biddle's pocket.' " He chuckled. "Am I right?"

"No." Biddle sounded surly.

"You know I'm right, Mr. Biddle," said Clifton Ross, and his voice started to get mean. "I want some o' that widders' money and I want it now. You been keepin' my furs, and I ain't got no money."

"You can have some credit at the trade store."

"I don't want no credit at the trade store!" cried Ross. "I want my beaverdam furs, and I want some o' that widders' and orphans' money."

"No."

"No?" repeated Ross.

"No."

"Just no?" Ross sounded incredulous. "With what I know about you, about the widders and orphans, why I could go to that Chief Factor McLaren or whatever-his-name-is and—"

Dorie listened to the loud crack, then a thud between them. Then a moan. She shivered.

"And that's nothing compared to what you'll get if you try to blackmail me again!" snarled Biddle.

The cat purred and rubbed its head on Dorie's knee where she crouched. The purr seemed to echo through the whole shed. Dorie prayed that the two men did not hear it. Suddenly the cat leaped away and Dorie sighed with relief. They didn't know she was there.

The cat bumped against the rake and knocked it into two more rakes and a shovel and an axe. They crashed against the wall and slid to the floor.

"What the hell is that?" cried Biddle.

"Came from the shed," said Ross.

They peered in the window. "Lookee there," said Ross with malicious satisfaction. Dorie could see that his cheek was scraped raw. "If it ain't *the* Miss Primfield."

Biddle poked his head into the window and glared at her.

"She heard us," said Ross unhappily. "Probably heard every word."

Biddle eyed her, considering. She met his eyes and saw the hate and anger in them. She couldn't speak, could only crouch there, looking up at him, fear flooding through her. He was a ruthless man, worse than she'd thought.

"Get out," he snarled at last, and she'd never felt such relief in her life. She jumped up and ran from the wooden building as though it were afire. She raced back to the safety of Prue's house and slammed the door behind her. She was safe. This time.

Clifton Ross and Clarence Biddle watched Dorie Primfield flee across the yard.

Biddle turned to Ross. "There is a way you

can earn your furs back, after all," he commented. "Interested?"

"Only if it involves some money from the widders' and orphans' fund too." Ross's jaw clenched. This was the last time he'd work for Biddle. The man was like a mad grizzly bear and untrustworthy besides.

"Sure," said Biddle easily.

Ross gaped at him.

"Not too much, mind you," amended Biddle hastily, "but a few pounds. Say, twenty?"

Ross gasped. "Twenty pounds sterling?"

Biddle nodded, his glasses flashing in the late afternoon sun.

"What do you want done?" asked Ross suspiciously. Twenty pounds sterling! That was a man's wage for a year!

Biddle took off his glasses and pulled out a white handkerchief from a leather sack at his waist. "What I want," he said, blowing on the lenses, "is for you to escort Dorie Primfield back to Missouri."

"Awww, hell no," answered Ross. "I don't want to do that. I don't even like her. Me and Billy Bow already escorted her out here all the way from Missouri. Cain't the woman make up her mind?"

"Evidently not. And Dorie Primfield knows too much," said Biddle, holding up his glasses

374

and peering through them. He started to polish them again.

Ross shrugged. "She'll forget."

"I can't take that chance." Biddle stopped polishing and peered through the lenses one more time. Satisfied, he popped them onto his nose. "She heard about the widows and orphans fund, thanks to your big mouth. She probably heard about the Durban murder attempt, too." For a moment Biddle's glare caused Ross to shrink. But just for a moment. "I want you and your partner to escort her away."

"Aww," Ross started to protest.

"And *then* you'll get your furs back."

Ross was silent.

"And you'll also get," continued Biddle with a grand air, "Edward Cecil's furs. There's a hundred of them." He added slyly, "You see, I haven't paid him yet."

"Not paid?" said Ross in surprise.

"A man has to *pry* his furs out of me," boasted Biddle.

How well Ross knew that! He asked cautiously, "And I'd get the widders' and orphans' money, too?"

"Yes. That too." Biddle smiled.

Ross thought about it. "All right," he said after a while. "I guess me and Burke can escort her back."

"Good." Biddle smiled. "And you don't have

to go all the way back to Missouri, either."

"We don't?"

"No. You see, while under your escort, Miss Dorie Primfield is going to suffer a grievous accident—a most grievous accident. Why, she won't reach Missouri at all, I'm sad to say." He laughed.

Ross stared at him; Biddle's meaning dawned slowly. "She won't?"

"I want you to kill her."

Chapter Thirty-one

Zander leaned forward in the saddle and winced. Each step that Shadow took jarred his back, which was still not completely healed.

But Father Bartholomew's efforts had certainly helped Zander. The Jesuit had changed the bandages several times a day and given him that horrible-tasting tea to drink. He spat—even the memory was foul. God, it had been awful tea. But the knife wound in his back had healed, and he was cured. More or less.

He glanced at the sky. He should be reaching Fort Walla Walla later this day. He nudged Shadow to a trot and ignored his aching back.

Dorie was at Fort Walla Walla. He had to find her. He had to hear from her own lips that she carried his child. By now, perhaps she had cooled down and realized she loved him. He could convince her to marry him. Then she and the child would be his, and he wouldn't have this terrible loneliness in his heart.

Unfortunately he was wrong about how long it would take to reach the fort. He had to camp overnight because the screaming pain in his back would not allow him to be jostled on horseback for even one more step.

So it was early the following morning when he rose and stretched his cramped muscles. He saddled the horses and pack mule and started for the fort.

He rode through the open gates of Fort Walla Walla at mid-morning. A trapper wandered along the palisade walkway and scanned the grounds outside the fort. At Fort Walla Walla, there was a constant alert against Indian attacks.

Zander rode over to the corral and unloaded the mule and packhorses. He brushed the tired animals down and fed them some corn and hay. That done, he set off, whistling, to find out where Dorie was.

It was her last morning at the fort, and Dorie was slowly getting ready to leave. She'd breakfasted with Prue, Leland, and the children. It was very difficult to part from her sister, but part she must. It was time to go home to Rochester, Missouri. She'd forced herself to pack and at last she was ready.

She was just about to step off the porch when she caught sight of a man leading a string of packhorses through the gates of the fort. He rode a large black mare, and she easily recognized that confident, lean figure. Zander Durban!

She ducked back into Prue's house, her heart pounding. Her fist flew to her breast. Zander! Here! What was he doing here? She'd been frightened for him when she'd first heard Clifton Ross and Clarence Biddle talking about their murder plans, but she'd convinced herself that Zander had somehow survived their evil plot. Once her worry for his safety had died down, her old anger at him flared up. She gritted her teeth. And now he was here! In Fort Walla Walla! She wrung her hands. Oh, what should she do?

She peeked out the door.

Yes. It was Zander, all right. Alive. In the flesh. At the fort.

She closed the door with a soft click. What was he doing here? Why had he come? Here. Now. When she'd put him out of her mind and out of her heart. She stood just inside the door, her hands clasped tightly together, the knuckles white.

No one noticed her. Prue was changing the baby and the two girls, Susan and Peggy, were arguing over who was supposed to clean the breakfast dishes off the table.

The nerve of the man, she fumed. How dare he come to the fort where she was! At least he could have waited until she was gone! Oh, but she was good and mad at Zander. It still rankled that he'd kidnapped her and seduced her and allowed her to think she was his wife. His wife! Her cheeks burned at the very thought.

Then she hesitated. Perhaps he'd come for her! Perhaps he loved her and was searching madly for her. . . . *Stop it!* she commanded herself fiercely. *He doesn't love you. He never did.*

Her good sense restored, she opened the door a crack and peeked outside again. He was unsaddling the black mare. No one would miss her if she sneaked down to the corral. Just a closer peek at him was all she needed. Prue was busy with the baby, and the two girls still argued.

She picked up her black cloak. It was big and comfortable and hid her well. "I'm going out for a minute," she called to Prue.

Prue wiped her sweating forehead and nodded. Dorie slipped out the door.

What was she going to do? she wondered as she walked slowly along, keeping her face averted from the corral. Her heart pounded with excitement. What should she do if he saw her? She glanced Zander's way, but he did not notice her.

He was walking toward the men's quarters while she was on a course for the corral. Disappointment surged through her. Had she truly hoped to meet him? Speak with him? Yell at him? What?

She reached the corral and spotted Lightning. Softly, she called the old horse and walked up to him. He nosed her hand for a treat. She patted him and he snorted. She glanced around, alarmed at the sound. Had Zander heard? Did she want to see him or didn't she?

Lying against a shed by the corral were Zander's saddlebags and trade goods, all in a neat pile. She spied seven of his rifles. The sight of his familiar possessions suddenly raised her ire again. He'd hurt her, hurt her terribly. The rat.

An idea came to her, wicked perhaps, but just what he deserved! And it would make up, in some small part, for all the heartache he'd caused her.

With a grim little smile, Dorie picked up an old nail that was on the ground. "I'll spike the piece," she muttered to herself. She hefted up a flintlock and wedged the nail into the vent near the pan. This plugged the vent so that no spark would get through to light the black powder. It wouldn't hurt Zander, and the gun would fail to fire.

Pleased with her work, she picked up another nail. Working quickly, she plugged the next rifle. Soon all seven guns were done.

Ah, revenge is sweet, she thought as she tiptoed away. Now she could return to Rochester, Missouri, knowing she'd done her best to avenge herself upon the man who'd used her so terribly.

With a tiny little smile of satisfaction, she returned to Prue's house. Her smile vanished when she saw who awaited her there.

"Time to go, Miz Primfield," said Clifton Ross laconically.

Her dismay must have shown on her face, for he added, "When Mr. Leland Pomeroy found out me and Burke were traveling to Missouri, he hired us to escort you. 'Course, there ain't no one else available," he added, cutting off her possible protest. "If'n you want to go to Missouri, you go with us."

Mouth open, she stared at the man. What a wretched surprise, she thought. Then she noticed that Ross did not bother to introduce Ian Burke, who sat on his horse and grinned down at her. Although she already knew Burke and had no wish to be reintroduced to him, Ross's carelessness about polite introductions further irritated her.

"First I must bid my sister farewell." She hurried inside.

Dorie hugged her nieces and kissed Baby Peter good-bye. Then, tears in her eyes, she hugged Prue.

"Do you have to go?" whispered Prue.

Dorie saw the sadness in her sister's blue eyes and knew it mirrored her own. "I must," she choked out. "I—I've tried to live here. I've failed."

Prue nodded her head slowly and Dorie felt even worse. Even Prue saw her as a failure. Shoulders slumped, she picked up her carpetbag and opened the door.

Prue and the children followed her out onto the porch. Dorie walked down the steps and glanced around the big fort. No, she scolded herself, she was *not* looking for Zander. She was—well, she was just seeing Fort Walla Walla for the last time, that was all.

She turned to Prue.

"Let's go, Miz Primfield."

Dorie ignored Clifton Ross. "Farewell, sister."

"Farewell, Adora." Prue's eyes were bright with tears.

Dorie dragged herself over to the emaciated white gelding her escorts had provided. She hooked her carpetbag over the saddle horn and mounted the animal. Then she followed Ross and Burke out of the fort gates.

*   *   *

It was dusk. "Anton! Good to see you, Anton." Zander grinned at his friend, glad to see someone he knew at this unfriendly fort. Every one of his questions about Dorie had led to grunts and muttered "don't knows" before the trapper or trader hurried off to find something more important to do than to talk to Zander Durban.

"Perhaps you can tell me why the hell no one in this fort seems to know where Dorie is?" He didn't need to hide his irritation from his best friend. Anton would understand.

But Anton only glared at him. "Where the hell have you been?" he answered. "Mary just told me that Clarence Biddle sent Dorie back to Missouri. Clifton Ross and Ian Burke are her escorts."

Zander stared at his friend, aghast. Not those two would-be murderers! He whirled and raced for the corral. He threw a saddle on Shadow, slung three of his rifles over the saddle horn, and jumped on the mare's back, heedless of Anton or anyone else in the fort.

He'd kicked the mare to a full gallop before he even reached the open fort gates. "Heeyah!" he cried to the mare. "Oh, God, will I be too late?"

Chapter Thirty-two

Clarence Biddle tapped his quill pen as he sat at his plank desk in the trading room. Today the numbers did not console him or delight him—even when he added up the figures in the Widows and Orphans column.

No, something was on his mind. Something nagged at him as he sat there. He tried to think it through.

With a sigh, he set down the feather quill. Usually numbers were so satisfying. One added them up and one got a total. So simple. So reasonable. Unlike his life, which was messy of late. But that was about to change. He would take control of his life again. Then everything would be clear. Simple. Just like numbers.

He sat there pondering, trying to figure out what was bothering him. It was like a debt someone owed him that he'd forgotten to write down; like some figure he was not accounting for. But what?

There was a knock on the thick wooden door. He ignored it. He was in no mood to trade today.

The knock came again. "Go away," he called. "The trading room is closed."

But whoever was on the other side of the door did not seem to care if the trading room was open or closed because now they were pounding on the door.

With a sigh, he heaved himself out of his chair and walked over to the door. He peeked through the iron grill.

Aww, beavershit. "Go away, Mrs. McKay."

She croaked at him, "My Charlie told me that if he ever died—"

"Yes, yes, Mrs. McKay, I believe I've heard that story a time or two."

"I don't have anything to eat!" she screeched at him.

He sighed. "Eat with the rest of the widows at the big table. You'll get plenty to eat."

"I have nothing to wear!" she yelled. She tore futilely at her ragged dress, as though trying to pull it off her skinny frame. "I have no shoes to wear!" She kicked up a naked brown foot.

"Go ask a trapper for an old pair," he suggested.

"Winter's coming," she screeched. "My feet will be cold!"

"Well," he said, reaching for the little iron door that he could pull over the grate and end this irritating interview, "maybe we'll all be lucky and you'll die of frostbite." He chuckled to himself at his humor. He had lowered the iron plate halfway. "One more thing, Mrs. McKay."

"What is it?" she asked pitifully. "Please, some money? Just a little. I want to buy—"

"You are a spendthrift, Mrs. McKay. And you've had enough money for the month." God, he couldn't stand to look into her pathetic brown eyes. Begging, all the time, begging. And how was he supposed to make his profit of nine pounds sterling on her account if she was always hounding him for more money? "Get out of here," he said and slammed the little iron door on the grate.

She yelled and kicked and pounded on the thick wooden door, but it did her no good. He had the iron cover safely in place. After a while she grew hoarse and went away, and he returned to his numbers.

But still, he couldn't concentrate on the tidy little columns that he loved so. What was wrong?

With a sigh, he rose from his chair and wandered over to the window and peered out at the fort. What was bothering him? He pulled out his handkerchief and removed his glasses. What was it?

He began to polish his glasses. At last he realized what it was. It was Clifton Ross. And Burke. Ross had already tried to blackmail him once, when he found out about the Widows and Orphans fund. And now Ross knew even more. He knew that Biddle had ordered Primfield's death as well as Durban's. There would be more blackmail from Ross. That was certain.

Elated, Biddle polished harder. Now he knew the problem. It was that Ross knew too much.

And what about Burke? He lifted the glasses to the light and peered through them.

Burke. He'd watched Burke at the fort; the man talked loudly when he drank. And he drank frequently. Not a good combination in a trapper who knew too much about one Clarence Biddle.

Biddle put his glasses back on his nose. Yes. That was what had troubled him. Ross and Burke. And, come to think on it, he, Biddle, would soon owe the two trappers a large number of furs and quite a sum in pounds sterling once they'd completed the little job on Primfield.

He smiled to himself. There was a way that

he could keep the furs for himself *and* shut up
Ross and·Burke.

Excited now, he hurried over to his desk and
closed his account book and put it neatly in its
place. His account with Ross and Burke would
soon be settled. He must leave the fort at once.

All he had to do was find Ross and Burke and
kill them.

Chapter Thirty-three

The uneasiness had been with Dorie all day. Something was very wrong.

She slid a glance at Clifton Ross, who sat on a rock and glared at the fire. Across from him, Burke muttered into his tin cup of whiskey. Dorie leaned a little closer to the fire and pretended to warm her hands, but it was actually to hear what Burke was saying. Perhaps his drunken murmurings would tell her why she felt so uneasy.

Ross had remained silent through their evening meal of cornbread and bacon and coffee. Once she had turned abruptly and caught his cold eyes upon her. What was the matter?

"Biddle's cheap," muttered Burke.

Ross eyed him. "What the hell do you mean by that?" He took a swig of whiskey from his own tin cup.

"He's damn cheap," repeated Burke. "Thass what I mean. Damn cheap." He took a drink.

Burke was drunk, she realized. He would not be making sense this night.

Disappointed, she withdrew into herself, hunching on the rock, her arms protectively crossed over her stomach. But she couldn't relax. Not with these two. They'd been acting strangely toward her ever since they left Fort Walla Walla.

How could she ever have agreed to let Ross and Burke escort her? She knew what they were like. But she'd been so anxious to leave the fort and get away from her failures that she'd given little thought to her escorts. Now she was beginning to regret her haste.

Burke and Ross were acting oddly. Earlier in the day, when they'd passed a trapper and his wife on the trail, Ross had barely spoken to the man, and he'd hurried Dorie along before she could even say a word. It was customary to socialize and exchange news at such happenstance meetings. Dorie was gaining the impression that it was almost as if—well, as if Ross and Burke didn't want anyone to recognize them.

"Cheap. Damn, damn, beaverdam cheap,"

continued Burke. He waved his cup around. "More."

Ross glared at the fire and kept silent.

"And he's no' payin' us enough furs for what he wants us to do." Burke wagged his head. "Och, no. No' near enough. I havena kilt a—"

"Shut your mouth, Burke." Ross's hard voice interrupted whatever else Burke was going to say. Ross got to his feet and said, "Time to turn in, Miz Primfield. We'll be gettin' an early start in the morning."

She watched Burke, wondering what else he was about to say. He remained quiet, however, and drank his whiskey. Ross was still staring at her, waiting. Slowly, she got to her feet. "Very well, Mr. Ross, but first I must . . ." She paused delicately, hoping he would understand.

He didn't answer and there was a long silence between them. She felt compelled to explain, "I must go—uh, into the forest, and er—that is . . ." her voice trailed off. Couldn't he understand she needed to relieve herself?

"Well, hurry it up then," Ross said and turned away.

Her face burning with mortification, she hurried off toward a stand of big pines with boulders scattered here and there.

Her mocassined feet trod quietly upon her return, and she paused behind a large pine. Burke and Ross did not hear her.

"How long do we play this game?" demanded Burke in a slurred voice. "How much longer afore we kill her?"

"Soon, soon," answered Ross. "We gotta get her away from the trail. Maybe head into the hills tomorrow."

"I suppose ye want *me* to do the killing," said Burke belligerently.

"Yeah." Ross laughed. But his voice was serious when he added, "You talk too much when you been drinkin', Burke. Anyone ever told you that?"

"Naw."

"Well I'm tellin' you. Ain't healthy for a man to talk so much."

Burke spat at the fire. "I dinna give a good goddamn what ye think."

"You watch your tongue," warned Ross. "You say too much, and that gal's gonna figure out what we're up to. She'll run. Make our job harder to do."

Burke wagged his head. "Naw, she willna figure it out. The lassie's no' too smarrrrt. . . . " He leaned his chin on his chest and snored.

Shaking, Dorie tiptoed back to hide behind a pile of boulders. They planned to kill her! Her whole body trembled. They planned to *kill* her! My God, how had this happened?

What was she going to do? Where could she go? Who—? *Stop it*, she warned herself. *You*

*must remain calm. Think! You can outwit them.
They're both drunk. You can do it. You must do
it!*

Calmer now, she stepped out a second time
from behind her hiding place. She took a few
steps toward the fire, then gave a little cough so
they'd be sure to know she was there. She made
herself amble slowly to the fire, her legs quivering. Head high, she forced herself to glance at
the men who intended to murder her.

Burke leaned against a rock and snored.

Ross watched her. Tentatively, she smiled at
him; her lips trembled in her effort, and a
strange copper taste emerged on her tongue.
She had to get away from them. Tonight! When
they were both asleep, she'd take one of the
horses and run.

Ross glared at her.

"I—I don't feel very sleepy yet." She wasn't
lying. Alarm pumped through every limb of her
body and kept her wide awake. "Would you like
more whiskey?" She had to get Ross to sleep.

"Turn in, Miz Primfield. That's my advice to
you."

She couldn't. He might kill her as she slept.
She sat down by the fire, wondering how she
could convince him to drink more. That way he
would fall asleep before she did.

Finally she took his tin cup and walked over
to the whiskey keg that was lodged beside

Burke. She filled the cup, brought it back, and wordlessly handed it to Ross. He watched her through narrowed eyes, but the lure of the whiskey proved too much for him. He took the cup from her with a grunt and tossed back a swig.

She smiled to herself. *Drink more*, she urged him silently.

And he did. Soon he was swaying where he sat. "Time to go to sleep, Mizzz Primfieeeel'."

"Very well," she replied obediently and got her blanket and lay down across the fire from him. She pretended to sleep but watched him until she saw his eyelids flutter closed. Good! He's asleep. To be certain, she forced herself to wait a while longer, until deep, rhythmic snores issued from both Burke and Ross.

Carefully, Dorie crept out from under her blanket, snatched up her carpetbag, and tiptoed over to the horses. She wished the moon were not so full and bright. If Burke or Ross saw her trying to escape, she was sure they would kill her right where she stood.

She studied the horses. The thin white gelding she'd ridden earlier had been bone-weary by day's end. She wouldn't steal him. All the horses had been hobbled, and she went about swiftly unhobbling each one. The only decent-looking horse appeared to be Ross's gray gelding. She unhobbled him and patted the animal's nose to calm him, then put a bridle over his head. There was no time to put on a saddle.

She patted the gray one more time, then led him over to a low rock. She stood on the rock and from there she climbed onto the gelding's back. She clutched her carpetbag in one hand, the reins in the other.

No sooner was she astride the gray than Ross awoke. He cried out, "Halt! Halt!"

He got shakily to his feet. With her carpetbag, she slapped the skinny rump of the white mare and the rumps of the chestnut packhorses. Horses bolted, scattering in every direction.

Dorie dug her heels into the gray's sides and they sped out of camp.

"Come back!" cried Ross.

She thought she heard a second voice— Burke's—join in. "Faster," she yelled at the gray. "Faster!"

The gelding burst into a gallop. Dorie peered at the blurred ground. She tried to guide him along the rocky path. "Faster!" she urged.

Behind her she could hear Ross's and Burke's gruff shouts to stop.

She smacked the gray on the rump one more time. Cool wind brushed her face. She was alive!

Chapter Thirty-four

The gray horse raced along the trail. Dorie could hear his flagging breath, feel him stumble now and then. She had to stop soon. The animal was exhausted and so was she. They would never make it to the fort this night.

She glanced over her shoulder. By the moon's light she could see no sign of pursuit. Her plan to scatter her escorts' horses had paid off.

She reined in the gelding to a walk and patted his neck. Her hand came away wet with sweat.

Suddenly her head came up. Was that smoke she smelled? She sniffed the air. Yes. Wood-smoke.

She halted the gray and slid off his back. Her legs shook so badly, she had to lean against the horse for support. Nervously she glanced around, straining to see in the moonlight. First, a deadly race from her murderers, and now a new threat—a fire. A fire meant someone was nearby.

She could only pray it was a harmless trapper!

Exhausted, frightened, she stood in the middle of the gravel trail and glanced around, seeking the source of the smoke. What should she do? Should she stay silent and pass by? Or should she seek out whoever was there? Perhaps they would help her.

She shook her head. No, she couldn't be certain that safety lay with whoever was at the fire. Better that she continue on her way, swiftly and quietly.

Encouraged by her reasoning, Dorie tiptoed along the trail, leading the gray. She had to find a place to rest him and soon. Perhaps over the next small hill.

Suddenly a man's shape appeared before her, his face hidden in the shadows. She gasped.

"Dorie?"

Her mouth dropped. He knew her!

And she knew that voice! "Zander?"

"Yes."

She dropped the gray's reins and ran to him. "Zander!" Her voice held all her terror, all her fear. All her gratitude. He was safety. She hurled herself into his arms. "Oh, Zander, I'm so glad to see you!"

She felt his hard body surge against hers. His warmth. His strength. "Oh, Lordy, Zander!" She sagged against him.

Then she remembered. "Zander," she cried and clutched his shoulders fiercely. Tears stung her eyes. "They're going to kill me!"

Chapter Thirty-five

"They're going to kill me!" She stared into his darkly rugged face. Fear and hope warred within her. Would he help her? "Clifton Ross and Burke. They're after me. . . . " She laid her head on his chest and held on to him, then jerked her head around, peering into the blackness. "What was that?" Her grip tightened.

"Shhhh, easy, Dorie," whispered Zander. "It was nothing."

She squeezed her eyes shut, reveling in his closeness. Her heart finally slowed its frantic pounding. "Oh, Zander," she moaned. "I'm so afraid."

"Shhhh, Dorie, you're safe now," he murmured, and his arms tightened around her. "I know the likes of Ross and Burke. That's why I'm here. I followed you as soon as I learned they were your escorts. Thank God I wasn't too late!"

He squeezed her once more, then reluctantly let her go. "We've got to get you off this trail," he warned. "Ross and Burke will come along soon, and I plan to be ready for them."

Numbly, she gripped his hand and followed him. Relief swept through her. Zander was here. Now she'd be safe. She refused to let go of his hand as he took the gray gelding's reins and led him off the path.

"My camp is over here," he said as he strode along between rocks. She had to run to keep up with him.

They reached his campfire. "It got too dark to follow you, so I made camp," he explained.

"I smelled the smoke from your fire," she said.

"If you could smell it, then Ross and Burke will too," he answered. "Let's build up the fire so they don't miss us."

"Don't miss us? But Zander," she wailed, "I don't want them to find me!"

He chuckled. "They won't find *you*. They'll find me." His voice turned grim. "Or perhaps I should say, I'll find *them*."

"What are you going to do? Where are you going?" she clutched at him unashamedly. Now that she'd found him, she wasn't going to let him go.

"Help me gather wood," was his answer.

They picked up branches of dead wood. Here, in the forest of big pines, there was no lack of firewood. He hobbled the two horses, then put more wood on the fire. When the flames leaped high, he smiled in satisfaction. "That ought to get their attention."

He picked up his blanket, then turned to her. "Come. I've got to hide you away safely."

She grabbed her carpetbag and followed him through a thick stand of pines and past some large boulders. She could hear a rushing sound from a river flowing a little distance away.

She felt him pull away from her. "Wait," she whispered, grasping his hand one more time. "Tell me where you're going. Please." She knew she was begging, but she didn't care.

He met her eyes, and she wanted to throw herself into his arms once more. Zander! Lord, how she loved him. If anything were to happen to him . . . She couldn't finish the awful thought.

He halted near a boulder flanked by pines.

"I'm setting a trap for Ross and Burke," he said. "With you safely hidden away, I can go after them." His dark eyes were grim. "I've got my rifles. I'll be back as soon as I can." He kissed her lips.

She clung to him. "Oh Zander, be careful," she whispered. "Be very, very careful."

He kissed her again, then reluctantly pulled away. "I have to go, Dorie. I have to be ready."

He slipped away into the darkness, leaving her wrapped in a warm blanket, the taste of him still on her lips. "I love you," she whispered into the darkness after him. And she did. Oh yes, she did! Country wife or not—it didn't matter. Not anymore.

She nestled into a contented huddle under the blanket. She was safe; she was hidden. Drowsily, she yawned and snuggled down into the blanket. Rest at last.

Then she remembered that she had spiked his guns.

Chapter Thirty-six

"Where do you think the Primfield lass got to?" Burke turned around in his saddle and glared at Ross. They were riding into denser pine woods now.

"How the hell should I know?" snarled Ross, kicking his horse to go faster. "It's all your damn fault. You should have been watching her."

"Me? Oh, no, *partner*," sneered Burke. "Ye canna blame me for what happened. Ye're the one who was on watch when she skedaddled."

"You beavershit," answered Ross irritably. He wished he'd never partnered up with a beaverbrain like Burke. And once they found Primfield and Durban and killed them, Burke was next. Ross would kill him. Then Ross could have *all* the money and furs of the reward. None of this sharing with a partner for him!

"Well, leastways we saw her ride off down the trail. Probably tryin' to get back to the fort," Burke guessed. "Too bad she took the best horse. . . . "

"Shut your beavertrap," growled Ross. He kicked the emaciated white horse he'd been reduced to riding. "Damn that Dorie Primfield."

Burke galloped ahead. Then he pulled up his horse and waited for Ross. "Canna ye make that horse go any faster?"

"You ride him," snapped Ross, "and give me your horse."

"Oh, no, ye don't. Ye're no' gettin' yer hands on my nag." Burke patted the chestnut. "Bonny horse, this one."

Ross grunted and rolled his eyes.

"I'm gonna ride ahead," announced Burke. "I'll be scoutin' for Primfield."

He galloped off and Ross plodded doggedly after him.

Later, Ross drew abreast of Burke.

"Took ye long enough," chortled Burke. "Why, Primfield's probably at the fort by now."

"What makes you so beaverdam happy? You

like to lose out on all them furs Biddle was gonna pay us?"

Burke grimaced. "Och, no." He spat chewing tobacco on the ground. "It's just so funny to see ye ridin' on that skinny white nag, is all."

"Yeah? Well, find someone else to laugh at." Ross glanced around. "Why are we stopping here?"

"I smell smoke."

Ross sniffed the air. "Where's his camp?"

"Who?"

"The trapper that lit the fire, you fool."

"Camp's over there," Burke pointed.

Ross grimaced. How had he missed seeing such a bright fire?

"Probably not Primfield's," observed Burke. "She wouldna make a fire announcing her presence now, would she?"

"No. Load your rifle," Ross ordered Burke. "Let's see who it is."

They dismounted and tied their horses to a pine tree. Then, both carrying loaded and primed rifles, they stalked over to the fire.

"Nobody here," said Burke as he walked the periphery of the fire and peered past boulders, surrounding pines and into the night. "Some fool set a fire and wandered off." He squatted and studied the ground. "Canna see any tracks."

Ross glanced around, uneasy. "Don't seem

right to me," he muttered. The hairs on the back of his neck tingled.

Zander stepped out from behind a big pine tree and into the circle of the fire's light. "Drop your weapons," he ordered. It felt good to be holding a rifle in each hand. One was pointed at Ross and the other at Burke.

Ross jumped when he heard Zander's voice. Burke slowly got up from where he squatted, peering at the ground.

"Throw your weapons down," repeated Zander. "If you don't, I'll shoot."

Ross snorted. "We both got a gun on you. Not likely we'll throw down our weapons." He sneered. "Besides, them two guns you're holdin' are gonna get heavy. Can see them shaking already."

Burke's eyes glittered with suppressed anger. "Why, lookee here. It's Zander Durban! Durban, how are ye, lad?" he asked in a falsely jolly voice. His flintlock pointed directly at Zander.

"I'll be better once you lay your weapons down," answered Zander soberly.

"Och now, we're old friends. Remember? At the Indian village and all. Ye and me, and *Campbell*!" Burke's voice was cold and menacing. "Ye didna have to kill him, ye bastard!"

"I killed him in self-defense," said Zander

wearily. Damn, his rifles *were* starting to get heavy. He rocked on his heels, legs apart in a firm stance. "If you don't drop the guns, I'll fire."

"Go ahead," taunted Burke. "I been wantin' to kill ye for a long time. And before I shoot ye daid, I want ye to know that the bullet in this rifle is in memory of a damn good partner— Campbell!"

Chapter Thirty-seven

Clutching her pistol, Dorie brushed aside a pine branch as she hurried through the night. Her panting breath sounded loud to her own ears. She must get to Zander, she must! The light from his campfire was a beacon, guiding her onward. She could hear voices now. Someone was with him!

She winced as she stubbed her toe on a rock. Then she pushed past another large pine tree. Finally she saw him. Zander!

She ducked behind a boulder. Ian Burke and Clifton Ross stood to one side of the fire, in front of several large pines and two boulders. Each of them held a flintlock pointed steadily at Zander's heart. Zander was in terrible danger!

Gripping her pistol tightly, she crept forward. Zander ordered the trappers to drop their guns.

"Oh, Lordy," she whispered to herself, guilt knotting her stomach. "I sabotaged his guns. Zander doesn't know they won't fire!"

There he stood, the man she loved. In each arm he held a useless flintlock, pointed at his enemies. And they meant to kill him!

"Zander," she hissed. She had to catch his attention. "Zander!" He didn't turn. A little louder, she whispered, "Zander, your rifles won't fire." Then, despairingly, she tried again. "Zander!"

But he didn't turn. He didn't hear her. His attention was solely on the trappers.

"Oh, Zander," she moaned desperately. "What do I do now?" She glanced around. Burke raised the barrel of his gun. He was saying something to Zander, and he looked angry.

Her pistol! Fortunately, the small gun was loaded and primed, and the powder was dry. She peered at the gun in her hand. She had one shot in her pistol. One sure shot. And there were two trappers.

She watched Ross and Burke, sweat running down her forehead and into her eyes. She had to stop them, she had to!

She glanced at Zander, her beloved Zander,

then back at Burke and Ross. She had only one shot in her pistol. One.

Suddenly, she grew very still. She loved Zander. She would do anything to save him. It didn't matter now about his making her his country wife. It didn't even matter that she was a better shot than he was. She was his only hope. She had to save him!

She wiped her forehead to get the sweat out of her eyes. She must be very calm, very careful. She raised her little pistol. Fortunately, Zander stood to the side of her, and the boulder she hid behind was almost parallel with him.

Across the clearing from him stood the two trappers, a few paces apart, side by side. She had a clear shot at them, and she had the advantage that they had yet to discover her.

Which one should she shoot? Should she wound them? Kill them? What? They were both deadly in their intent to kill Zander. When she peeked around her boulder, Ross was actually the closer to her, but Burke, standing on the other side of him, looked very angry. She decided that he was the bigger threat to the man she loved.

One shot. Two trappers. She could never reload her little gun and tamp down the bullet with the ramrod and refill the powder in time to shoot the second trapper.

She brought the gun up, peering down the

short single barrel, taking careful aim. She closed her eyes tightly for a second. "Zander," she whispered, "I love you."

She opened her eyes. A heavy pine tree limb hovered above the trappers' heads. Holding the pistol steady with her other hand, she squeezed the trigger. The gun went off with a loud report. Then there was a second *crack* as the pine branch above Ross's and Burke's heads broke and fell. It landed on both trappers' heads, stunning them.

They dropped to the ground as if pole-axed.

She darted out from behind the boulder. "Oh, Zander!" she cried.

"Dorie?" he asked in astonishment. "Did you do that?"

She ran up to him, breathless. He still held the two rifles. But she had to touch him, had to stroke his arm, had to feel his face, had to reassure herself that he was alive. "Oh Zander!" she cried. Her whole body trembled in the aftermath of the shot.

"That was a mighty fine shot," he said. "You saved my life!"

"Zander, we don't have time . . ." she glanced nervously at the two prone trappers. "They might wake up."

He smiled, confident. "Doesn't matter if they do. I have my rifles."

"Zander," she cried, "that's the problem.

Those guns don't work. I—I sabotaged them!"

"How?" he demanded, staring down at the rifles. "My God," he cried. "You did!"

"I stuffed a nail in the vent," she said humbly, wishing guiltily that she'd never had the fool idea to fiddle with his rifles in the first place. "When I did it," she explained, "I was angry with you. I wanted to make things difficult for you. I didn't know you'd almost be killed." She put her hands over her face as she started to cry. "Oh, Zander, I'm so sorry."

He dropped one rifle and was working frantically with his fingers at the pan of the other.

"I wedged a nail in the vent," she repeated in a small voice. "Oh, Zander!"

He ignored her as he intently tried to pull out the jammed nail. "Damn it, Dorie," he gritted between his teeth. "I see that you know exactly what you're doing with a gun. You stopped it up very effectively. If I'd pulled the trigger nothing would have happened. No spark would get through the chamber and the gun wouldn't fire!"

She winced. "I know," she moaned guiltily. "Oh, Zander."

He finally pulled out the nail and flung it aside. He reached for the second rifle. Just as he was about to touch it, Burke spoke, "I wouldn't go for that gun if I was you, laddie!"

Zander froze. Dorie went still.

Beside Burke, Ross shook his head groggily and sat up. He glanced at the other three, then he too picked up his rifle.

Zander and Dorie slowly moved to face the two angry trappers and their two primed and loaded rifles.

"Oh, no, Zander," whispered Dorie. "They woke up too soon!"

Zander didn't answer. He stepped protectively in front of her. *At least his rifle works now*, thought Dorie dismally, *even if he does have only one shot.*

Chapter Thirty-eight

The next thing she knew, Dorie was flung to the ground. She landed with a thud and a mouthful of dirt. She spat out the dirt. "Zander," she cried. "What—?"

Two loud shots rang out, deafening her. Then Dorie's whole body flattened from the impact of Zander careening onto her. She lay on the ground, Zander on her back. She tried to lift her head. Moans greeted her ears.

"Zander?"

He stirred.

"Zander, what happened? Get off me!"

He moved off her and she sat up, looking around. Ross stood staring in dismay at his mangled rifle on the ground. Burke lay on the ground, writhing and moaning. He held one buttock and bright red blood seeped between his fingers.

"What happened?" asked Dorie in dismay.

"I shot them," answered Zander. Just then, he lunged for Burke's gun, the only rifle still loaded and primed. Ross lunged for it too. The men wrestled for the rifle, rolling over and over, the rifle wedged between them. Suddenly the rifle fired, and Dorie heard the bullet thud harmlessly into a tree. Finally Zander got hold of the barrel and hit his opponent on the head. Ross didn't move.

Dorie ran over to them. "Oh, Zander," she moaned, kneeling beside Zander and hugging him. "Thank the Lord you're safe!" She peered at the prone Ross. "Is he dead?" she asked.

Panting, Zander answered, "Knocked out." She saw then that Ross's chest rose and fell. He was breathing. "I hope he stays that way for a long time!"

Burke was still clutching his rear and moaning.

"What happened?" demanded Dorie. "What did you do, Zander?"

Zander sat up and winced. "I had to keep Ross from getting Burke's rifle."

"Not that," she said impatiently. "Why did you throw me to the ground?" She glanced at the tormented Scotsman. "What did you do to

Burke? Why is Ross's gun all mangled?"

"Ricochet shot," explained Zander with a groan. "I had only one shot, so I pulled the trigger and bounced the bullet off Ross's rifle and it shot Burke in the butt." He gave a weak chuckle.

Dorie stared at him. "You planned that shot?" she gasped.

"Yeah." He reached for her. "Help me up, Dorie. My back is still a little stiff."

Hastily, she aided him to rise. He leaned on her and she smiled to herself. "Zander," she said slowly, "that was a very good shot."

He shrugged. "It kept them from killing us," he answered.

Dorie shook her head, marveling to herself. Zander had just outshot her! How ironic that she'd given up her main requirement in a man—that he be a better shot than she was— just before Zander pulled off that trick. She pulled him closer. "I don't care if you're the best shot in the world," she said. "I love you."

He glanced down at her, puzzled, as he limped beside her. "I love you too, Dorie. Let's go sit on that boulder." She helped him over to lean against the large rock. "Ooh. That's better," he groaned, settling on the rock.

"Help me," croaked Burke from the ground.

Dorie glanced over at the Scotsman. "He's hurt, Zander. What'll we do?"

Zander closed his eyes. She could see that he, too, was in pain. "I know a place he can get some goddawful tea to drink," answered Zander. "And bandages. They can patch him up there."

"But Zander, is it safe? He tried to kill you."

He shrugged and opened his eyes. "I don't want to kill him, Dorie. Do you?"

She shook her head. "No."

"Well, then, we'd best get them to the Jesuit mission."

"Oh." She walked over to Burke.

"Lassie," he moaned, his face contorted. "It hurts very bad. Do ye have any whiskey? A wee droppie?" He moaned. "Tell Durban he's a lousy shot if he was aimin' for me heart." Then he closed his eyes. He'd passed out, too, she realized. She hurried back to Zander.

"He needs that goddawful tea, that's what he needs," snorted Zander. "It tastes like beaver p—" He stopped. "Never mind what it tastes like." He winced again and she moved closer. "Dorie, let's get married."

She gasped. "M-Married?"

"Yeah."

"Well, now, Zander," she said. "I'm very glad you mentioned this. I am very angry with you for not telling me what a country wife is. I thought we were already married!"

He met her eyes and she saw the remorse in

his. "I should have told you I wanted to marry you, officially, before this," he murmured.

"Yes," she exclaimed. "You should have!" Then she hugged him. "Oh, Zander, you could have been killed. Those awful men . . ." She began kissing his face, his hair. "I'm so glad you're alive!"

He reached out a hand to stop her. "Dorie," he said softly, "you are the wife of my heart. I love you. I want to marry you. In front of any priest or minister or whoever you want me to marry you in front of. We'll make it official. Say you'll marry me!"

She looked at him, at this strong, brave man who had risked his own life to save her. She touched his face, her hands trembling. "I love you too," she whispered. "I love you so much! And yes, I'll marry you!"

"Are you carrying my child?" Zander asked softly.

She nodded. "I am."

He pulled her to him. "Good."

She clung to him as they kissed. With every beat of her heart, she loved him more. "Oh, Zander," she whispered. "I'm so glad you're alive."

They embraced and kissed again.

"How touching," snarled a sarcastic voice.

Dorie whirled.

Out from behind a tree stepped Clarence Biddle, his round glasses catching the early dawn light. In his hands, he held a single-barreled flintlock, pointing squarely at them.

"What the hell do you want, Biddle?" Zander's voice was cold as he moved Dorie aside. He was moving her out of the line of fire, she realized.

"Your display of lust sickens me, Durban." Biddle turned a sneer on Dorie. "Hah! And I see you saved me the trouble of killing Burke and Ross."

Chapter Thirty-nine

Dorie stared at the intruder. He watched them both with huge, glittering eyes behind his glasses.

He prowled closer until he stopped beside the unconscious trappers. "Neither one of them could do a job right," he sneered at the bodies. "Looks like you saved me the trouble of paying out good furs for your death, Durban."

"It was you who paid them to kill me?" asked Zander casually.

Dorie remembered the conversation between Ross and Biddle that she'd overheard.

"Yes." Biddle glared at them. "You and your soiled dove made me a laughing stock at the fort!"

Dorie felt Zander's hand squeeze her arm as he moved away from the boulder and placed himself in front of her.

He means to shield me from Biddle's gun, she realized. Once again, he was protecting her.

She put her hand on her stomach. "You have a fine father, little one," she whispered to their baby. Sadness overcame her. She knew that none of the rifles in the clearing was loaded or functional. Except for Biddle's. Zander had nothing to defend her and the baby with. Nothing but his bare hands and his bravery.

Pride in him mixed with her fear and sorrow. "I love you, Zander," she whispered to his back. "And nothing can take that away. Nothing! I love you now and I'll always love you. Even in death I'll love you, Zander. Even in death!"

His shoulders tightened beneath her gaze. She touched his back. If this was all they had, so be it. She loved him and she had this moment, this heartbeat, when the three of them— her, the child, and Zander—were together. "I'm glad we met, glad we made love, glad we had the time together that we did." She faltered. "I'll always love you, Zander. Always." She bowed her head.

"You don't have to kill her, Biddle," she heard Zander say. She wiped at her tears.

"I'll kill both of you," answered Biddle angrily. "She made me the laughingstock of the whole fort! Everyone knows I paid one hundred furs for her safe return! That's too many furs for a woman. A woman you ruined, Durban!"

"That's no reason to kill her," said Zander.

"Reason enough," snapped Biddle. He raised his gun.

Dorie said over Zander's shoulder, "He's lying, Zander. The reason he wants to kill me is because I know he cheats people out of their money."

Biddle laughed. "She's right, the little eavesdropper. She knows too much. She heard me and Ross arguing. With her dead, and you dead, there'll be no one to interfere with my plans."

"Plans for what?" asked Zander.

Dorie knew he was trying to keep Biddle talking so he could think of some way to stop him. But there was nothing he could do, she thought sadly. Yet she loved Zander all the more for his vain attempt.

"Plans for more profit, of course," sneered Biddle.

"Of course," answered Zander. He turned to Dorie. "I love you, Dorie," he said.

"Turn around and face this gun," ordered Biddle.

Dorie's eyes squeezed shut. She felt Zander kiss her one last time.

"I love you," he whispered.

She opened her eyes and nodded, her eyes

blurred by tears. She knew he loved her. She could see it in his eyes, feel it in his heartbeat, taste it on his lips, smell it in his scent. He loved her and she loved him. They had their love. Only their love.

Zander turned to face Biddle.

Biddle smiled grimly, dawn's light glinting off his round glasses. He raised the rifle and pointed it directly at Zander's heart.

"No!" screamed Dorie. "Oh, God, no!"

A shot rang out.

Chapter Forty

Dorie watched in horrified fascination as Clarence Biddle plunged to the ground. She clutched Zander's arm. "Is he—is he—?"

"He's dead," Zander said flatly. Slowly he pulled her to him and groaned, kissing her deeply. "And we're alive."

She could feel his warm flesh under her arm. The blood coursed through her veins. "Yes," she murmured, "we are alive." They kissed again. "I love you," she said.

He held her tight and nuzzled her hair. "Mmmm." He lifted his head suddenly. "Wait." He drew back as though pulled suddenly from a trance. "Who the hell shot Biddle?"

Dorie glanced around in alarm; she could see

a little better in the dawning morning light. Boulders and the thick pine trees provided many hiding places. Her grip tightened.

"I'll get the loaded rifle that's still on my horse," said Zander. Reluctantly, she released him. He strode to the pine tree where he'd tied Shadow.

He returned with the gun and pulled the nail out of the vent. Then he swiftly began to load the rifle. "Whoever shot Biddle might have been aiming at me," he explained, turning to Dorie. "No more surprises. I want to be ready."

"Zander!" came a low voice.

"Who—?" began Dorie.

Zander's warning hand squeezed her shoulder, and she immediately fell silent. They both peered around.

Out from behind a boulder stepped a man.

"Anton! What the hell are you doing here?" demanded Zander.

Dorie gasped.

Anton walked up to them, his face solemn. His dark eyes focused on Zander. "Once you saved my life. Now I have saved yours."

"You have," agreed Zander, gripping his friend's arm. "You certainly have!" He released Anton and put his arm around Dorie.

Anton stepped back, but he kept his eyes on Zander. "One night when I was drunk at the fort, I told Clarence Biddle where to find you," said Anton. "That's why he sent Clifton Ross after you. Ross knew to look for you at the cabin. I betrayed you. I was drunk."

Zander's expression changed. The grim look he shot Anton spoke of Zander's love for his friend mixed with his sadness at the betrayal. "You endangered Dorie too!"

Anton nodded. His jaw worked. "I stay away from firewater now," he said remorsefully.

Zander's anger and Anton's shame hovered between the two men, and Dorie wrung her hands. She didn't know what to do. Anton had saved Zander, but had nearly cost him—and her—their lives as well.

At last Zander said, "You saved my wife and my son's life. For that I will forgive your betrayal."

Anton's face remained impassive, but Dorie thought she saw a flash of relief in his dark eyes.

Dorie put her hand on her stomach. "What son? Perhaps it's a girl."

Zander said wryly, "It's a boy. It's got to be a boy after what we went through."

She smiled when he met her eyes and she saw the love flicker in those black, black eyes. "Now that I think on it, a girl would be fine, too." He grinned. "But now we must go to the Jesuit mission. We'll find a priest there and get married officially for those who don't know we already have a marriage of the heart!"

Dorie beamed at him and clung to his arm. "I'm so happy to be marrying you, Zander!" Then, suddenly aware of Anton watching them, she added graciously, "You are the first person to be invited to our wedding, Anton."

He nodded solemnly. "I will attend."

As the morning sun rose in the east, they helped Anton load the unconscious trappers onto horses. That done, Dorie and Zander galloped swiftly towards the Jesuit mission. It was the start of a new day.

Epilogue

June 3, 1827
Fort Walla Walla

Zander ignored the men around him. Why the birth of his child should be so amusing to them, he didn't know. But to him, it was not amusing. It was deadly serious.

They had set up an impromptu party on the fort's grounds. Men were drinking and carousing and gambling. One intrepid trader was taking bets on whether the baby was going to be a boy or a girl. Down on the flats, not far from the fort's palisade, Zander could hear the faint yells of the crowd as they urged on the participants in a horse race.

Zander Durban sat outside the Pomeroy residence by choice. He did not want to be inside the log house with Dorie and Martha Whitley and Prue and the other women. He did not want to watch his wife's labor or hear her groans. He did not want to do so because he'd already been in there and had tried to help her. But seeing her in labor had, unfortunately, caused him to faint to the floor.

Which was why the men were so damned amused. And he was so damned scared. He'd rather face two Biddles with loaded guns than watch Dorie go through whatever she was going through. Another of her deep groans came through the closed door, and he clapped his hands over his ears.

A nearby trapper laughed so hard that he choked on his whiskey. Zander got up and thumped him on the back until he stopped choking. Then Zander returned to his vigil.

Anton sauntered by. "How is Dorie doing?" he asked.

A loud groan from the Pomeroy residence answered him. Zander glanced nervously at the wooden walls that hid Dorie. "She—she's doing fine."

Anton looked at him pityingly.

"How's Mary?" asked Zander, anxious to change the subject and pretend Dorie wasn't lying abed in agony.

"She's gone back to the village," answered Anton. "After Biddle's death, she wanted to go home to our people." He paused. "She told me the money you gave her is helping out."

Zander met his eyes and nodded. A loud shriek cut through the air. Both Anton and Zander shuddered. "I cannot take this," said Anton. He left.

Zander closed his eyes. He wished he could leave, too. But he couldn't. He couldn't leave Dorie.

An old woman walked up to him and gave him a small leather sack. "For the baby," she croaked.

Inside the sack he saw two gold coins. Where did an old woman get so much money? he wondered. Then he studied her lined face. Now he remembered. She was Mrs. McKay, one of the four old widows who had each received a generous settlement from the Hudson's Bay Company after Biddle's death. Dorie had gone to Chief Factor McLaren, who had authority over several forts, and she'd told him of Biddle's double-dealings. The chief factor had thanked her and swiftly set things to right.

Zander nodded at Mrs. McKay. "Thank you," he said. "The baby will be very happy to receive such a fine gift. His mother and I are honored." He still stubbornly clung to the belief that it would be a boy.

The old woman nodded and shuffled away in her new moccasins.

Zander clenched his jaw. When would Dorie be done? When would he know she was safe? "Please, God," he prayed. "Let her be strong and survive this birth. Let our baby be healthy." He wondered if he should also say an intercessory prayer to Mary, Our Lady of Compassion. She was a mother, after all; she knew what birth was like. . . .

"Have a drink," said the trapper, waving around his tin cup. "Good whiskey."

Zander shook his head. He'd wait.

At long last, Martha Whitley opened the door and stepped out onto the porch. "Mr. Durban?" she called, looking disdainfully at the drinking trappers and carousing men.

Zander stood up and staggered a little. He'd been waiting a long time. "Is she—?"

"You needn't make a drunk of yourself," she reproached him sharply. "Just because a babe is born is no reason for a man to get drunk!" Her back stiff, she led him into the house.

Dorie lay on a big bed, the covers almost up to her chin, though it was a warm evening.

"Dorie?" He tiptoed over to her. "Are you asleep?"

She turned her head and he saw that she was smiling. Relief crept through him so great he thought he would collapse to the floor. No, he mustn't. He'd already done that once this day.

He cleared his throat and took her hand. "You look—you look beautiful," he said at last.

She smiled at him softly. "See, Zander." She gently moved aside a blanket flap to reveal a tiny bundle at her side. The shiny gold wedding band on her left hand glinted.

Zander crouched by the bed and stared at a little pink head with the thickest, blackest hair he'd ever seen. "Is it—?"

"It's a boy," she said. "And he has all his fingers and toes."

Zander closed his eyes and gave a swift prayer of thanks to God.

He perused the little head, scarcely daring to breathe. The baby's mouth made sucking movements even as he slept.

Zander squeezed Dorie's hand. "He is a fine son," he said at last. He met Dorie's blue eyes, gleaming with love. They kissed. "How I love you, my country wife," he whispered.

"Oh, Zander!" And she hit him on the head with a pillow.

Dear Reader:

In researching this fur trade book, I realized how fraught with hardship and danger those times really were—danger from animals, men, raging rivers and deep canyons, and violent storms and starvation. A traveler's horse dying could mean, at best, being stranded; at worst, a miserable death for the traveler. The brave men and women who lived in those times had to face dangers we never even think of. Like grizzly bears.

To better research this story, I dragged my husband and two daughters off to Fort Vancouver in southern Washington State. We walked through gardens and cabins and houses that were reconstructions of the original fort established in 1829. There I had the opportunity to browse through beaver pelts, twists of tobacco, and buy beads, clay pipes, and all sorts of interesting things. Talk about dangers! I was lucky to get out of there while my checkbook still had checks in it! Now do you see how our modern dangers differ from those in the bad old days? No comparison. I'll take the bad old days anytime.

I hope you enjoyed reading this story as much as I enjoyed writing it!

Best regards,
Theresa Scott

P.S. For those readers who want to write to me, please send an SASE to: P.O. Box 832, Olympia, WA 98507.

References

Brown, Jennifer S.H. *Strangers in Blood: Fur Trade Company Families in Indian Country*. The University of British Columbia Press. Vancouver, B.C., Canada, 1980.

Chittenden, Hiram Martin. *The American Fur Trade of the Far West*. Vol II. The Press of the Pioneers. New York, 1935.

Cole, Jean Murray. *Exile in the Wilderness. The Life of Chief Factor Archibald McDonald, 1790–1853*. University of Washington Press. Seattle, WA, 1979.

Combes, John D. *Excavations at Spokane*

House—Fort Spokane Historic Site 1962–1963. Washington State University. Pullman, WA, 1964.

de Voto, Bernard, ed. *The Journals of Lewis and Clark.* Houghton Mifflin Co. Boston, 1953.

Garth, Thomas R. "Archeological Excavations at Fort Walla Walla." *Pacific Northwest Quarterly,* Vol. 43, pp. 27-50, 1952.

Irving, Washington. *Astoria. Adventure in the Pacific Northwest.* KPI Limited, 11 New Fetter Lane, London, England. First pub. 1839. Reprint 1987.

Laycock, George. *The Mountain Men.* Outdoor Life Books. Danbury, CT, 1988.

Pambrun, Andrew Dominique. *Sixty Years on the Frontier in the Pacific Northwest.* Ye Galleon Press. Fairfield, WA, 1978.

Ruby, Robert, and John A. Brown. *The Chinook Indians: Traders of the Lower Columbia River.* University of Oklahoma Press. Norman, OK, 1976.

Russell, Carl P. *Firearms, Traps, and Tools of the Mountain Men.* Alfred A. Knopf, Inc. New York, 1967.

Sandoz, Mari. *The Beaver Men: Spearheads of*

the Empire. Hastings House Publishers. New York, 1964.

Stern, Theodore. *Chiefs and Chief Traders: Indian Relations at Fort Nez Perces, 1818–1855*. Oregon State University Press. Corvallis, OR, 1993.

Walker, Barbara M. *The Little House Cookbook: Frontier Foods from Laura Ingalls Wilder's Classic Stories*. Scholastic, Inc. New York, 1979.

Webber, Bert. *Indians along the Oregon Trail*. Webb Research Group. Medford, OR, 1992.

Whisler, Frances L. *Indian Cookin*. Nowega Press, 1973.

Hunters of the Ice Age
Theresa Scott
Broken Promise

BESTSELLING AUTHOR OF *DARK RENEGADE*

Among the tribes warring at the dawn of time, the Jaguars are the mightiest, and the hunter called Falcon is feared like no other. Once headman of his clan, he has suffered a great loss that turns him against man and the Great Spirit. But in a world both deadly and treacherous, a mere woman will teach Falcon that he cannot live by brute strength alone.

Her people destroyed, her promised husband enslaved, Star finds herself at Falcon's mercy. And even though she is separated from everything she loves, the tall, proud Badger woman will not give up hope. With courage and cunning, the beautiful maiden will survive in a rugged new land, win the heart of her captor, and make a glorious future from the shell of a broken promise.

_3723-8   **$4.99 US/$5.99 CAN**

FORBIDDEN PASSION

THERESA SCOTT

Bestselling Author Of *Bride of Desire*

"More than Viking tales, Theresa Scott's historical romances are tender, exciting, and satisfying!"
—*Romantic Times*

Ordered to Greenland to escort his commander's betrothed to their Irish stronghold, Thomas Lachlann is unexpectedly drawn to the beguiling beauty he was sent to find. Bewitched and bewildered, Thomas knows that if he takes Yngveld as his beloved his life will be forfeit—but if he loses the golden-haired enchantress his heart will break.

_3855-2 $5.99 US/$7.99 CAN

Dorchester Publishing Co., Inc.
65 Commerce Road
Stamford, CT 06902

Please add $1.75 for shipping and handling for the first book and $.50 for each book thereafter. NY, NYC, PA and CT residents, please add appropriate sales tax. No cash, stamps, or C.O.D.s. All orders shipped within 6 weeks via postal service book rate. Canadian orders require $2.00 extra postage and must be paid in U.S. dollars through a U.S. banking facility.

Name_____

Address_____

City _____ State _____ Zip _____

I have enclosed $_____ in payment for the checked book(s).

Payment <u>must</u> accompany all orders.☐ Please send a free catalog.